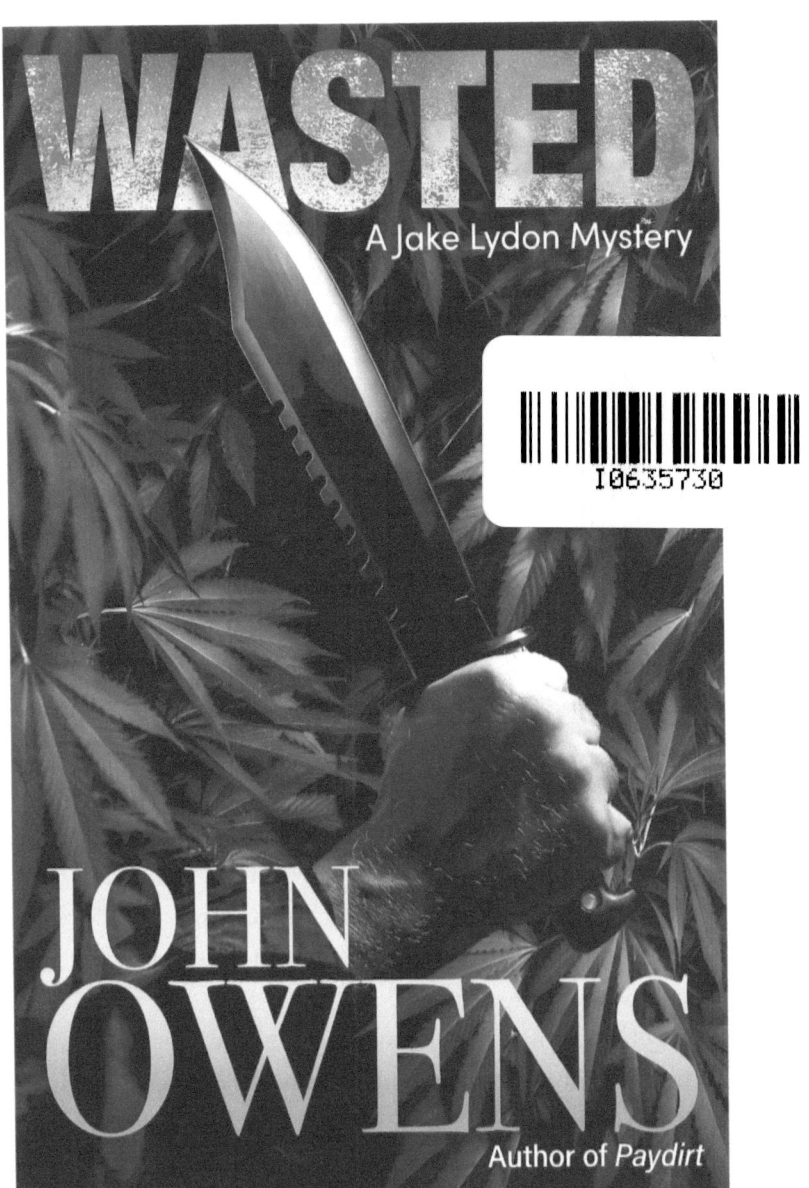

WASTED

A Jake Lydon Mystery

JOHN OWENS

Author of *Paydirt*

I0635730

OTTAWA PRESS
AND PUBLISHING

MYSTERY

ottawapressandpublishing.com

Copyright © John Owens 2024

ISBN (print) 978-1-990896-26-2
ISBN (epub) 978-1990896-27-9

Cover design: Glenn Torresan
Page design: Glenn Torresan, Joanna D'Angelo
Cover photography: Glenn Torresan and Beth Clark
Author photograph: Sara Owens
Plants courtesy of Corey and Phil the Pharmer

ALSO BY JOHN OWENS

For JoDee and Lou

WASTED

A JAKE LYDON MYSTERY

JOHN OWENS

I'm a joker
I'm a smoker
I'm a midnight toker
I sure don't want to hurt no one

— Ahmet Ertegun / Eddie Curtis / Steve Miller

There's lots of shady characters, lots of dirty deals
Every name's an alias in case somebody squeals
It's the lure of easy money, it's got a very strong appeal

— Glenn Frey and Jack Tempchin

PROLOGUE

G od, he hated cities.

He wanted to be anywhere but here—a side alley off the busy boulevard, away from all the self-conscious hipsters and befuddled tourists crowding the many patios that lined the avenue. Yet here he was, out of sight behind a dumpster, for Christ's sake. It all felt so seedy, so unnecessary, so unlike the civilized way things were done at home.

He was, he concluded, way too old for this shit.

He knew he, at least theoretically, was taking a huge risk. Florida treated this crime seriously and an arrest would ruin him, his business, everything. But what are the chances of getting caught? Slim, he'd decided, while he waited in the narrow alley for the stranger, as they had arranged inside the restaurant minutes earlier.

When the well-dressed man joined him, he seemed far

more nervous than he had been inside the restaurant. It was infectious; now he got jumpy.

Jumpier still when the seller almost suddenly, fixed his eyes on his. C'mon, c'mon, he silently urged the man standing close in front of him. Let's get this over with.

At last, the deal was done. He almost sighed out loud. Cash was handed over in exchange for the plastic bag. Its contents seemed overpriced to him and a little under the promised weight, but what the hell, he thought. It was enough to last him until he was approved.

He knew his anticipation went beyond weight and price. His purchase, he had been told inside the restaurant, was reputed to be Joy Blaster, a premium strain of bud he'd heard about back home but never tried. He could imagine its glorious high, just as every addict imagines his next score.

He slipped the baggie into one of the pockets of his cargo shorts and looked down as he patted the lump as flat as it would go.

That's when he saw the blur of the knife produced from the stranger's belt. The blade flashed upwards, ripping into his gut. Searing, electric pain in the second it took the sharp steel to travel deeper, up and into his body, now in his chest. Then the agonizing, wrenching twist of the knife. Stunning, wordless, soundless shock.

A second of release, a thought of his wife. Blackness enveloped him, and then the pain went away.

CHAPTER 1

WHAT I DID OVER MY SUMMER VACATION BY JAKE LYDON:

L et me see here.

I almost finished *The Sixth String*, my second novel. A couple of more passes cleaning up the stupid shit and I'd be done. And I had started the hunt for an agent, a publisher, anybody who would do me and the reading public a huge favour. My first book—a Depression-era coming of age novel—was published by a small regional press whose owner admitted he had done so against his own advice. No way would he put to print my second outing—about a Roma flamenco guitarist caught up in wartime Nazi Germany. Not when his most recent offering was the best-selling *Fun Facts About the Trent-Severn Waterway*.

My soul-destroying search was well underway. Unless

you're Nordoff and Hall, you write a book alone. Then, suddenly, you have to venture out into the real world searching for someone to believe in it even half as much as you do.

Lots of people exist in the real world. I don't. I spend an inordinate amount of my time with my head up my ass. I don't join any writers' forums; I don't go to literary festivals. I do nothing to cultivate any connection to anything or anybody in the publishing world. So, there I was, starting from scratch, compiling lists of names and addresses of agents and publishers, fending off pitches from promotions and PR outfits, editorial services, and self-publishers (I liked it better when they were called vanity presses). Then sending out an e-armada of sample chapters with craftily persuasive cover letters.

What else did I do in the leafy green season? Well, I finally quit smoking. Boy, that was fun. Especially for Alexandra. Champix took away my craving most of the time and replaced it with wild, surrealistic dreams that I actually enjoyed and remembered. But in the waking time, I was even more surly than I normally am.

It was and, for my last fifty years of puffing away, had always been an insanely stupid habit. I was a kid when I first heard Bob Newhart's absurdist phone conversation between Sir Walter Raleigh and a friend who wants to know all about the shipload of dried leaves Raleigh is bringing back to England from the Virginia colonies. "No, don't tell me, Walt...

you stick it in your ear. No? Between your lips and…and…you light it on fire?!" So even in my mid-teens, I knew that, logically, smoking was dumb as fuck. For the record, I never felt cool smoking either; I just liked doing it.

And I didn't quit for health-related reasons—especially after my surprising all-clear result from my lung scan the summer before. I quit solely because it had become expensive as hell as governments taxed the fuck out of it the way they usually do with any fun things.

After two or three shitty weeks in June, during which Alex was a solid-gone champ, both my urge to light up and my grouchiness subsided. But I missed smoking and suspected I always would. It had been one of the few things I was good at it.

What else? What else happened? Oh, yeah. Alexandra and I got married.

It seemed like the obvious, natural thing to do. Without ever talking about it, both of us acted like we were in this together for the long haul. Even though, at the identical age of sixty-five, that long haul would be shorter than it is for most newly married couples.

Want to hear about my grand, romantic proposal? Tough bananas, I'm going to tell you anyway.

We were sitting side by side in our Adirondacks on the deck for our near-daily evening ritual of watching the sun set over Mississauga Lake. It was mid-July, the sweltering time in Central Ontario cottage country. The air had cooled somewhat from the furnace of the day, but the temperature was still in the mid-80s. Mercifully, the swarms of mosquitoes had fucked off until the following spring.

She had her glass of Pinot; I cradled a (surprise, surprise) frosty Molson Export as we sat in silence and the lake went to full glitter before the sinking sun slipped behind the wall of pine, spruce, whatever the fuck, on the far shore.

As darkness descended and the spell broke, Alex, as is her wont, started talking about some projects around the Hovel she'd like to see completed.

"Listen," I more or less blurted out, "After I rebuild the front porch, do you think we can get married or what?"

Silence returned as we looked at each other and grew massive grins.

"Yeah," she finally said. "I think we can squeeze that in."

Alexandra then wanted to swing into planning mode but there wasn't much to do or haggle about. Mercifully, there was no quibbling over the guest list. I have two dear friends: Steve Golding, a Toronto crime reporter turned successful true crime author and Carl, my neighbour who lived on an island a couple of hundred yards from my back deck. Alex didn't have anyone close enough, she felt, to invite with the exception of Jessica Hackett, a Vassar college buddy with whom she had remained tight for more than forty years. Except for Halley, my daughter, Alex and I have exactly the same number of immediate family members: zero. Beyond that, every parent, every aunt and uncle we once owned was deceased. Nobody's disconnected cousin made the cut either, mostly because we couldn't even remember the majority of their names.

There was no dissension in picking a date either. Mid-August—about a month away—seemed right. Likewise, the venue—the Hovel's back deck, and the menu—grilled steak and salmon—were proposed, seconded, and carried unanimously.

There was, however, some to-ing and fro-ing about a few things.

I got the ball rolling with the strong but jokey suggestion that she should be legally known as *Mrs.* Alexandra Lydon, figuring that would appeal to her feminist sensibilities. She countered with her assertion that, since I was a man-child in constant need of protection and adult supervision, it was only fitting I should adopt Mr. Jake Simpson.

The debate ended in a standoff when I agreed to her proposal but only on the conditions that I legally change my first name to Homer and that she would henceforth be called Marge, dye her hair blue and pile it up on her head like a big stack of IHOP pancakes.

Likewise, there was a bit of a tug of War of 1812 as to where the official Lydon-Simpson residence would be—the States or Canada.

"We can be in Florida for more than six months," she had reasoned. "And I might be able to get you a Green Card."

"Yup, you sure do know me, woman. I'm chompin' at the

bit to get working again. And I'm really keen to live in 'Merica so I can give up free healthcare, just as I get free drugs too. I won't need any of that as I slip into my dotage and go full decrepitude on you."

But she was adamant about not giving up her tastefully restored mid-19th-century home in Framingham, Mass-achusetts and I was fine with that. 'Twern't any of my business.

"You can Airbnb the hell out of it," I suggested.

"Fuck that," she said. "It stays empty until I need a place to escape from you."

So, when we filled out the marriage application at the township office, we listed both places of residence.

Then Alex and I got down to the nitty-gritty.

She wanted me to sign a pre-nuptial agreement. At first, she was cuter'n hell about it, all embarrassed and shy for bringing up the dicey subject. But then, the proceedings became real businesslike, as she quickly produced the ten-page pre-nup document as though she routinely walked around with it stuffed in her back pocket. I had zero problem with signing my John Hancock. She asked that I scratch it out and write my real name.

It's not like I had waited until I was sixty-five to spring an elaborate gold-digging scheme on anybody. Nor did I think I was anybody's idea of a trophy husband. I had no idea what kind of money Alex had made and stashed away. I figured that amount was substantial because she was smarter than hell, her boutique ethical investment firm had grown wildly in recent years, and she lived expensively. But never for a goddamn second could I imagine that I had or would ever have any claim to a dime (slightly higher in Canada) of it.

In that tit-for-tat way we have, I told her I wanted her to sign one too. But I was too lazy to get a fair-value estimation of both the summer Hovel here in cottage country Ontario and our southern one in Indian Rocks Beach, Florida that I'd recently inherited from my absent, dead father. Then there was my priceless collection of Hawaiian shirts, (sixty-five and counting). She liked my shirts and both the homes, so why shouldn't she have them if I kicked?

When I called to invite Halley, my Toronto homicide detective of a daughter (engraved invitations for seven people to come to what amounted to a small, casual barbecue seemed goofy) she surprised me when she suggested a double ring ceremony—that's how serious it had become between her and fellow cop Ron Farisi, a fraud detective.

"Does he know about this yet?" I asked. "Or is this just another egregious example of police entrapment?"

"It was his idea, dad." [Sidebar: Although I could tell she wanted to, she's not allowed to call me an arsehole the way all my friends and wife-to-be did; it just didn't seem right].

"Smart man," I said. "And a lucky one."

I was thrilled for her, but I nixed the idea of joint nuptials when she revealed her grand plan for the marriage(s). We're talking caterers, elaborate decorations on the deck, scores of cop friends, a live band, flower arrangements 'til hell wouldn't have it, and even a port-a-potty or two.

"Hal, sweetie," I said. "You should absolutely have all those things if you want them, and you're entirely welcome to transform the Hovel into a fairytale wedding palace. We'll even help. Well, Alex I'm sure will. And I can guarantee you I'll shout words of encouragement while you're getting the joint ready. It's just not what we saw happening for us." She understood.

My dear—well, only—friends, Steve and Carl, were appointed my co-Best Men, while Halley and Ms. Hackett would share Maid of Honour duties. We never found out what those duties ought to have been. We dispensed with usher selections as there was nobody to ush.

MERCIFULLY, IT WAS A SUN-DRENCHED AUGUST DAY WITH THE air clearer and less humid than it had been in sweltering July. As she stood on the deck surrounded by a motley crew, the rookie Justice of the Peace appeared more nervous than we were. It was her first wedding. With one apiece, Alex and I were old hands at this marriage thing.

Alexandra was stunning in a swirling floral summer dress; I went Hawaiian formal, swapping out my customary shorts for long pants. The oddsmakers took a beating as Carl won in the Most Overdressed category as he'd dusted off his only suit for the occasion. In particular, the judges praised his suitcoat lapels for being as wide as the Pearson Airport runways.

After all the legal stuff was read, Alex started sniffling about half-way into her self-written vows—I'm pretty sure the idea of her saying all those nice things about me out loud had horrified her. Or maybe it was the realization she'd made a terrible, terrible mistake.

I fell apart too. And I had all of seven goddamn words to say.

I had picked a simple quote from Twain's *Diaries of Adam and Eve* that summed up everything I felt and thought of my bride-to-be:

"Adam: Wheresoever Eve was, there was Eden."

I didn't plan on blubbering and the sneak attack of emotion shocked the shit out me. I got overwhelmed, a supercharging of how I *felt* about Alexandra, even as we spent little time over the last three years *talking* or even *thinking* about it. It just *was*. And felt like it always had been and would always continue to be.

The warmth and goodwill of our little group was almost tangible and elating, despite all the cheap shots I took from my so-called friends for being so undeserving of my bride. Like I didn't know that already.

For sure, it was warmer than the BBQ that ran out of

propane as I was cooking five thick bone-in ribeye steaks as well as two massive hunks of salmon for our non-red-blooded vegetarian visitors from the US. Carl saved the day by paddling over to his island offshore from me and retrieving his tank.

And then, except for Halley, we all got shit-faced, high-light of which was watching Carl and Steve pile themselves into the canoe in the dark for the tippy trip to Carl's island/crash pad where unconsciousness lay before them.

The next morning, our bleary-eyed band of less than magnificent seven reconvened at the Buckhorn Inn where Halley and Ron were staying. We had a delightful breakfast on the deck and a re-cap of the previous day's events. General consensus: the simple ceremony ranked near or at the top of any they had attended while the post-nuptial antics were unmatched.

The rest of our summer passed pleasantly, despite the Alex-directed activity. Both of us decided that being married had changed things in some way, but we just couldn't explain how.

I did a darned smart job on re-building the front porch steps—OK, it's serviceable—alright, alright, it hasn't collapsed yet. We had already decided to spend the tail-end of September and all October in Framingham after I learned that, apparently, Massachusetts had maple trees that changed colour just like ours.

I got some writing in, polishing the novel, even as I

endured the incoming torrent of "Fuck off" notes from agents and publishers. There were a couple of nibbles but not one of the sons of bitches asked me how I wanted my multi-million-dollar advance cheque made out.

Alex had not completely retired—and I suspected never would—so she busied herself writing op-eds, papers, and articles extolling the virtues of investing with companies who didn't act like complete dicks wherever they operated.

All in all, a wonderful summer.

But in early-September, we got a telephone call from Florida that we weren't expecting, one that would change a lot of the upcoming winter for us.

CHAPTER 2

It was Laura Harding, one-half of the duo that comprised our swell neighbours in Indian Rocks. The Colorado couple were easily my favourite legal pot growers, mostly because they were the only legal pot growers that I knew. They wintered in a one-bedroom condo next door to us, and we had instantly hit it off, one of those random encounters that generates immediate connection. Plus, they loved tequila almost as much as I did. Wait, now that I think of it, maybe that was the connection.

They were about a decade older than we were and their varied, unconventional history together marked them as true authentic hippies in their younger days—five years living on a Mexican beach after college graduation (in accounting, no less), then goin' up the country in Colorado to buy 200 acres on the Gunnison River, dead-centre in the middle of hilly fuck-all. There they set to work, applying the agricultural tips they'd picked up in Mexico on growing the bags of marijuana seeds they'd smuggled in their VW Westfalia. In short order, they built a booming outlaw pot business that, decades later, was now legal.

Generally, they'd maintained their idealism of the peace-love-understanding era but were markedly different in their characters. Laura was pragmatic, even-tempered, and a keen observer of just about everything while Stan was the feistier of the pair, scrapping like a bantam rooster with anybody who pissed him off or against anything that struck him as unjust.

When I found out that Laura edited textbooks as a sideline, I had asked if she would pull out her red pen for my new book and what would she charge.

"Of course, I will," she had answered. "And my fee: unlimited margaritas."

I had sent her the e-manuscript of *The Sixth String* a month earlier but hadn't heard back and was loathe to chase her for her free services. So, I was a bit surprised when she called.

"Stan's dead," she said in a quiet voice.

"What?!" I said, putting the phone on speaker so Alex could hear.

"Stan's dead," Laura repeated.

"Oh, Laura," Alexandra said. "I am so sorry!"

"What happened?" I asked, expecting to hear about a

health misadventure. After all, Stan was in his mid-70s, easily within the range of the time when mortal coils are routinely shuffled off.

But how do you push a conversation like the one we were having when you know there is absolutely nothing smart or helpful you can possibly say? You can't. So you wait.

"He was murdered," she finally said.

My turn for a stunned silence. Until Laura pressed on.

"Stan's older brother, Duncan, passed three weeks ago. Heart attack. We went to St. Petersburg for the funeral. Duncan had retired there. Even though Stan and he weren't that close, it's one of the reasons we bought in IRB; he sold us on the area. So, we decided to drive and start our Florida Winter early; our boys had the business well in-hand.... It was four days ago when..."

Her voice trailed off. I could hear her getting choked up and sniffling.

"Stop, right there, Laura," I said. "You don't have to tell us anything else."

"No...I need to. I want you to look into this, Jake. Please. I don't think the police are serious about it."

That took me aback. She did know of a couple of my previous crime clown jobs, not because I'd told her about them, but because the two shitshows had led to gunplay at the southern Hovel next to her building. And it's been my experience that that sort of loud exchange of bullets tends to attract attention.

"I will find out what happened," I offered. "I promise. Just not now. We'll talk later."

"Laura," Alex quickly added. "Go home. Be with your boys."

"Yeah, we'll make sure the place is alright."

"I...I can't come back here," Laura said.

Alex and I looked at each other.

"Laura, we'll handle it," Alex said.

"Get us the keys and legal permission and we'll take care of it," I suggested.

"Your only job is to fly home. Right now," Alex insisted. "We'll get your car to you."

We got off the phone and just stood there, stunned and saddened. In the past, people we'd known and cared about had died. Just not as homicide victims.

"What should we do?" I asked.

"Not entirely sure," Alexandra said." I guess we get a jump on our Florida winter."

I WENT LOOKING IN THE *TAMPA BAY TIMES* ARCHIVES FOR THE story about Stan's death. Here's the headline I found: *Tourist Killed in Suspected Drug Deal Gone Wrong in St. Petersburg.*

The article was lengthy but relatively light in detail.

Name, date, time, location. Stanley Arden Harding, 75, of Gunnison, Colorado was stabbed to death in an alley beside Benny's, a local restaurant, in the 200 block of Central Avenue in downtown St. Petersburg. The police said that "At this time, we have no suspects" but they did have a description, probably supplied to them by Laura.

The reporter seemed miffed that she couldn't get a direct quote from Laura at the scene when she wrote that "the grieving, blood-soaked widow, Lara (sic) Harding refused comment."

A spokesperson for the Sheriff's office said that they had found "a quantity of illegal substances on Mr. Harding's person. It has been confiscated." The reporter then had a local politician quoted as saying: "We must put a stop to the scourge of illegal drug use that threatens to tarnish the image of our great city." There was more blah-blah-blah bullshit from various "community leaders" that together all sounded like the Mayor of Amity trying to downplay the danger of a huge animatronic shark.

The article stopped short of declaring that "the guy had it coming" but it was implicit in its tone.

All in all, a shitty public eulogy for such a fine man.

I don't remember much from our trip down to Fla-fla-Land. Whirlwind packing. Carl, my stalwart neighbour, re-iterated his promise to properly close the joint up before the winter deep freeze, in exchange for the contents of my regular and beer fridges and liquor cabinet. Then we were on the road.

Early September and precious few snowbirds had started their migration, so the highways were easy driving at first. We made an eight-hour detour to Framingham so Alex could check on her house and put in an appearance at her company's head office. I could have kept the car running while she made both those brief stops.

And then we pushed it for what turned out to be thirteen hours a day behind the wheel (Curse you, construction and the American inability to master zipper merging!). While one of us drove, the other watched for state troopers as we completely abused the posted speed limits whenever we could.

Unlike the fall before, there wasn't too much in the way of elation as we pulled into the southern Hovel's driveway.

Michael, the guy we'd hired for some basic gardening, watering, and lawn cutting, had done an admirable job on all the living things. Not included in his job description was anything to do with the groundcover.

I had built meandering raised beds for some forty-odd tropical plant species and covered the beds with thirty bags of red mulch that looked swell in Florida but dorky up north.

I'd then laid down a ton of river rock as a border leading up to our patio. The heavy summer rains and subsequent flooding of streets and backyards had floated a great deal of the mulch onto the river rock. It looked like shit. Note to self: Find the rookie snowbird idiot who thought that that particular groundcover combo was a swell idea in low-lying Indian Rocks (a whole nine feet above the Gulf of Mexico).

Because of our involvement in fixing up, de-cluttering, and selling Stan and Laura's place, there wasn't much time to focus on ours. Which was just as well. I did not relish the idea of working in that September heat to separate the fucking mulch from the fucking river rock and then add about thirty more fucking bags of new fucking mulch to refresh the fucking beds.

It was weird as hell going through their one-bedroom condo. Alex with her camera phone walking and talking around the place with Laura voting yea or nay on the items and me slapping post-it notes on the keepers. The whole process was lengthy and sad as she described why certain things held strong sentimental reminders of Stan.

We carted the stuff she wanted to keep over to our tiny place which could look overcrowded with the addition of a single extra case of beer, let alone half a condo's worth of new stuff. Our tiny eight-foot by nine second bedroom resembled a garage sale or a hoarder's storage locker.

Finding a real estate agent wasn't an effort. They were hungry like the wolf [Sidebar: I swear to Christ, that'll be the only Duran Duran reference I will ever make!]. At that time, homes—especially those within brick-throwing range of the Gulf of Mexico—didn't stay on the market for days or weeks. It was a matter of hours before they were snapped up, meaning new listings were at a premium.

Jim the Agent was scarily upbeat when he toured Laura's condo. He praised the decorating and the layout as well as the common area outside with its communal BBQ, lush gardens and large patio. He set a price on the spot. A big price. Then he turned his attention to our place. We had no intention of selling, but after a quick walk-through he was almost drooling. Our almost completed renovations that Alex had directed inside were tasteful as hell, as was my landscaping artistry [Sidebar: Sorry, folks, I'm not going to be humble about that]. [Sidebar to the sidebar: Wait a minute, I'm not humble about fucking anything].

Jim decided to hold exactly one open house, that on the day the condo was listed. Twenty-nine people turned up and he had eleven offers by sundown—seven over asking. The winner was a widow from Minnesota who hadn't even seen the condo in person, just on a video her agent had taken while doing a walk-through of the place.

Jim the Agent dealt directly with Laura for all the paperwork, but she did call us when she was close to making a decision. She wanted to know if we thought it was a fair offer. Like we had a clue. But 210K more than they paid for it four years earlier struck me as a good deal.

Laura was laser-focused on the condo sale, even though, at the same time, she was making funeral arrangements, comforting her sons, and burying Stan. I admired the hell out of her for somehow being able to compartmentalize her grief and was all business. She had recovered from—or at least tamped down the initial shock of her husband's death and, as near as I could tell, was dealing with the sadness that accompanies such a terrible loss.

I decided to venture a conversation about just what had happened to bring us to where we were.

"If you're up to it, Laura, can we talk about the events? I've got a bunch of quest—"

"—I've been waiting," she said, cutting me off. "Go ahead; ask away."

"Alrighty then. First off, I'm assuming the 'illegal substance' was cannabis-related and not anything harder."

"Yes, he was looking for marijuana."

"You're surrounded by pot at home. Why didn't you just bring some or send it to Florida?"

"Both are illegal. Driving through the South, the last thing we needed was to get busted by a state trooper. Three years ago, we stupidly tried mailing our best weed here from Colorado before we left, but it never got to us in IRB. We should have known better. An arrest would destroy our business."

"What happened?"

"Don't know. Likely, somebody at a post office found it and did us a favour by not reporting it."

"Because they realized they had just scored themselves a weekend bonus."

"Probably. In any event, nobody came back at us, nobody raised a stink."

"Why weed? Why not gummies or something else?"

"Stan was old school. He liked the social aspect of smoking it—even when it was just the two of us."

"Why didn't you just get approved for medical marijuana prescriptions? Judging by all the weed stores—sorry, I mean medical pain clinics—I've seen around here, you'd probably find a prescription-happy doc pretty quick."

"That's exactly what we did. Right after Duncan's funeral. But it was going to take at least two weeks to get approved and have the card sent to us. Sounds bad, but Stan didn't want to or couldn't wait that long."

"So he risked buying from a stranger."

"He didn't see it as dangerous. He sold like that for years without any problem."

I gently warned her that this questioning was now going to get detailed and painful but unavoidable.

"For God's sakes, Jake, don't dance around."

"Alright. How did you meet the seller?"

"After wandering around the Dali Museum, we stopped for lunch at a restaurant on Central Avenue. The place was crowded. He had the table beside us."

"Did he arrive after you or was he there already?"

"Maybe ten minutes after us."

"Alone?"

"Yes."

"Tell me about the guy," I said, knowing that Laura was a keen observer of the world around her —birds, flowers, traffic patterns, weather. She was a damn good artist and she noticed things. I could visualize her closing her eyes and going into something like a trance.

"Middle-aged guy, maybe late forties, not a big guy but bigger than Stan, smaller than you, longish black hair but neat, face stubble, again neat. Wore sunglasses. Casually dressed, light sports coat, red Henley t-shirt, slacks not jeans, polished brown loafers, but no socks."

"Kinda looked like the *Miami Vice* guy?"

"Exactly," she answered, maybe opening her eyes, "but a couple of decades after the fact. Oh, and he had big scar on his cheek."

"Why did Stan approach that guy in particular?"

"Sounds silly. He was wearing a small green and gold marijuana leaf lapel pin. That's like a signal, I guess."

"Had you ever seen him before?"

"No."

"OK, how did they strike up a conversation?"

"Pretty easily. Stan sort of pointed at his lapel pin. The guy nodded and gestured to go inside. I guess they had a chat in the washroom."

"But they didn't do the deal there."

"No. Stan came out and went to the alley alongside the restaurant. The guy followed a couple of minutes later."

"Then what?"

Here, Laura's voice became quieter as she re-lived her horror.

"When he was taking so long, I went back there to see what was going on. I...found him....so much blood. He wasn't breathing....so much blood...."

"That's enough for now," I quickly said. "We'll pick it up later, OK?"

"OK, Jake."

"Wait. One more thing. Did you see the guy come out of the alley?"

"No."

"Alright, that's it for now. You've given me a lot. Thank you."

After our call ended, I recounted the gist of it to Alexandra, ending with a fucking stupid editorial comment: "I just don't understand why Stan would take the chance instead of waiting for the medical clearance. He must have had some kind of strong addiction to weed of all things."

"Gee, Jake, how long could you wait for a cigarette...or a beer?"

CHAPTER 3

In my relatively brief time being exposed to major bad things being done to good people, I've learned that it's helpful for me to visit the scene of the crime, not in the hopes of finding new evidence, but to get a feeling for what could've happened there. The setting gives me the detail, the physical dimensions, that form the background of the movies I make in my wee mind. I yell "Action!" to myself and watch how I think it might've played out in real life. Then, usually, I have to yell "Cut!" when the scene makes no logical sense. That forces me to tear down the set and construct another for a new scene, moving the players involved into more realistic situations. The editing and music come later. The finished product becomes my idea of what happened and, more importantly, it normally raises a host of questions that demand answers.

All that to say: I found Benny's restaurant and the alley beside it and presumably the dumpster. I stood behind it, amazed at how quickly the environment changed. About a hundred feet from the sidewalk and in the shelter of the dumpster that was taller than I was, traffic on Central Avenue was barely audible. There was no sunlight because of the building heights on either side, no laughter and no background noise of servers and cutlery from the row of open-air patios that had claimed the sidewalks.

There was a faint dark rust blood stain running intermittently down the brick wall. Stan was a slight man, maybe 140 pounds. The knife would have been huge to completely pass through him. He must've been backed up against the wall. My first thought: Why? Why would he do the deal with a stranger when he was cornered like that? Before Colorado legalization, he would've made hundreds of sales like that— as the vendor—with no injury, no problems, according to Laura. Was it just the hangover of the vaunted peace, love and understanding ethos in hippie-infested Colorado or was he just smart? I voted for smart.

Why did they find the weed on him? Why wouldn't the killer have picked his pocket and walked away with both the cash and the product?

And why had Stan made no sound? A knife isn't a particularly guaranteed killing tool. Despite Hollywood, it, more often than not, wounds, not instantly kills; it's messy, imperfect. Grievously hurt maybe, Stan could still make the effort to cry out or crawl or stagger towards the street looking for help. Unless the killer knew what he was doing to end him quickly. But how would a low-level weed seller know what he was doing? Or did he just get 'lucky'?

To settle that last question, I called Quentin Purdy, the behemoth of a St. Petersburg police ballistic expert who had nearly died trying to help me with the previous winter's shit-show. Although he was retired, he immediately wanted to know if somebody had taken a shot at me or Alexandra again.

"Sorry, Quentin," I said. "No gunplay this time. I'm calling to see if you know somebody in homicide or forensics or the coroner's office who I can talk to about the stabbing that happened just over a week ago in downtown St. Pete?"

"That guy in the drug deal by Central Street?"

"That's the one. Something's off about this."

I described the questions that were nagging me.

"Jake, why are you even looking at this case?" he asked. "Out-of-towner meets the wrong guy, drug deal goes south? Not that unusual."

"First off, the victim was a friend of mine. He was my winter neighbour in IRB. Secondly, does it sound like it was 'not that unusual'? Small amount of weed, and, in a matter of seconds, he dies?"

"Damn. Sorry to hear that...I do know someone, but she probably won't talk to you. What do you want to know?"

"Just what the fuck happened."

Conscientious as hell, Quentin called back the next day to tell me he had seen the coroner's report.

He skimmed the clinical description of Stan's death.

"Single stab wound. Entering just below the sternum then upwards at an approximately 60-degree angle through the right ventricle and into the left ventricle, followed by a 45-degree twist. Big knife, long, broad blade, point of which exited the back. Extensive internal damage."

"Like a hunting knife?" I asked.

"Yeah. Or one like the military uses. The blade used was serrated."

"Why would they make those?"

"For maximum tearing."

"Was the wound instantly fatal?"

"Close enough, we're talking *maybe* a few seconds, if that, before death would've occurred. The victim likely would have died before his initial shock wore off."

"Anything about the killer?"

"Looks to be about average height, say five-foot ten. Probably left-handed. Or used his left."

"Why do you say that?"

"Rib cage extends down past the sternum. From the upward angle of the thrust, a righty would probably have hit bone first and missed the heart."

"Lucky jab?"

"Maybe. But if I had to guess, it was a pro job."

I thanked him and promised that if I got anywhere near a

bullet lodged in something or somebody, he'd be the first person I'd call.

I got off the phone shaken. A professional hitman killed Stan?! Holy shit, that added a new dimension. What the Christ could a 75-year-old, small, legal pot farmer have done to warrant murder by a paid assassin two thousand miles from home?

The question was driving me nuts because there was no obvious answer. But it had to have been connected to his crop on the other side of the country, unless there was something in his past, some side to him that I didn't and even his wife of fifty years didn't know.

A detail in Laura's description of the event had nagged at me but now made sense. The reason the dope deal didn't happen in the restaurant bathroom—where it could've easily been concluded—was now clear.

The killer wanted Stan in that alley.

"WELL, MRS. LYDON, WHAT DO YOU WANT TO DO?" I ASKED, after I filled her in on the startlingly new hitman angle.

"I don't know, Mr. Simpson. Any ideas?"

"How about a road trip to return Laura's car?"

"We can just have it shipped."

She was right, but I explained that the reason Stan died in Florida was because of something that happened in Colorado. If I—we—were honouring Laura's request, we'd have to go looking there.

"Fine with me," she said.

"But let's not tell her we're coming. Surprise the hell out of her."

"I thought you hated surprises."

"When they're done to me."

"Alright, a road trip it is."

"And bonus: we might miss a hurricane or two."

Hurricane season was still on, so the decision wasn't that hard. You'd want to visit your property after it's taken a smack from a Category-Five, but you don't want to be in the building when it huffs and it puffs and it blows the house down. The Hovel was built in the 1920s of concrete blocks and so had withstood all manner of weather over the last century. I'm glad we had installed "hurricane-proof" windows last winter, but the trusses and roof weren't so sturdy. With the weather getting more intense these days, a major storm coming in at a certain angle would rip it off. Once inside, the roaring wind would function as a giant blender liquifying everything it touched.

As it was, two days after we got down there, we got hit by what looked like, on the weather website radar map, a non-threatening, fast-moving little blob of orange and yellow that was dwarfed by all the giant blobs to the south-east and north-west of us. But for twenty minutes, it was fierce as hell, with a howling wind that drove the rain almost horizontally and flooded the streets.

That flash storm served as all the compelling evidence we needed to prove that we ought to light out to the Colorado territories as soon as possible.

CHAPTER 4

Before we struck off for drier points west, I was determined to find out as much as I could about the apparent reason Stan had been killed: the pot business. I really had no idea about what kind of industry it was, beyond my general sense that it had become a helluva lot more sophisticated, commercial, and dangerous than it had been in my naïve, dumb-as-a-bunny days a half century earlier.

I've always had a benign view of weed use, from the time I was an active inhaler in my teen years to the present day. To me, pot was just a built-in feature of North American life. For many, it was a rite of passage, for others, a fifty-year habit, and for still others, mainly seniors, a relatively recent cure or at least a mask for a host of physical ailments since its legalization in Canada and in a growing list of US states.

It was impossible for me to learn about the pot industry

in the 2020s without looking back at my own experience involving "the heathen weed with its roots in hell." In a word, my experience for a few years had been extensive.

Over a four-year period in high school starting in grade ten (we used to have a grade thirteen), I was all in. From my first toke. I loved everything about it—the anticipatory ritual of rolling, the first sparking up, the passing around the joint, the expert dabbing of the joint with a wet fingertip when it was burning lopsided, the laughing at everything, the effort to hold your toke, and, best of all, the high when it really hit.

At peak stone, I believed I was incredibly witty, perceptive, and the funniest goddamn kid in the room.

I didn't stray much from the orthodoxy of regular pot. I did acid once (I could picture myself on a boat in a river, but I didn't see the tangerine trees and marmalade skies and all the other trippy bullshit), cocaine once (waaaaay too pleasurable to not come at a very high literal and figurative cost), and mescaline once, which I liked but, unless your Aldous Huxley, who's got that kinda time to endlessly stare at minute stuff for hours?

It didn't take long for me to winnow down the list of people I liked to get fucked up with. One person: Dave Williams, a grade 12 student. We just sort of gravitated towards each other at house parties and cemented our friendship through weed and music.

Dave was just two years older—but two crucial years back then. I was kinda flattered that he had broken high school convention by hanging out with a lowly grade tenner. He had an older brother who was really into music. Consequently, he exposed me to older records, so that by the time I was fifteen, I was a full-fledged LP collector with pretty advanced musical tastes. I mention this only to note that music was a really big deal back then, creating a bond between people with similar likes and dislikes.

I designated a subsection of my collection as Best When Wasted. The list of records in this niche included *Caravenserai* from Santana, John Mclaughlin and the Mahavishnu Orchestra's *Birds of Fire*. Cream's *Disraeli Gears*. Other than somebody having to get up three times to flip the records, Hendrix's double LP, *Electric Ladyland,* was a favourite. Or we played the same song over and over until the grooves wore out. Prime examples: the Stones' *Moonlight Mile* and *Time Waits For No One.* If we were keen to wallow in atmospheric gloominess, it had to be *The End*, with Morrison exhorting us to "ride the snake' and "walk on down that hall." Or Steppenwolf's *Monster* with its mesmerizing album cover of intricately arranged human bones and skulls.

I started out liking all seventeen minutes of *In-A-Gadda-Da-Vida* when I was fourteen but, you know, you grow. Truth be told, we'd get so fucked up, even the ukulele solo in *Tiptoe Through the Tulips* sounded great.

Dave, bless him, always had pot and a desire to get high with about the same frequency as I did. We happily smoked away behind the gym, in the vice-principal's car with the windows rolled up, at high school dances, but mainly in my parents' half-finished basement rec room.

Way back in the Stoned Age, you took what you got and were never all that fussy. Seeds, leaves, stems and all—who forgets the startling pop when a seed blew up about a half an inch from your nose? The herb was plentiful, and we didn't even mind if the promised Acapulco Gold was really Huatulco ditch weed. Smoke enough of it and you'd get your brains fried for a while.

Back then, the level of paranoia struck deep, amplified by all the public warnings from law enforcement and the weed itself, until we imagined we were surrounded by black-clad, Ninja SWAT teams stealthily closing in, about to bust down the doors, guns blazing. But let's face it, that fear added to the fun.

Financing my recreational obsession was not problematic. Despite my offers, Dave only occasionally asked for a contribution. My father, a professional gambler, would, from time to time, give me generous cash handouts when he was winning. I supplemented that with odd jobs in the neighbourhood—cutting lawns, cleaning pools and such—when Pops was on a losing streak. Just like now, I never needed a lot of money because I didn't want much. Records and a decent sound system, that was it. Oh, and Levis. And KFC when I was baked.

I didn't get into the commercial end of things, but some of my friends, including Dave, dealt weed which sounds like a lot more criminally sinister act than it was: They sold tiny quantities to a few of their friends. It was like somebody joining a pyramid scheme—sorry, multi-level sales organization—only instead of selling yourself tons of make-up or diet supplements to reach bonus cheques, you got high more cheaply. And especially in the jumpy 70s, you weren't eager to see your grinning photo from some glitzy, rah-rah Las Vegas event in a company newsletter.

My mother, bless her, was either willfully ignorant or just ignorant of what was going on in her basement, apparently buying our excuse that we were burning incense. She didn't press me after my shrug and non-answer to her question about how her butter knives had come to be blackened or why we were looting the fridge at two in the morning.

My father, when he was home, knew exactly what was going on but, on the plus side of his character ledger, said nothing. "Let the boy figure it out on his own" seemed to be his motto. Maybe he fretted and lost sleep over my many questionable choices or maybe he didn't give a good goddamn. I never had the chance to ask him.

Toss me onto a shrink's coach and I could claim that my father's aloofness, which led to his eventual abandonment of the family, was the cause for me to essentially self-medicate throughout high school.

But really, I thought then—and still think—I just liked getting high.

I could always focus my wee brain—even wrote some

pretty good high school essays and bad poetry while fried. But the more pot I inhaled, the more I could feel myself becoming less inclined to do anything that smacked of ambition or hard work. Even though my famous iron-willed self-discipline forbade me partaking in the morning, I spent an ungodly amount of time wasted through my latter high school career. I just wanted to listen to music, giggle, and eat KFC. As worthwhile as these pursuits were, (and still are), I found myself smoking more and enjoying it less. I became concerned when, for a while, I felt I needed to suck down half a joint before I went to bed just to help me sleep. With university looming, I got worried. So, I just quit. I didn't find it difficult to give it up; I had beer as a perfectly good fallback.

I was eased into my abstinence by a summer at the end of high school. Three months hitchhiking around England and Scotland were mostly non-high times.

OK, I dabbled a bit at university—usually in social settings—but found out that a lot of Liberal Arts majors become even more pretentious when they're high. And Beth, who eventually became my wife, wasn't a big fan, so I gave up even occasionally getting bent.

I remember my weed days with neither pride nor regret. It was just something I did that was fun and then I stopped. That's it, that's all.

Things turned out differently for Dave. I lost touch with him after he graduated from high school but knew he had decided to forego university in order to experience "the real world." I went looking for him after a couple of years not hearing from him, armed with a possible address in Toronto's hippie district of Yorkville. This was after the "glory" hippie days and before the neighbourhood had morphed into the current gentrified, expensive hipster enclave.

The seedy, old fourplex was dismal. The scrawny, vacant-eyed dude who answered the apartment door was instantly depressing. And the words he said: "Dave died, man. Last month. Smack OD" were horrifying.

In retrospect, Dave had experienced a sort of "real world." And it had been nothing but tragic.

AS WITH EVERYTHING ELSE, I HADN'T REALLY KEPT UP WITH ALL the developments in the pot business starting with the product. Completely unimaginable back then, the weed was all bud now. Hundreds of different strains coming in all sorts of delivery systems—edibles, smokeables, bakeables, inhaleables, drinkables, salveables. What's your pleasure? We got Bubba Berry, Nigerian Haze, Death Star, Sour Diesel, Gandalf OG, and the ever-popular Purple Monkey Balls. All of them promised different kinds of highs.

This product variety has begotten a legion of experts and

connoisseurs who claimed the talent to distinguish the subtle differences among hundreds of strains. They come off with the same level of pretension as fucking wine snobs. Want to know how crazy it's getting? This level of bullshit over weed is fast approaching the absurdity of fucking "gourmet" water where you have your choice of "dozens of infused water varieties, designed to fit your needs and moods." Those preceding quotation marks are there because, verbatim, that's an actual goddamn sales pitch.

Jesus H. Christ.

With legalization, the floodgates opened. A myriad of companies were hastily formed and just as hastily they scrambled to go public, hoping to reap the cash benefits from wildly overpriced share offerings. I don't know what the pot companies were smoking, (fuck, that's a lazy joke) but the demand never came close to their crazy, self-serving projections which, if you added them all up, more or less predicted an entire continent of stoned citizens wandering around dazed and confused every fucking second of the day. Never mind the imagined market for medicinal pot that, would eliminate the need for doctors and hospitals. Oh, and faith healers.

Scores of cannabis companies were set up to meet this alleged new bonanza of stoners. It was the same as with any brand-new industry. They go from zero to a hundred in a split-second, then fall back to a more sensible speed limit. Remember pocket calculators? There used to be over 60 manufacturers trying to capitalize on the craze of having automatic arithmetic machines you didn't have to haul around in a wheelbarrow. Now there's about three. The same is going to be true for Artificial Intelligence. Now, everybody's a fucking AI company, even though only a handful of people truly understand what it is, does and, more scarily, what it can and will do. All those companies either will go out of business or be snapped up by bigger companies and we'll wind up with a few monster corporations making money by fucking with reality.

The pot companies did what every company does—they grossly inflated the potential market size to include pretty well everybody with a nose and/or a vowel in their name. They neglected to consider that regular potheads already had their own established illegal sources, especially now that possession penalties might be a fine, as opposed to jail sentences that destroyed people's lives.

Despite the claim that legalization would put all the illegal operations out of business, the opposite had happened. While illegal growers and importers—for obvious reasons—don't report their sales to the IRS or the Canada Revenue Agency, estimates put the black market for weed as being at least two to five times larger than the regulated shit. One of the reasons for its size is the different state laws. I learned that, at the street level, $1000 worth of weed grown in California is worth four to five times as much in Florida.

In Canada, where weed had been nationally legal since

2018, there's no big inter-province price disparity, but there remained the violence and mayhem as the bad guys fight over their share of the still-thriving underground commerce.

All in the name of harmless fun for us consumers. Back then, no one ever thought of or talked about the ton o' harm being done just to get the dope to my basement Wrecked Room, as we had christened it. Thousands of people were dying every year as the cartels and gangs jostled over turf and distribution channels throughout Central and South America and across the Caribbean. "Well, how about we forget all that and fire up another blunt?"

The recent near-hysterical plunge into legal weed also attracted a gigantic predator. Government. Smelling the opportunity for windfall tax profits, governments stepped in to regulate how pot was grown, distributed, and consumed. Oh, and taxed.

But any government anywhere that gets involved in any kind of commerce is bound to fuck it up. It's a basic rule of nature.

On previous margarita get-togethers in IRB, Stan had described the host of challenges they faced after they applied and got their legal license to grow and sell. Basically, it was "Cry havoc and let loose the dogs of bureaucracy." Any spanking new industry now requires equally spanking new departments bolted onto the machinery of governing. Licensing stores, regulating THC content, inspecting for purity, evaluating criminal background checks for everybody that worked in the biz, and on and on.

If you're able to navigate the mounds of paperwork and miles of red tape, then you're ready to have government tax the fuck out of your brave new business. In Colorado, the excise tax on cannabis was 15% or five times the retail sales tax for beer. Add on another steep tax if you sent your pot to be converted into gummies and other edibles. And that's not counting local taxes. Nor does include the fact that the federal income tax system does not allow normal business deductions for pot companies.

The longer Stan talked about their government travails, the more amped up he became, to the point that he got red-faced and damn near frothing. Alex and I learned that, like politics and religion, some topics were off the table when tequila was on the same table.

I could see his point, of course. As part of the exchange for legality, he got complication. Nobody likes complication, and this new reality was a far cry from the simpler days when Stan and Laura ran their illicit biz. They built their reputation and repeat customer base by having good weed, accurately weighed, and affordable to the people who sought them out. No cartels had a role— including the biggest cartel of them all: government. No violence, no nastiness, no accounting ledgers, just a pleasant little pastime that paid all their bills—in cash. With enough left over to build a big house bit by bit over the years on the banks of the Gunnison River.

While they didn't run the risk of arrest and imprisonment anymore, they were, at the outset, handcuffed to compete against the illegal grow ops which didn't pay taxes and weren't subject to regulation or quality control of any sort ("Say, buddy, how about a little dab of fentanyl to juice up the proceedings?"). The black marketeers' main overhead expense, after growing or buying and being armed, was a car whose trunk was stuffed with merchandise.

So legals lost to the illegals on price.

Pure and simple. And obvious.

And, somehow for Stan, fatal.

CHAPTER 5

Alexandra, because she excels at these sorts of things, had planned and printed out a proposed route to Gunnison. All in all, just short of two thousand miles and 30-ramp directions. I got the printed version because I don't own a fucking cellphone. Alex went out of her way to point out that my hard copy would be the absolute last, last resort should her phone not work and the calmly confident voice in the car stop talking to us.

I studied the route anyway, knowing full well that I would forget every detail before we actually started driving.

Before we got our motor running and headed out on the highway, I went back to Benny's where Stan had died. Not to revisit the crime scene as my movie was already locked in, but to see if I could get anything useful by talking to people.

Often, I can pick up a scrap of info, some remembered detail, that contributes to the general storehouse of knowledge.

I made sure to go the restaurant at exactly the same time and day of the week when Stan and Laura had visited a scant two weeks earlier. It was a glorious day and the joint's patio was full, the interior nearly empty.

If you want to talk to restaurant staff, go the rear of the building. There's always a spot with a pail or coffee can for cigarette butts and a few staff on break from the hot, whirl-wind madness of a busy eatery.

I walked down the alley, past the murder scene and around the corner where an intersecting alley ran to a side street (the killer's escape route, I saw). Sure enough, there was a young, uniformed guy sitting in the doorway hauling on a lung dart.

"Hey, buddy, sorry to bother you on break but, can I ask you a few questions about the stabbing here a couple of weeks ago?"

"Yeah, OK," he agreed warily.

"Were you were working that day?"

"Yeah, the dead guy was in my section."

"Was it as busy as it is today?"

"About the same. It's always busy these days."

"Any single diners?"

"There was only one I remember."

"But you actually remember him?" I asked, surprised,

given the volume of customers he would have dealt with that day and in the intervening two weeks.

"Yup. Spiffy lookin' fella with a scar. Spent the whole time on his cell. But that's not the only reason he stuck out."

"What else?"

"Credit agencies regularly send out a list of stolen cards. I saw the list days after the killing and the card he used here was on it, with the amount charged and the date it was stolen."

"How the hell would you know that?"

"It was lifted two days before the day I served the guy; I remember the day 'cause it was my brother's birthday. And it was smallest bill any of us wrote up that day. Guy had garlic bread and water, fuck-all for a tip. Cheap bastard."

"Ever seen him before that day? Like, was he a regular?"

"No," he said. "Wait! Was that guy the murderer?"

"Looks like it, son."

"Cool."

Driving back to IRB, a whole new set of considerations sprung to mind. The only way the killer could've known that Stan and Laura would stop at that restaurant was if he had followed them from Indian Rocks Beach to the Dali Museum then up to the eatery. It was unlikely that Stan or Laura would've had any reason to think they were being tailed. Maybe he was even close enough to overhear their decision to grab some lunch on Central Avenue. On the spot, the killer would've improvised his plan and acted. It sounded pretty complicated. But, going by the fact that Stan was dead, it had obviously been doable.

But how? Tear it down, Jake. Look at the individual elements. Would a professional hit man have taken a chance by wandering out to the side street and just casually walking away, certain that no one would give chase? Doubtful. Especially because the killer would've likely been splashed with blood. More probably, a car was waiting on that side street. Now how would the driver have automatically known to park there? He wouldn't. That had to have been arranged *after* Stan and Laura were seated. What had the waiter just told me? The guy was on his phone the whole time. It had to be that the killer was talking to his accomplice about where to position the getaway car.

Conclusion: we were going to be looking for a two-man hit squad.

Back home, I called Quentin again, admitting that it was a long shot but hoping he could reach out to someone in the police department who could tell me about the stolen credit card.

Quentin got back to me that afternoon. The card had been stolen on September 8 in an armed robbery. The cardholder/victim was a William Wayne Fontenot who lived in Tallulah, Louisiana where the robbery took place.

Tallulah, Louisiana. Why did I know that name? Because of Ms. Bankhead, it was a small town that stood out to me along the route that Google picked for us as the quickest way to get to Colorado. Why, the same small Louisiana town that would've been on the reverse of the route that Google would've offered up to Stan's killer, if he was an out-of-towner looking to drive to St. Pete from, say, Colorado.

So that cinched it for me. Stan was dead because of something that happened in Colorado. The killer knew when and where he was in Florida, then followed him to the restaurant in St. Pete where he decided to make his murderous move.

We packed up all of Laura's stuff into her small SUV and struck off.

After a pleasant night in Mobile, we got away early and headed north then west. William Wayne Fontenot was not difficult to find. Shortly after we got on the road, Alex called the number she'd e-found. Above the din of at least two and perhaps ten or more crying children, the beleaguered voice told us that 'Dubya' was at work at Gracie's.

On the I-20 at Vicksburg, we crossed the wide, serpentine Mississippi River into northern Louisiana around noon. Less than a half hour later, we found the exit ramp to Tallulah. Gracie's Storage and Moving was only a few of hundred yards off the highway. In the high-fenced yard filled with rows of low buildings fronted by garage doors and delivery trucks, I parked and entered the regular-sized door with the hand-lettered 'Office' sign.

A formidable-looking woman eventually looked up from the sheaf of papers she was studying. She was a large woman with meaty arms and an unadorned a face that reminded me of a bulldog's, all set off by a faded print dress.

"Hep ya?" she asked, as she rose and labouriously walked towards me at the counter.

"I'm looking for William Wayne Fontenot, ma'am."

"Shoot, nobody calls Dubya that. You one of them process servers?" she asked with suspicious menace.

If I *had* been one of them, I would've instantly denied it.

"No, ma'am," I quickly said. "I was asked to look him up by a mutual friend. Is he here?"

"No, sir. He's where he's always at for lunch: the parking lot behind McDonald's down on Bayou."

"What's he driving?"

Gracie looked at me as though I had just asked how many noses Dubya had.

"Pick-up. F-150. Black, got brass balls."

I was going to ask if her testicular detail was meant to describe the truck or William Wayne, but instead thanked her. Before I could skedaddle out of there, she spoke/growled: "You see him, you tell him to get hisself and his fat ass back here."

I feared for Billy Wayne's physical safety should he

choose to disregard the message I had guaranteed Gracie I'd deliver.

The rear parking lot at McDonald's was almost empty; Alex spotted the truck immediately, not only because it was black but because it had the tell-tale metallic gonads hanging off the rear bumper below the license plate.

I approached the truck and heard music playing. Classical music, of all things—a quiet violin and flute piece. I rapped on the widow, startling the driver who had been reclining in his seat with his eyes closed, grinning like a madman Buddha.

"Dubya?" I said, through the window glass.

"Who's askin'?" was his reply, as he rolled down the window and hoisted himself into a sitting position, the effort of doing so being considerable as he had to have been carrying 350 pounds, maybe more.

"I'm Jake Lydon from the credit card company. We're trying to find the criminal who stole your card and, we think, several others."

He straightened up and, gosh, he was big. Well, big around. Bushy red beard that matched the colour of his thick belly hairs obvious below his stretched, too-short, black AC/DC t-shirt.

"You catch the fucker?" he asked.

"Sorry, not yet. I'm investigating. Do you mind telling me about the robbery?"

"Sure. But there ain't much to tell. I like sittin' here, not inside, so I can listen to my tunes, and I like to eat slow on accounta my doctor tellin' me it helps with the diabetes. It's peaceful and nice. See that?" he said, pointing at the foliage planted in the median by his front bumper. "That there's a banana shrub. Damn, but don't it smell like bananas?"

Dutifully, I walked over to the bush, bent down, and had a whiff. Damn, if it didn't smell like bananas.

"Shame I gotta keep my window rolled up on accounta what happened," he said, shaking his head.

"So, Dubya, can you tell me what went on?"

"Like I told the police, I was sittin' here, like now, and a car pulls up right beside me. Pissed me off 'cause the lot was damn near empty—"

"—What kind of car?"

"Hell, I don't know. Not a truck. Foreign shit all looks the same to me. Silver, one of them SUVs."

"So, what happened?"

"Guy gets out, leans in my window, all friendly like. Wants to know what I'm listenin' to. Then outta nowhere, he flashes this big ol' black huntin'-type knife, says I better hand over my wallet right quick."

"What did you do?"

"Whatja think? I hand over my wallet right quick. Weren't a thing otherwise I could do. He had a look, like he was hopin' I would try something just so's he could fillet my gut."

"Can you describe the guy."

"Ain't likely to forget. Young punk, long blonde hair, big fella. Crazy, hurtful lookin' eyes."

"Anybody with him?"

"Had to be. That big bastard come at me from the passenger side. Didint get a good look at the driver. Sunglasses, black hair mebbe."

"Plates?"

"Not from around these parts. Mostly turkoise with a black cactus stickin' up in the corner, that's all I seen. It booted on outta here. You think you can get him?"

"We're trying."

"Police found the wallet a while later in a dumpster over to the Love's gas station," Dubya continued. "Cash gone. Hardly ever use the sumbitchin' card so I didint know it was gone for a week after, so I couldint cancel it right off. Bunch of charges from Florida; I ain't ever been to Florida. You guys made good on the charges, so thanks for that."

"We aim to please."

"Nuthin' personal, but at 24 per-cent goddamn interest, your aim ain't that precise."

I couldn't argue with him about this modern-day usury.

"You catch up to that guy, you give me five minutes with him, hear?" he snarled.

"You got it, bud. Thanks. Oh, and listen, Gracie wants you back at work."

"Why the hell didint you tell me sooner?" he said, his mean-ass demeanour washed instantly away by a look of dread in his eyes as he hurriedly twisted his key in the ignition and the truck's massive engine roared to life.

"While we're here," I said to Alex, as we watched the black pickup—its testicles appearing to retract—peel out of the lot. "Wanna grab a bite to eat?"

"You barbarian," she answered. "We're in Louisiana, you know, Cajun territory."

"We Canadians settled in the South, if I'm not mistaken."

"All of maybe two hundred and fifty miles from here. For Christ's sake, there's a Cajun restaurant in Framingham, near my place; you really think Louisiana's famous cuisine didn't make it up here?"

To his credit, the teenager at the McDonald's cash seemed personally insulted when we asked for somewhere else to eat. Eventually, he reckoned some real Cajun food could be had at Trapp's, two towns west in Monroe.

Twenty minutes later, we sat overlooking a river in Monroe that, while not as big, was certainly muddier than the Mississippi. Alex had the Cajun salad; I went with a big bowl of Maw Maw's chicken and sausage gumbo, and we split an order of Josie's fried crawfish tails. All wonderful.

Back on my shitty laptop, I figured out how long the likely killers took to get to Tallulah from southern Colorado. About eighteen hours. Two guys driving in shifts straight through could make it in a day, with less than a full day more to St. Petersburg. So, I backed up and estimated—courtesy of, once again, the Google—that there was probably a stolen

Arizona vehicle—or just its distinctive turquoise plates—that had visited Florida recently. But over lunch, we voted to pass on the hunt for a silver SUV in Arizona, reasoning that if Stan's killer was willing to a) kill Stan and b) boost a credit card at knifepoint, he wouldn't likely have been too shy about carjacking.

Alexandra brought up a good point that almost had us change our route.

"If the SUV wasn't stolen, then the killer must be from Arizona. Maybe we should go there."

I thought about it and realized that if we just showed up in the Grand Canyon State, the first question would be: "OK, now what?" We agreed to stay on the road to Gunnison, reckoning that our paid assassin likely drove to Colorado first to get his marching orders and/or to pick up his big blonde killer-in-training.

We passed through the Pelican State and aimed for Dallas. We believed ourselves to be oh so fucking clever at skirting the likely busy downtown freeways by taking the southerly I-30 which looked to be on the outskirts of town. Big mistake. First-off, the highway was real busy with evening rush hour traffic and, secondly, that stretch of road had been christened the Tom Landry Freeway after the buttoned-down former coach of the hated fucking Dallas Cowboys. I contented myself with a discrete forefinger in the direction of their stadium, looming in the distance. I wasn't being all that brave because I suspected a full-fledged, arm-out-the-window gesture would likely have been met with a hail of gunfire.

EVEN THOUGH IT WAS LATE EVENING WHEN WE GOT OUT OF Dallas, we decided to press on, after stopping for a 9:30 pm take-out dinner at, surprise, surprise, a Tex-Mex joint. Alex wasn't in the mood for that cuisine and trotted across the parking lot to national sushi outlet. We were almost too tired to eat as we sat in the car staring at our Styrofoam clam shells.

"Dig in, girl," I said. "Before it gets cold."

That line got a wan smile when, ordinarily, it would've rated at least a polite chuckle.

Dining tip: Maybe avoid late-night take-out fajitas and, I understand from Alex, sushi from a chain restaurant about to close.

Alex was dead tired and willing to dispense with her usual pickiness over hotel choice in favour of a place, any place, with a mattress. For some reason—maybe it was all the dead cow I'd ordered—I was wide awake and wanted to keep going. So, she reclined her seat and instantly fell asleep. Thankfully, she was on the passenger side at the time.

I ploughed on into the largely empty dark West Texas

flatlands and, like the song, made Amarillo by morning (i.e. just after midnight). With my bride comatose, I stopped at a Super 8, figuring I'd bear her wrath the next morning. I led my dozy wife by the hand to our room the way I used to escort my sleepy daughter to bed when she was a toddler.

The next thing I knew, I was awakened by the smell of coffee and a less than gentle jab in the ribs. Alex was raring to go while I was raring to sleep considerably longer than the five hours I'd been granted.

In the light of day, Texas and the corner of New Mexico we nicked were overwhelmingly flat and dry and vast. Driving through what we guessed was Tornado Alley, we spent a good deal of time watching the sky and there was lots of goddamned sky to watch. But we didn't see any dark funnels or flying cows.

Finally, we entered Colorado. The high, craggy, snow-covered Rockies that I was half-expecting to drive through the instant we crossed state lines, were always in the distance.

Those Colorado highway planners sure were a bunch of slackers, I thought. They had always taken the easy routes through flatlands or marginally hilly terrain. But neverthe-less, navigating the twisty Colorado roads required focus after the arrow-straight highways for most of Texas and New Mexico. In those previous states, we just sort of aimed the car and looked around, although, truth be told, there was pretty much fuck-all to see.

CHAPTER 6

A lex was driving and I was gawking when her phone rang. "RMHH Enter" said the display screen. I recognized the number from all the condo sale-related calls between us and Laura. I picked up.

Laura, in the politest way possible, wanted to know if we'd made any progress in arranging shipment of her car because she wanted to lend it one of her sons. I said we were working on it and would let her know the details as soon as we had them. After the call, we stopped and asked the Google where RMHH Enterprises might be located.

They grow the states big out here, I thought. It took longer than I expected but, at last! Signs of civilization (sort of). An Arby's and a McDonald's, that looked the same as they would in Patterson, New Jersey or anywhere else. Traveling through two-stoplight Gunnison, we did see businesses with a more local flavour. The one that stood out as being Colorado as hell was Traders Rendezvous. Its doorway was wreathed in a jumble of white antlers, with rows more of them on the sidewalk in front of the long, low building. It looked like a bleached-out, tangled formation of dead elkhorn coral. I could imagine that some store clerk didn't have much fun bringing in that pointy pile every night at the end of business.

About ten miles west of town, we turned onto an unpaved side road, then passed a row of huge McMansions that were locked in mortal combat with each other to see which was the most ostentatious. Finally, we came to a gate with a wrought iron sign over it reading RMHH Enterprises. We started down the long, dead-straight driveway.

A true compound greeted us at the bottom of a slight hill. There was a sprawling main house, two other smaller homes a few hundred feet away on either side and surrounded by a bunch of outbuildings, sheds and such. At some distance were two very large white Quonset huts, elongated domes that looked like mammoth versions of those maggots you get inside your garbage can on hot summer days.

Our initial reception party consisted of three huge dogs which, as one, had risen from under a tree where they'd been napping and charged the vehicle. One was a German shepherd —Rin Tin Tin's big, crazy uncle. The other two were slightly shorter, squatter, black fuckers with huge heads, jaws, and appropriately large teeth. Apparently oblivious to their size and weight disadvantage, the Hound of the Baskerville times three crowded around our slowly moving car, barking their heads off in unison.

Fearful of hitting one of them, I braked, and we sat there, debating our next move as the dogs, now two-legged, danced around us, flinging spit, pawing at the windows, and still yelling their doggie their heads off.

"Now what?" I asked.

"I think they're friendly," Alexandra said. "I can see their tails wagging."

"It's probably because they're overjoyed to see the big meals Door Dash for Dogs just delivered unto them."

The front door to the main house opened and Laura appeared. As she shouted at the dogs to shut the fuck up, she looked mystified, before she connected her car with her friends from IRB and moved from mystified to completely gobsmacked.

"What the hell are you doing here?" she demanded with a big, big, smile.

"We were in the neighbourhood and we thought we'd drop in with the car that you were on my back about a couple of hours ago," I said, as we staged a clumsy, three-way hug. The dogs wanted to horn in on the action and celebrate with us because that's what dogs do even though they don't know what the fuck's going on. Laura pulled away with tears in her eyes.

"Thank you for coming! You'll stay here with us...me," she said. "Grab your bags!"

We did just that and followed her into the house, after making buddies with the canine monsters.

If you remember *Bonanza*, that great old TV series, then you can picture the main house/shooting set at the Ponderosa ranch. Laura's house was a lot like that (only not in black & white). Honey-coloured logs everywhere you looked, inside and out. Massive, open great room with an equally massive stone fireplace, just like the living room where the Cartwright family spent a whole lot more time than they did ranching. But there was nothing local-looking or rough-hewn about the furniture, which was an eclectic mix of antiques that, thanks to Laura's artistic eye, turned the house into showcase material. Any cheerful colour in the room was supplied by the vibrant colours of the artwork adorning the walls. A chandelier made from white antlers hung down on a heavy chain from the sloped ceiling twenty-five feet above us.

"Get that in town"? I asked.

"You saw that store, did you?"

"Hard to miss. Not a lot like them in Florida."

"We got the raw material there; Stan made the light. He worked his ass off over the years, designing the house, doing a lot of the interior finishing, the plumbing and electric himself."

"Bet he first spent a lot of time watching *Bonanza* re-runs."

"Not a lot of people get that," Laura chuckled. "It was Stan's dream house. We added bits when we could afford it. Took close to thirty years to complete and here it is—more or less. Now leave your stuff by the stairs," she said, pointing the direction through an archway, "And go out to the porch. I'll get drinks."

"I'll help," Alex said, because of course she would.

As instructed, I went through to the large wide screened-in porch. I settled into a comfortable captain's chair and did what I always do: stared at big water. In this case, the Gunnison River lazing along about a hundred feet from the house. Obviously, it was shallow in parts as evidenced by the slight waves and ripples it formed as it coursed over submerged rocks. It was a different story upstream, I had read. There, the river narrowed, creating a powerful current and a series of treacherous rapids that made aquatic travel nearly impossible, except to whitewater rafting tourists eager to die on vacation.

I pledged to myself to get up early and come down to the river where I half-expected to spot Brad Pitt and Craig Scheffer standing knee-deep, casting their fishing lines illuminated golden by the early morning sunlight.

Laura and Alex came out with two big ol' glasses of wine and one regular-sized Coors Banquet and an ashtray.

"I won't be needing that," I said.

"The beer?" she asked in surprise.

"Don't talk crazy, woman! The ashtray."

"Good for you!"

"Maybe. Jury's out."

Then I remembered something.

"Excuse me," I said. "I'll be a while, so bear with me."

From our cooler, I extracted limes, limeade and bottles of Cazadores Reposada and Triple Sec. I went into the kitchen —one of those designer-cook's affairs that Hop Sing wouldn't have known what the fuck to do with—found ice, wine glasses whose rims I salted, and a blender that soon was noisily grinding away after I squeezed the limes and poured the booze in. I poured out the cold, green Mexican fuck-you-up.

Laura was all smiles when I announced that Jake's mobile margarita canteen was open for business and presented her drink.

"God, this reminds me of Indian Rocks," Laura said, after her first sip. Then she started to quietly cry.

Alex got up and hugged her. She pulled herself together.

"I just don't understand it," she said, as much to herself as to us. "Stan could always talk his way out of a jam."

Alex and I looked at each other. Clearing up Laura's confusion was about to get real painful.

"Laura, there's no easy way to say this," I began.

"But we think that Stan was murdered," Alex, the ol' band-aid ripper, quickly added.

"What?!"

"It wasn't a simple dope deal gone bad for no reason," I said. "It was planned."

There wasn't much for us to do beyond look concerned as our news sunk in.

"Who? Why?!" she sputtered.

"We don't know. But somehow, it all starts here," Alex said.

It was difficult not to feel like we were just cruelly piling on with this second announcement.

One of the things I had come to like about Laura was her no-bullshit attitude. She was a lot like Alex in that regard. Visibly, she shook off her stunned disbelief, narrowed her eyes, and insisted on facts, the proof for our hurtful news. I gave her what we had, the unusual goings-on in the alley, the stolen Louisiana credit card used in the restaurant by that alley, the waiter's remembrance, Dubya's statement, and the Arizona license plate.

"Doesn't seem to be much doubt, does there?" she said.

"I'm afraid not. A favour to ask. Well, two. Would you be up to going to the cops here to let them know about what I just told you? It will matter more coming from a local, especially the wife of the victim."

"Certainly. What's the second one?"

"Can you not tell the boys about our suspicion for a bit?"

She got her back up over that, as I expected her to.

"My sons have a right to know what happened to their father!"

"Of course they do, Laura," Alex said. "But they also have the right to the facts. And we don't have them yet."

"So how do you get those facts?" she demanded.

"By getting answers to a whole new set of questions." And for that, we have to poke around here."

"I did ask you to look at it. I just thought it'd be limited to Florida."

At that moment, I figured was as good as any to further question her.

"Are you sure this guy was alone?" I asked.

"Yes. Why?"

"Did you see any tall, long-haired blond guys around?"

"Jake, it's Florida. There are lots of those surfer-type beach boys around. Hell, my son, Johnny, looks like one."

"Here's the standard question I bet you were asked by the cops. Did Stan have any enemies?"

"No...I mean yes. No, the St. Pete police never asked me that. I suppose once we established that we were from out of town, just tourists really, they made their minds up that it was, like you said, a drug deal gone bad. But yes, he had some people pissed at him here."

"Who and about what?"

"We don't exactly know who, but we do know Stan had been creating waves in the industry. He was obsessed with the big illegal growers and astounded they couldn't be rooted out and shut down. The tighter our margins became, the angrier he got."

"I'm betting he just didn't sit around and stew about it."

"Not a chance. At first, he focused on the pop-up stores operating outside the law. He'd drive around to different towns and cities and visit stores. It was easy to call them out. If they didn't have a state license posted in the retail area, they were illegals. And he'd then summon the state or local cavalry to bust them."

"OK, that had to have helped the cause."

"It did. But the operators would just show up with a new store in a matter of a few weeks. What pissed Stan off was the slowness of the response by authorities."

"Why so slow?"

"Because the state police are understaffed and the local cops either looked the other way or didn't consider it all that important. What *really* pissed him off was the fact that these illegal shops were either illegal growers themselves or they were buying from illegal growers. We were told by the Colorado Bureau of Investigation that opening an investigation consumed a lot of money, time, and people, and would only be undertaken if the CBI got a solid lead on the grow ops."

"Stan must've taken that well."

"Nothing happened fast enough for Stan. Jake, he was so frustrated; he wanted the government to do more. I could see his point. After all, the state wants the tax revenue—last year they took in almost as much from cannabis as they collected in booze and cigarette sales tax *combined*. But they don't do enough to crack down on the illegals who don't pay taxes and there's no check on quality, while we have to jump through hoops and pay a lot of tax."

"Seems pretty obvious to me," I said, "that if they choke off that illegal source, it'd drive more people to the legit outfits and produce more tax for them and better profits for you," Alexandra observed.

"Exactly! Not a lot of people know or care that the illegal pot business has exploded; it's probably four or five times larger than all the licensed growers and sellers put together. Storefronts either grow their own like we do, or they buy direct from licensed growers. But not everybody follows the rules. If they can get inventory at half price and their customers are happy, why not? And I don't really blame the consumers. Bargains are bargains."

"Wait, it couldn't be that tough to shut down the grow-ers." I said. "Just sweat the store operators with stiffer penal-ties if they don't give up names."

"Jake, you have to understand that things are different now. The illegal growers are getting nastier and nastier. The store owners know that they could hurt them and their fami-lies far worse than anything the state could do. So they shut up."

"But Stan wouldn't let it go at that, would he?"

"No."

Laura went on to describe the hours Stan would spend finding recent aerial photography in the state, cross-referencing the photos with property records when it looked like there was a possible grow op on the land. Through property records, he'd come up with the landowners' names then call the CBI's Illicit Marijuana Team. Recently, he had been posting those names on social media sites dealing with the industry."

"How'd that go?" I asked.

"He was pleased that shit got stirred up and the police did close down a few grow ops and stores. But then he gave them a bad tip about some storage companies being fronts for weed grows. I think government agencies tuned him out after that. But, overall, he created quite the stir."

"Any threats?"

"A few late-night phone calls over the last couple of months."

"Saying?"

"Saying nothing. Just silence."

"Could Stan have been hiding more direct threats?"

"I don't think so, but he hated to worry me. I do know that."

"Surely, Stan wasn't a lone crusader."

"No, but I bet he was one of the most persistent. And we have an industry association, the Marijuana Industry Group. We pay dues and they lobby government on our behalf. MIG are good folks but, in Stan's opinion, they haven't really pushed the enforcement side enough to seriously hunt down all the illegal growers. Above all, they and us want more investigators, greater police abilities to monitor water or power use, put more eyes in the sky. That sort of thing."

"Through all this," Alex said. "How's your biz doing?"

"Good, I think. I don't have much to do with it, frankly. I'm 75 damned years old and the boys have all jumped in."

"We need to talk to them."

"You suspect one of them?!" she asked, alarmed.

"No, no, no! I just want to get a handle on what they do, who they might have had contact with, what they might have heard on the street...or rural road."

She seemed mollified by my assurances.

"You'll meet Johnny, Greg, and Joe today."

"Those are some kind of all-American names."

Laura explained they were christened in honour of Messrs. Winter, Lake, and Walsh, respectively.

"Stan really liked good guitar players," she said.

"Did you tell them why we're here?" Alex asked.

"*I* didn't know exactly why you were here. I'll tell them I invited you and you wanted to bring the car back."

"Before the meet n' greet, can you tell us about them?" I asked.

Unconsciously I'm sure, Laura provided us with character sketches of her three boys in descending order of age.

"Joe's the eldest. He's always been the studious one, smart as a whip. When he was just a teenager, he used to follow his father around, learning how he did things when, you know, we were... a little outside the law."

"A little?"

She smiled.

"That's how I like to remember it. Anyway, Joe earned his four-year business degree in three. Passed the exams—first try—and became a full-fledged Chartered Public Accountant. His dad and I took three shots each at getting our papers. He hung out his own shingle in town for a while and did very well for himself. But soon after legalization, Stan asked—begged, really—for Joe to come out here and sort through all the new things we had to deal with. I'm not criticizing the other two, but Joe's the brains of the operation. There's no detail, big or small, that he doesn't have his eye on. And he frets over all the government red tape and paperwork. Sometimes, I worry that he worries too much, but he's proud we're fully compliant with the law.

"We were delighted," she continued, "when he decided to join us out here and build beside us. He's got a wonderful wife, Cynthia—she's a teacher—and my two precious grandchildren, Scarlett and Zoe. I take care of them in the afternoons; they just started half-day kindergarten in the morning."

"How about Greg?"

"Ah, Greg, our middle boy. I don't know where he gets it from, but he's a natural-born salesman. That boy was always selling something. When he was a kid, he conned me into making sheets of cookies and pitchers of lemonade. He set up a stand near the big shed and sell his products to the potheads who Stan trusted to come out here to buy our weed. In junior high, we caught him "borrowing"—as he put it—some pot we were growing to sell to his classmates. He was always popular and the class clown, but not very serious about his studies. After high school, he left home, saying he was going to Denver. I'll always remember his line when we asked him why: "More people to sell more shit to." Hard to keep track of all his jobs he held over those seven or eight years. He was a bartender. He worked in an electronics store, sold insurance, timeshares, TV advertising, he even leased luxury aircraft. Overall, I think he was doing well, but he jumped at the chance to come home and work with us. We were thrilled when he built out here last year. He's married to Elena, a local girl and a real sweetheart. No kids yet, but I'm pushing."

"And Johnny?"

"My baby. He was lost for a bit. After high school, he went to Hawaii on vacation and stayed for about six years."

"Like you and Stan did in Mexico."

"Yes, smartass. We didn't really have an idea what he was doing there beyond just bumming around. We didn't have much contact with him. The odd e-mail or phone call. He always sounded upbeat, said he was doing well at the University of Hawaii, but the truth was he had dropped out in the middle of his sophomore year. I know we had to send him money from time to time while he did whatever it was he did. We thought he had grown tired of that life but when he came back to Colorado, he was equally shiftless, you could say."

"Fell in with the wrong crowd?"

"Jake, I'm not that blind. He *was* the wrong crowd. But eventually, he got his life together. He worked hard at Colorado State to finish the Horticulture degree he'd started in Hawaii, then he passed a series of tests. Now he's allowed to call himself a Master Grower. That isn't just a proud mama's description of her youngest son; it's an official designation, a high-status rank in the business, like Master Brewer. You have to know what you're doing. Johnny lives in town near the store. He lives with a woman."

"Who has a name, I bet."

"Charlize. Honestly, I don't much care for her; she's so… flighty. But he seems happy."

"Why hasn't he moved out here?" Alex asked.

"He's a sociable person. He likes being around people, especially because he's out here all day alone with *his* plants."

"Doesn't he spend much time with his brothers or his mother?" Alexandra asked.

"Not really. He was always close to his dad; they spent a lot of time together with the farming before Stan became obsessed with his hunt for illegal growers. But now, Greg's on the road a lot or at the store and Joe has a family. And Johnny knows I have my art—and my grandkids."

I ASSUME THEIR PRESENCE WAS REQUESTED BY MOMMA AS ALL three sons showed up that evening, all looking none too pleased to be there, as if they were children being forced to go to church or meet a long-lost great aunt.

Like every family everywhere, the siblings were far from similar.

Joe was the eldest and the spitting image [Mid-Sentence Sidebar: What does gobbing up saliva have to do with close resemblance?] of a younger Stan. Like his father, he was slight, about 5'8", maybe 145 pounds. He seemed quiet and reserved, peering through thick, round glasses. To a fan of stereotypes, it would be no surprise that his job in the family business was running the accounting function. Dressing in different tones of brown didn't exactly scream wild man either.

We then were introduced to Greg, the middle child. Like his name, he appeared to be gregarious as hell, with a big, welcoming smile and a powerful handshake. About the same height of Joe, he was far stockier and a whole lot better dressed. Again, true to form, Greg constituted RMHH's Sales

& Marketing department. He also was in charge of the farm's storefront operation in Gunnison.

Johnny, the youngest, was the least similar of the three. Broad-shouldered and large, a couple of inches taller than my six feet, he had a boyish round face and long blonde hair, unlike his brothers who wore theirs dark and short. Johnny was the company's head of production, a department that consisted of him.

"Our Master Grower," Laura said proudly of the baby of the family.

"Cool shirt," Johnny said as he shook my hand, but I was humbled. My pale orange and white number did have an intricate floral design, but the overall effect was muted next to his, a bright red number with a wild collection of colourful lizards and parrots.

"Cooler shirt," I said.

All three boys were polite. I couldn't read Greg through his perpetual half-smile and Johnny seemed intrigued by us. Joe, on the other hand, wore the expression of someone who had been weaned on a pickle.

After the boys left, we had a nightcap with Laura. Judging by the rounds of infectious yawning, we were all exhausted and packed it in quickly. Laura showed us the guest room and Alex and I were soon enveloped in the soft mattress and thick comforter.

"So, what's the plan?" Alex, keener that she is, wanted to know.

"Sleep."

"Tomorrow, ya big goof. What are we going to do tomorrow?"

"Steal Johnny's shirt."

"Anything else?"

"We have to get more out of Laura."

"You think she's holding something back?

"Probably not intentionally. Could be a detail she didn't think mattered. You want the job talking to her."

"Yeah, I do. I'm pretty sure she won't want to murder me. But you....?

"Yeah, that's a coin toss. We also have to interview the boys in depth. And their wives or girlfriends. All separately. Wanna pick one?

"I pick them all. How about you focus on the illegal pot business and go charging off. I'll stay around here and do something useful."

Why not, I thought. Alexandra is smarter than me, a helluva lot more tactful, and people like her.

"Fine. But, only on two conditions," I said.

"Which are?"

"One: about the interview subjects. I want to talk to Johnny because there's something appealing about him, and I need to understand the agricultural ins and outs. Oh, and I just changed my mind about Laura; we should talk to her together."

"And the second condition?"

"When you can, record the conversations, like you did with that hedge fund asshole last year."

"You don't trust me."

"Well, of course I do, touchy one. But I've done a bunch of these. They have a shape. It depends on who's answering. Their tone, their pauses, what they emphasize, some details they leave out that beg for follow-up, on the spot or later. We need to be sure of what *exactly* was said and how it was said."

Just before sleep arrived, I thought of Stan. Intelligent, feisty, and fearless sprung to mind as top-line descriptors of the man I knew. The man who died two thousand miles away from his beloved compound and the comfortable life that he had built with his family.

And that led to contemplation of the sons of bitches who had snuffed out that life. Back up, Jake. Why would they go to all the trouble of sending hitmen to Florida when they had to know where Stan lived in Colorado? The answer was simple and smart: kill on your home turf and the first suspects the police would look at would be the names on Stan's published shit list or anybody else he was needling. Stage what looked like an unrelated one-off dope deal on the other side of the country, and you deflect attention.

Whoever we were dealing with was, for sure, goddamn cunning.

The next morning, Alexandra got up and, after a quick cup of coffee, was eager to go walking. I was eager not to, as I needed at least two cups to join the living, maybe ten to charge me up for any sort of exertion. I never completely understood this compulsion of hers to march all over the goddamn place, especially first thing in the morning, and when there was always a good car around.

But so I didn't understand it? So what? I didn't need to. One of the beauties of getting married late in life was that each of us were completely set in our ways. Neither of us had a to-do list that included changing their partner "for the better." We might make small concessions to our spouse but, in the main, we respected—or at least tolerated—the other's choices, habits, and character quirks, while mercilessly mocking them. One rule: Just be funny. I could never get enough of Alexandra's deep, rich laugh, even if the joke was at my expense.

With Alex having a full slate of interviews on her agenda, I decided it was time to dive into the illegal pot business. I might find a way into it. At the very least, I'd learn something. But maybe I could work my way into the operation, rise to become the right-hand man, all the while collecting solid evidence to turn my mole operation into an explosion of arrests that grabbed national headlines and eventually would be featured in a Netflix true crime series.

Nah.

That's not quite what happened.

CHAPTER 7

First up on the agenda was a cover story. If I was going to be asking a bunch of questions, then I had to assume a bunch more would be coming back at me in return. I couldn't just be an aging hippie looking for a cheap stone.

I hit on the notion that I represented a small out-of-state operation looking for enough weed to make it financially appealing to them but not so much they'd smell competition. It had to be based in a state they likely would have no presence or interest in.

The internets suggested North Dakota as my likely fake origin. Tough laws, tough punishment and far enough away as to be inconsequential.

I couldn't see going undercover in Gunnison (population: 6695). About an hour west of Gunnison, the town of Montrose was three times the size.

With cash in my pocket, I drove to Montrose, parked near the downtown section and just kinda loitered, looking for a likely prospect.

For decades, I hadn't approached a stranger for anything more than the time or directions to the nearest bar or bathroom. On vacation, it cuts the other way. You can't go to an island without being incessantly approached by someone selling weed [Sidebar: Asterix for Cuba. Yeah, it happens, but not often and even then, it's often a local cop looking to put the *mordita*—the little bite—on tourists who fork over cash because they have the imagination to visualize what the inside of a Cuban prison looks like.]

I walked up to a guy smoking and hanging out against a brick wall near a street corner. I figured he might know where to score. He was average build, well-dressed, maybe forty. What stood out was his long curly brown hair—about my length—at a time when men his age often start losing theirs and either keep it short or shave it all off. Or they get shorn of their locks because they're trying to "act their age," whatever the fuck that means.

Also noticeable was what he didn't have. A ball cap. All the males and some females walking by him and all those I'd seen passing through Gunnison seemed to be sporting different ball caps. That gave me the impression that the local amateur baseball and softball leagues were incredibly well-organized and popular.

"Say, man," I whispered. "Sorry to bother you, but I'm new to Colorado. Know where I can get a puffy?"

"Try the store about three blocks up, that way. It's called Buddy's. You can't miss it."

"I don't want to pay those goddamn prices, man. What a rip-off!"

"How much you looking for?"

"A couple of hundred bucks worth."

"That'll get you an ounce of primo bud. You got the money?"

"Right here," I said, patting my pants pocket.

"I might know somebody. Give me your phone number."

"Don't have a cell. They can track you with that, you know."

He thought for a bit.

"Go over to that park over there. Have a seat and wait."

"For how long?"

"Long enough to get what you want."

"Alright. Look, if it's good, how can I get some more?"

"Oh, it's good. And I'll be around."

"No, I mean *a lot* more."

"What are we talking about?" he asked, staring a little more intently now that I appeared to be a notch above the aging slacker/stoner category I had originally presented as.

"Twenty pounds," I said. "To start."

That got his attention right quick. His eyes narrowed. I was about to be vetted.

"Where you from?" he asked.

"North Dakota."

"Canada's just north of that. Why bother with Colorado?"

"I got a buddy pulling five years at the state pen in Bismark after he got caught at the border making a run down from Winnipeg."

"Where exactly are you from?"

"Grand Forks."

"What the hell is in Grand Forks?"

"Absolutely nuthin'."

"So how are you gonna move that weight?"

"There's nuthin' in Grand Forks except North Dakota State. And ten thousand college kids facing a fucking long cold winter. It'll move."

"And you have access to them?"

"I work on campus—heating and cooling division. Word got out. Now, I can't meet demand. Put it this way: A lotta kids seem to show an interest in the power plant. They know where to find me."

He wanted to know how in hell I wound up in Montrose looking for quantity. And why I picked him for a connection.

"Pretty well chose Montrose by putting a pin in a map. I was looking for someplace way out of the way in a legal state. And you kinda look like somebody who might know where to get pot."

"Alright. You head over to the park; I gotta call to make."

"Before I do that, can you actually get twenty pounds?

"I think so."

"Price?"

"Fifteen K per."

"Ouch. Maybe it's smarter for me to go somewhere else."

"Good luck with that. We're the only game for at least two hundred miles around."

"OK, how about a volume discount? Say, thirteen thousand?"

"Fourteen and we have a deal."

We shook hands, all proper and normal.

"Name?" he asked.

"Jeff."

"Jeff what?"

"Jeff's good enough for now. And yours?"

"Be here Monday, Jeff," he said as he turned and walked away.

It was pleasant sitting in the park. The day was chilly, but the sun beat bright. I was there for maybe twenty minutes, watching what few people and pigeons were hanging around, when a young clean-cut guy in a dark grey suit and carrying a briefcase meandered up to me. He sat down at the other end of the bench.

"Jeff?" he asked.

I nodded and asked him his name.

"Benj-" he started to say in that automatic way we all trade basic information. He caught himself and stopped. He snapped open the briefcase on his lap.

"Put the money in this folder," he instructed, as he slid a lumpy file folder over to me.

I made the exchange, trying to hide the flattened baggie as best I could with my hand. For a nano-second, it struck me that this was the kind of deal that had cost Stan his life, but I relaxed because we were out in the open and Benjamin's face didn't feature a facial scar.

"So, that guy I first talked to—what's his name again?"

"I bet he didn't say."

"Right. Anyway, that guy. He a heavy hitter around here?"

'Benj' sort of laughed. "Have a nice day," he said, which wasn't close to being an on-topic answer to my question. He got up to leave and I said thank-you. He looked at me puzzled. Apparently simple consumer etiquette hadn't made it to the world of illegal weed deals.

I was oddly exhilarated and not oddly self-congratulatory by this successful piece of business as I had resurrected a behaviour I hadn't practiced in almost fifty years. Like riding a bike, I thought, only high.

As I drove back to Laura's, I realized that it hadn't exactly been a back alley of a transaction. Deals were bound to be a little looser in a legal state. But it was scripted and controlled, and I was sure my original unnamed contact was watching. A phrase the guy used also bothered me: "*We're* it for about two hundred miles around," he had claimed. Had he built a monopoly for that huge area or had he been given a sales territory by whomever was the other part of the "we"?

Back in Gunnison, the first thing I did was go out to the grow houses and ask Johnny to test it.

"Did you try it?" he asked.

"No."

"Where'd you get it?"

"Guy in Montrose."

"Long brown hair?"

"That's the guy."

"Fuckin' Pete," Johnny said after he sort of harrumphed.

"You know him?"

"Yeah, but not really. We were pretty tight a while ago, when I first got back from Hawaii. We got high a lot, went hunting or just hung around. A few years ago, I gave up weed, hunting, and just hanging around, while Pete got more and more into selling. So that was that for our friendship. I haven't talked to him or seen him for must be four years, maybe five. And I'm good with that."

"There's a line in *Tequila Sunrise* that sort of sums up your situ-"

""Maybe friendship just wears out*like*everything else.*Like tires*,"" Johnny recited with a huge grin.

"Great film."

"No keeding, bud-dee," he said, doing a swell impersonation of Raul Julia's Mexican drug lord in that fine movie.

My turn to grin. Shared enthusiasm with a stranger for a book, an obscure album, an underappreciated film always delights me. It's like a secret code that lets you circumvent all the bullshit small talk by creating an instant connection, some commonality that you both appreciate.

Johnny readied his testing apparatus then fed a sample into his pro-looking equipment. But first, he weighed my purchase.

"How much do you think you bought?"

"I asked for an ounce."

"You got just over three-quarters of an ounce."

"Fuck."

"What'd you pay?"

"$200."

"Ouch."

We shot the shit while waiting for the test results.

I always like listening to someone who loves their work. Their enthusiasm and conviction impress me. It was pretty plain that Johnny was that kind of person. Class was in session as Johnny delivered a tutorial for Cannabis 101 in thorough, mind-numbing detail.

I said I liked listening, not that I ever actually absorb much knowledge. My eyes glazed over, as if I had been smoking weed instead of hearing Johnny talk about it. Sativa versus indica strains, how he culls male plants in favour of the more productive females. How he prunes for a bigger bud yield or how he gets maximum THC levels, optimum light and water and on and on.

His test machine beeped, and Johnny withdrew the printed report.

"Inferior," Johnny sniffed. "Really low THC content—less than 8%. You'd have to smoke a lot of this stuff just to get a little buzz. If I had to bet, it was an outside grow in shitty soil and harvested too early."

"So, all the way around, Pete fucked me."

"Looks that way. Happens all the time. Should I point out that there's a lot more and better stuff right outside your door or should I just shut the fuck up?" he asked with a smile.

"I'm a moron. It was an experiment. And, yes, you should shut the fuck up."

He laughed, not a polite chuckle but a genuine, warm laugh.

"Mind if I keep this...for further testing?" he asked.

"Sure...Listen, is this Pete guy dangerous?"

"He is, if you listen to him tell it. I never saw it. But he does have a temper."

So, I had been ripped off. Bummer, as we used to say, and I still do. Not only did I get zero information, but I had also spent a couple of hundred bucks for something with about the same kick as oregano. I was surprised, because this Pete guy knew I was looking to buy a pile of the stuff. Do I go back to Montrose on Monday and confront him? Maybe, I thought, he sold me shit to see how savvy I was. And if smoking this weed was slightly more powerful than smoking lawn clippings, why did Johnny want to keep it?

Christ, I've got a suspicious mind.

As I was leaving the grow house, Laura was just pulling

into the yard. I greeted her when she got out of the car. Boy, oh boy, was she pissed off. She'd driven to Montrose after I had. Apparently, the local cops didn't jump when she laid out the evidence that Stan's death was a deliberate homicide and that the likely killers came from Colorado. All they said was that they'd look into it.

"Waste of time!" she fumed. "I got a desk sergeant who just went through the motions of taking down the statement. She looked so bored, for God's sake! Four hours total there and back and...and...I got a fucking speeding ticket on the way back!"

I then reported to Alex about the entire fruitlessness of my adventure and Laura's tale of police disinterest. She bore the brunt of my frustration.

"We're not getting anywhere with this," I groused. "And it's pissing me off!"

"Take it easy, Jake. We just started. And you got me on the case."

"Answers, we need answers."

"Maybe we haven't asked all the right questions."

"I know, babe. You figured out the mining scam last winter, remember? That was a big deal because if you don't get to the 'why' of a case, you got shit."

"But we already know the 'why' this time out," she noted. "To silence Stan mouthing off about the illegal grow ops. And we have the 'how'—a paid killer with a knife."

"Fine, but what kind of business were they protecting?

How big does a business have to be that somebody decided to eliminate Stan and then gave the order to someone else to do it?"

"Maybe it was the same guy."

"Doubtful it was the guy doing the growing. Unless he was a former Navy SEAL. Quentin more or less confirmed that it was a pro. And we know, through Dubya in Louisiana, that he had a partner."

"About that..."

"I was wondering who was going to bring it up first."

"I hate to say it, but Johnny does fit Dubya's description," Alex ventured.

"Not a chance it was him!"

"It's easy enough to check if he went missing for a few days recently."

"I wouldn't even bother. Dubya said the guy with the knife had "crazy, hurtful-looking eyes." That ain't Johnny. I just spent some time with him. No way he's having a hand in his father's death."

"So, we're going to trust your hunch?"

"Not a hunch. The eyes have it."

"OK, so how do we find two professional hitmen?"

"Beats me. What kind of circles do you move in that you can even get close to these people? Because you sure as shit don't leaf through the Yellow Pages and look under Professional Assassins?"

"Sorry, but you really are out of touch," she said, laughing. "There are no yellow pages anymore."

"Really? That's terrible! I suppose next you'll tell me they're phasing out rotary phones or that brightness switch for your headlights on the floor beside the brake pedal."

I thought for a bit; it didn't take long for the questions to start tumbling out of my wee brain.

"What kind of money is at stake? How many people are involved? Did Stan have specific information on one particular operation? Who did he tell? Where are the cops in all this? Who might we be up against? Are they as big as Pete suggested they were? For those answers, we gotta talk to people...and not get hurt while we're doing it."

A thought then occurred to me. An obvious one that should've turned up in my wee brain a long time ago, one that I'm almost embarrassed to tell you about.

"How the hell did the killers know Stan was going to be in Florida? And how did they know exactly when and where in Florida?"

"That's fine if you want to sit around all day asking yourself questions. But while you were out getting ripped off, I actually did something," Alexandra said. "I had a nice long chat with Joe."

"Oh, do tell."

"It's probably better if you just listen to the recording I made, as you instructed, sir."

But first, she set the scene. Apparently, Joe seemed

harried, almost irritated, when he answered the door. He led her through his showpiece of a house to his office. Like the rest of the place, it was neat. Really neat, with not so much as a loose piece of paper on his big oak desk.

"You think *I'm* OCD about tidiness," she said.

"You are."

"Joe seems to agree with me that everything has its place."

"Hey, I think so too, lady. And that place is wherever the fuck I decided to put it down."

Oh, she wanted to argue; I could tell. But then she realized the complete and utter pointlessness of debating my habits—honed over sixty-five years to slovenly perfection. She started the recording instead.

The first ten minutes or so of their conversation were fucking boring. They talked about business in general. Alexandra spoke his language and after some apparent initial reluctance, they were soon jibber-jabbering away about losses caried forward, interest swaps, currency exchanges and so forth.

But eventually, talk turned to the pot industry when Alexandra asked how, specifically, RMHH Enterprises was doing.

"It's tough out there," Joe admitted. "We have a series of threats that seem to be compounding all at once."

"Such as...?"

We supply three dispensaries. Ours here and stores in

two other towns. If we have a bad crop year—a disease or something—like we did three years ago—they buy somewhere else. The indoor quality slips, word gets out, and we're in trouble. And always there's the price point. Other wholesalers are just as squeezed as we are. This product of ours doesn't last forever—even frozen. Two years, tops. If there's a glut, like there is now, prices go down and the vise gets tighter."

"Has there been a decrease in market demand?"

"Some. We used to have pot tourists coming up from New Mexico, Nevada, Arizona. Now, they can get it in their own state because it's legal. Why would they drive here?"

"So, you've lost all your weed tourism?"

"Not yet. We still get a trickle of them from up north or east—Wyoming, Nebraska, Utah, and Kansas—but they're pretty small markets. Not enough to make a big difference."

"What are the other threats?"

"Do-It-yourself-ers who grow and cure their own. The law allows them to grow six plants per adult. More than enough to fill your needs for a year if you know what you're doing. With the Internet, they can figure it out. And if they're growing their own, they aren't shopping with us."

"On the expense side, it can't be cheap for you to run the store with rent, salaries, pot accessories, inventory, taxes," Alex noted.

"You left out compliance costs and business license. I've been trying to convince mom to close the store. Its overhead costs are a drain, and, in its best years, it barely breaks even. But she wants to keep it. So does Greg; we have to be seen, he claims. Neither he nor Johnny understand the numbers, except the ones on their pay cheques. We were among the first to open. We had great margins back then, but that kind of profit is long gone. Across the state, there's a glut of product and stagnant demand for it. Right here, there are now five legal pot stores in a town of seven thousand people. So, the predictable has happened and everybody hurts, until the newcomers fail. Or we fail."

"It's that serious?"

"It's that serious. Even employee theft has become a factor. Typically, it's 2 to 3% of gross sales. We need it to be zero. Our margins are getting smaller so losing 3% of our revenue hurts."

"What about all the government red tape and paperwork?"

"Sometimes, it's a pain in the rear end and it takes a lot of my time, but we're happy to comply. After all, it is law."

"I'm surprised you haven't mentioned the effects of the illegal growers on your business," Alexandra says.

"They have their customers; we have ours. That threat is overblown."

There's a lengthy pause in the recording. Alex stopped it and told me that she was expecting Joe to say more but he didn't, so she prodded him.

"So, your father was wrong in going after the illegals?"

"Let's just say, he was...misguided."

"What has to happen to improve the business?"

"It's clear to me—and I've always had a better handle on the business than anyone else, including dad—that we control our own future. As long as Johnny ups the quality and Greg increases the success rate of his sales and marketing, we'll be fine."

Alex stopped the recording again to tell me that at this point, Joe became distracted, staring at his computer screen. Alex said she took the hint that the discussion was over. She got up to leave.

She re-started the recording.

"Now let me ask you a question," Joe said. "Mom told us you were here to look into my father's death. How is that going?"

"We're just starting really. We wanted to get a handle on the situation here first."

"Well, good luck. Now if you'll excuse me..."

Alex thanked him for the chat.

She stopped the recording again and put her phone away.

"So, overall, waddya think?" she asked.

"Who says rear-end?"

"Anything else, master?"

"He wasn't being unfriendly, just reasonable, straight ahead. Him identifying the current squeeze on the weed market fits the research I did. Colorado was first out of the gate in North America, opening its first stores in 2012. Predictably, those were the days, my friend, when their bong overflowed with high margins and a lot of foot traffic. Did anything else jump out at you?"

"He doesn't seem to have a lot of respect for Greg or Johnny."

"Yeah, I found it odd to tell a stranger that his brothers weren't doing their part."

"And I'm confused. Joe doesn't seem to think the illegal growers are a big deal while his own father was obsessive about stopping them," Alex noted.

"It bugged me too. Let's side with Stan on this one. It wasn't just his personal "misguided" obsession. Some bad people thought it was a big enough deal to kill him over it."

CHAPTER 8

From a distance of two thousand miles, I still kept up my habit of tracking major storms in Florida. It was the height of the Atlantic hurricane season, and the skies were not quiet that month, my friend. Not that me fretting about it could have any impact on weather patterns (at least, I don't think it would), but I was unable to get beyond worrying.

The Indian Rocks locals always cited an alleged ancient Indian prayer being answered as the reason why the town had been spared from the ravages of big wind and water. They'd point to the fact that IRB hadn't been hit by a major hurricane in more than a century as evidence that the celestial pleading of the Tocobaga Indians in the late 17th century worked. This was just before that particular tribe of Native Americans was virtually wiped out by white men's diseases and Spanish guns. Apparently, their prayers to stave off those menaces hadn't been answered.

But whatever the reason, the Clearwater-St. Pete area had been lucky so far. A named storm made landfall two days earlier, south of Fort Meyers. It had rolled unopposed across the flat state before exiting on the Atlantic side. In its path, widespread flooding and a bunch of mobile homes turned to kindling. Another storm was now tracking across the Caribbean, forecasted to become a Category 2 hurricane as it took dead aim at the Florida panhandle north of us.

I breathed a little easier for the moment and felt more focused on the illegal business at hand.

I WENT BACK TO MONTROSE ON MONDAY, DETERMINED TO ACT the outraged consumer returning damaged goods to a manufacturer. But quietly. I didn't think either of us would appreciate a scene on a street corner. Pete was there, smoking and lounging around the same street corner. He wasn't alone this time.

Affixed to his arm was a slight, pretty woman with frizzy black hair, ruby red lipstick, and startling green eyes. Equally startling were the number of tattoos on her slender arms, hands, and neck, forming an inked tapestry of symbols and figures. There were Asian characters that I assumed translated to beef with broccoli in clam sauce. A green and yellow snake slithered down one arm while a black panther crept up the other shoulder, a front leg and paw extending up her neck and threatening to rip her face off.

As I'm in the midst of full-blown old fartiness, and I'm chauvinistic enough and shallow enough, I have yet to become accustomed to seeing all that ink on a human female canvas, regardless of how artistic the design. I'm old enough, to infer all sorts of sketchy things about heavily decorated human skin. Yeah, I know I was profiling her, something I hate when it happens to me.

"What the fuck was up with the bad shit you sold me?" I whispered angrily to Pete.

Instead of an argument, I got an apology.

"Sorry, dude, there must've been a mix-up with that guy in the park."

And with that, he produced a small baggie from his pants and slipped it to me.

"Hope this makes up for it," he said.

"It doesn't."

To my surprise, he took out his wallet and peeled off a hundred bucks. I nodded my satisfaction with the compensation package.

"I'm glad you showed up," he continued. "I wanted to tell you we aren't going to sell to you."

"Why not?"

"We made a business decision."

"What business decision?"

"The kind you don't need to hear about."

"Why don't I ask Benjamin if I can make a deal with you folks?"

"He told you his name?"

"Sort of."

"It doesn't matter. Benjamin no longer works with us. We're done here. Have a nice fuckin' life," he said as he pushed off from the wall and disappeared down the street, his unintroduced girlfriend still clinging to his arm.

Well, shit. That was a few days and two hundred bucks —well, a hundred bucks—wasted, I thought as I drove back while a bunch more questions ricocheted around my wee brain. Along with few solid assumptions, chief of which was, evidently there was some manner of an organization involved and not just a couple of guys selling home-grown. *We* made a *business decision*. Fancy talk if it just two guys and it sounded like he had been given a talking point. And why had they refused my business? Did they suspect I was a cop? Could it be because they couldn't meet my quantity request? Or was it the fact that they knew that most of their inventory was crap and a guy like "Jeff" was bound to find out right from the jump? And what the hell happened to Benjamin? Did he get fired for substituting shitty weed and keeping the good stuff for himself to sell on the side? If he had been canned for doing that, would he be worth looking up for more info on the operation?

Yet again, I had assembled enough questions for a week of *Jeopardy* and was still no closer to some answers.

"I'll take What the Fuck is Going On for $200, Alex," I said out loud.

I was also struck by what amounted to a genuine apology from Pete for doing the dirty on me. It was almost refreshing. Not enough people say they're sorry and mean it when they fuck up. I am puzzled why just about every well-known figure in sports, entertainment or politics who issues a public apology for their shitty behaviour can't finish a simple goddamned sentence. They say: "I am sincerely sorry," but they leave out "that I got caught."

Of late, they add some version of "This is not the person I am," when, in fact, it is *exactly* the person you are because... well, you did it! It's often followed by "I made a mistake." Stating that Bozeman and not Helena is Montana's capital is a mistake. Slugging a woman while the CCTV cameras are rolling or embezzling donor money from a charity is not.

Then comes the "I will immediately seek professional help for my gambling/substance abuse/anger management issues/criminal behaviour" because my PR handlers told me to say that. I do wish they'd conclude their public mea culpas with another honest statement: "Please forgive me as I will work hard to convince you to not reduce or eliminate my contract value/sales/acting career/electoral chances."

And yet here I was, getting an apparently sincere apology. And from a criminal, no less. Why didn't he just tell me: "Tough shit. Now fuck off"? It's not like I'd be running to the Better Business Bureau or Yelp. "Product not as advertised. Overpriced. Inferior quality. Surly customer service. Will not return. Half a star."

I took the compensation pot out to Johnny. He thought it was the real deal just by looking at it but agreed to test it after handling some urgent gardening issues that had just cropped up (a little horticultural humour there).

It seemed pretty obvious to me that approaching street level dealers wasn't the way into the renegade grow ops. If Montrose Pete wasn't bullshitting me, every low-level vendor within a three-hour drive worked for him. I could waste a whole lot more time trying find a way into that world with no guarantee of success. Or I could smarten the fuck up. Rather than wandering around blindly (my standard operating procedure), I should get a clearer general snapshot of what was going on in Colorado and what law enforcement was doing about it. And for that, I needed to talk to the cops.

I knew how this was going to go. I would be referred to their public communications department who would get a sign-off (hopefully) and call me back (hopefully) with an interview subject.

On my call, I was eventually referred to Alicia Witt, an extremely pleasant Information Officer. In the PR echelon, information officers rarely are allowed to decide to do things;

they carry out what other people with better business cards have decided to do. But I had to start there. And, as I said, she was extremely pleasant to talk to.

I explained that I was a field researcher for Stephen Golding, you know, that famous, best-selling true crime author. Mr. Golding was now investigating illegal cannabis growers in North America for his next book. His premise was to shed some light on just why the foreign cartels and organized crime were still in the marijuana biz when more and more states—and all of Canada—had legalized it. Mr. Golding thought it'd be a swell idea to start with the state that legalized it first, believing that they'd have the best idea of how these illegal grow ops had flourished, managing to build sophisticated operations with millions, perhaps billions of dollars at stake.

I obviously touched a nerve right off the bat in that charming way I have.

"What can I tell you?" she said, wearily. "We're doing all we can to stop them."

I quickly told her that I would play it any way they wanted: for deep background or for attribution. I assured her that this wasn't going to be a smear job on Colorado law enforcement. Rather, it was meant to publicize the lack of resources and provide a better understanding of what just the heck the realities were. I also offered up the names of FBI Agent Tasker in Tulsa and Special Agent Vanessa Turner in Tampa to at least note that they knew me, (regardless of how unpleasant their encounters with me had been).

The go-to these days with media relations departments is to ask that you submit a list of questions which they will allegedly answer within some undetermined period. If they do respond, there then will be the inevitable back and forthing, because no government department on the face of the planet *exactly* answers the questions you asked. Time passes with the secret hope on their end that the story will just fizzle out because a lot of government departments encourage their public information offices to not make information public.

So, Ms. Witt did just that, giving me her e-mail to send my questions that would, she assured me, be answered "promptly." I knew promptly was a government code word for "when hell freezes over."

"I don't want to be insulting," I said. "But I would much prefer to talk to an active officer from the Illicit Marijuana Unit within the CBI, anybody you might have in Southern Colorado—I'm calling from Gunnison. In my research in the past, I've found that the best approach is to talk to field officers. They're on the ground and can give me all the nuts and bolts of their operation, the day-to-day challenges. Mr. Golding believes his audience appreciates and expects this on-the-ground realism of police operations."

I fished out a business card from Jake Lydon Communications Inc. and offered to scan and send it to her. She declined, saying it wasn't necessary. Of course it wasn't necessary, Jake, ya big chowderhead. They're the cops; they find shit out.

Ms. Witt promised to get back to me "soon," which was more encouraging than if she had said "On the day after the Maple Leafs finally win the Cup again."

Now, all I had to do is get Steve to play along.

I called my writer buddy in Toronto. I've known Stephen Golding for more than thirty years. And I've always liked him, even though, during our early years of association, we were more or less adversaries. He was a hotshot business reporter at the *Globe and Mail* and I was the PR guy for a big publicly-traded computer services firm when we first got together over a bucket o' beer.

Our shared admiration of ale has remained constant, except for a brief period when he tried out sobriety (which didn't take), while everything else in our lives had changed. The deaths of all our parents, his bitter divorce, the birth of my daughter, the murder by cancer of Beth, my first wife, me quitting the corporate world, his newspaper career circling the alcoholic drain. We'd been there for each other through all them cha-cha-changes while respecting the three pillars of our enduring friendship that we established decades ago: sarcasm, apparent contempt, and the strict avoidance of sentimentality.

Some years back, Steve re-invented himself as a true crime book author and now was fast on his way to becoming a celebrity. And a rich man. His two books were based on my bumbling around, first, in the world of global ultra-hacking and, secondly, around a national effort to extort tribal casinos. He was a household name to the tens of thousands, nay, the hundreds of thousands who'd bought his books.

I held that same status with at least 600 Central Ontario residents who shelled out for my first novel. Any other notoriety I gained farther afield came from a few interviews where I played the clumsy antagonist who was just gosh-darned pleased that Steve accurately captured me and the events I caused or walked into. Oh, and a couple, no, several arrests raised some questions.

I was happy for his success and, of course, insanely jealous at the same time, even though I didn't want to write the books myself and he'd rewarded me well. Plus, I got to natter at him for being hot shit in the publishing universe.

"Steve, you old enema bag!" [A term of endearment. No, really.]

"Jake, you douche nozzle! [Same] "What's up?"

"Look, I feel bad about freezing you out on the hedge fund shitstorm last winter. Even though everybody else got the same treatment."

"You changed your mind?" he asked hopefully.

"No. But I may be onto something new that may interest you. All you have to do is agree to be you."

"What the fuck are you talking about?"

"You still at the *Sun*?"

"I'm leaving at the end of the month. Why?"

"There's something I may have for you."

"Whaddya got?" he persisted.

"For now, let's just say it's something big."

"What do I have to do?"

As you can see, Steve ends almost every answer to a question with a question. Fucking reporters.

"You'll probably get a call from the Colorado Bureau of Investigation, I said. "All you have to say is four measly words: "Steve Golding, *Toronto Sun*.""

"You better explain things a little better than that."

I laid out the semi-false story I was trying to peddle.

"I don't like lying to cops," he said after I finished my tale.

"Me neither. But—technically—you're not. You'll be hiring Jake Lydon Communications Inc. to do the grunt work field research again. About what you don't exactly know yet, but it will focus on the illegal cannabis industry. Look, I'm going to send you a contract. You scan, sign, and send it back. Then, we've got proof of our deal to show to the cops. I don't know when they'll call to check me out, but I'm sure they will."

"I'm not interested in writing about weed."

"You will be soon. Consider this as an appeal to your insatiable hunger for fame and money. I may be onto something. It's got everything you look for: It's based in the US for your bigger potential audience. A bunch of bad guys, hundreds of millions of dollars in ill-gotten gains."

"Anybody die?"

"Yeah, sadly, one I personally know of—but there's been others."

There was a pause.

"I want in," he announced.

"You are in. I'll give you everything I get as an exclusive. I swear."

"No. I want to be right *there* where it's happening."

"Respectfully, Steve, fuck off. I got Alex; nothing personal, but I don't need you going all George Plimpton on me."

"Want me to talk nice to the cops when they call?"

"You bastard."

I wrote out a simple, backdated, one-page contract between Jake Lydon Communications Inc (hereafter referred to as *The Contractor*) and J. Stephen Golding Communications Inc. (hereafter referred to as *the Smart Dipshit who decided to hire The Contractor*). I gave myself an hourly rate of $300 USD, plus expenses to undertake the field research. I signed it and sent it off with an accompanying note saying:

Here's the bullshit contract for our bullshit deal. Get it back to me pronto.

Pronto was within the hour. Now, the whole arrangement was approximately legal. I didn't feel bad about semi-lying to law enforcement. I was only sort of fibbing—in that self-justifying way I have.

Steve called me back two days later.

"As you predicted, Colorado police called and sent a confirming e-mail. I assured them that, even though you're a colossal dick, you were on the level. I told them they could read my Wikipedia entry or my books or my archived articles if they wanted to be sure I was me and you were you. They said they already had skimmed them. What sealed the deal, I think, was that dummy contract. But they also had checked out my police record, car registration, and passport. I presumed they did that for you too."

"Let's bet."

"Then they must've found out about all your lies. Plus, you've shot two guys, one fatally. Dunno why they would agree to deal with you."

"Yeah, you're right. I feel just terrible about it. I better quit snooping around."

There was a long pause.

"You won't give up whatever chase you're on," he said, calling my bluff.

"You, your publisher, and your bank account better pray I don't."

"Arsehole. Where are you again?"

"Huntsville, Alabama."

"RMHH Enterp... in Colorado?" (Fucking call display!). "I'll find it. See ya soon."

Click.

CHAPTER 9

While I was trying to set up a meeting with law enforcement, Alex interviewed Greg at the store on a rare day when he wasn't on the road peddling dope. In her professional life, Alexandra is mainly a numbers person. But when she's analyzing a company's market chances, she needs to be informed about all aspects of its operations, including what and how they sell.

Again, she had recorded her conversation and played it back for me that evening. After a bit of breezy chit-chat, she went for the heart of the matter.

"How do you market cannabis anyway?" she asked.

"The same way you market everything else," Greg said. "Press the flesh, be seen, and be prepared to deal."

"Yes but, with whom?"

"Direct to the retailers. There are a couple of larger chain stores in Colorado that I'm trying to crack. They're tough; they grind the growers the way Walmart or Costco does their suppliers. But if we can provide them with enough and if they like our product, then we're in. Just one big score would help a lot."

"Sounds like a deal might be a way off. What else are you doing?"

"Well, we're investing in expanding our production of gummies and other edibles. We're going to start a merchandising side hustle—you know, get some walking billboards on the street with T-shirts, ball caps, customized pipes and bongs and such. Oh, and also, we can advertise so we're getting into that."

"Really?" Like on TV? Hey, kids! Enjoy your breakfast cereal but don't forget to buy our weed."

"Hell, no. By law, we have to show that 70% our advertising audience is over 21, so that means no print, no billboards and such. We're left with late night radio and TV, like after midnight. But other than that, we can't use traditional media. So, I'm getting into social media, display ads on age-restricted websites."

"You mean like porn?"

"I mean *exactly* porn," he chuckled. "But also, fan media, aimed at aficionados. There are hundreds of sites. To stand out in that crowd, our marketing has to get edgier, more memorable. I'm fighting mom and Joe who want it toned down. I won on renaming the store. It was originally called

Gunnison Cannabis Company—exciting, huh?—but I got it them to change it to Bud-inski's."

"How is the store doing?"

"Pretty good…better than the others."

"Does the black market for pot hurt you?"

"It's a small issue; lots of businesses have to deal with a black market. Our target segment is the new cannabis user. They're either afraid to buy illegally or they can't be bothered finding a connection or they don't trust the quality. A lot of people just aren't comfortable with getting it on the street. They want cannabis in some form, and they'll pay the premium to buy it from legalized companies."

"I know it's a standard joke, but is employee theft a problem?"

"Not a big deal. But I did have to fire two girls in the last year for pilfering."

"Have you been approached by illegal growers to buy their products."

"Not to my knowledge. Why would I anyway? Our offerings are far superior. Around here, we market as "Gunnison's own." You know, shop local. Here's my line: 'We're best buds.' Like it?"

"That *is* good. Guess you need the store in town to push the local angle. Is there any chance of it closing?"

Alex interrupted the recording to explain that Greg's cheerful expression immediately clouded over.

"Joe talks about it all the time," Greg said as the tape re-started. "But mom wants to keep it; dad was real proud he got it up and running so fast after legalization. You can guess what side I'm on. I think it's a great thing to have."

"What's Johnny think?"

"Honestly, it doesn't matter what Johnny thinks. Johnny has one job: grow really good pot. To be fair, Johnny's convinced me that we should be going after a more elite market. You know, for the connoisseurs. They'll pay $400 for an ounce when you can buy field-grown weed for $400 a pound."

"How do you reach that crowd?"

"First, by selling top quality to cannabis storefronts all over the place. That's more time on the road for me. Denver, Pueblo, Colorado Springs, but it's promising."

"Speaking of the road, your mom says you were robbed going to Montrose."

"I'd rather not talk about that."

"And you bought a gun?"

"I did. Big deal. Lots of guns in Colorado. Now, as I was saying, when we start getting people talking about our strains by name—a buzz about the buzz, as it were—[here, Greg chuckled at his own less-than-new-joke] "we're on our way. We feature it on our website, so it gets more name recognition. That's really going to help as we build a mail order business."

"I thought you couldn't mail it out of the state."

"We can't. But we can ship it door-to-door—like FedEx or UPS."

"Wait, you can't mail it, but you can ship it direct?"

"Crazy, huh? But that's the law. Feds control the mail but not the couriers."

"All these plans, any chance you've started too late and other outfits are well ahead of you?"

"Not at all. We took our time and watched all the others make mistakes. Now we're ideally positioned to capitalize."

The recording ended.

"He skipped right over that highway robbery. Did you find that odd?" I immediately asked.

"A little," Alexandra said. "But he was in the middle of a sales job on me. Talk of robberies and guns would have interrupted his sunny shpiel."

"As you know, I am always suspicious of relentlessly positive people. Especially the ones who claim to be "ideally positioned"."

"A few of my *former* brokers would get that way. I'd hear them on the phone with clients. Whatever stock they were discussing was the absolutely best surefire bet they'd ever heard of. That's misleading, if not downright deceptive, and it made me nuts, so I fired them. The world's a little more nuanced than that."

"Your conclusion, Watson?"

"Well, Shylock, it's hard to have one. I got some detail, but not much in the way of realistic talk from him."

It was, for sure, a confusing picture. On the one hand, Joe seemed truly worried for the future of business—not just the store but the entire operation. Meanwhile, Greg was thoroughly optimistic that they were making all the right moves.

"Ya know, kid," I said, "it was as if you had two people looking at the same landscape. One says the sky is blue; the other insists it's grey."

"How about we let Johnny settle the tie?"

"Agreed. But I'd like to talk to him; we seemed to hit it off."

I wanted to wrap up my chatting with Johnny, so I wandered out to his magic garden centre. He seemed glad to see me which, believe me, doesn't happen a lot.

"Jake, before I forget, I tested the recent baggie you brought and most of the remaining shitty weed you originally got stiffed for."

"And?"

"The new stuff was top quality. But the weirdest thing with the rest of your original purchase: The THC readings were all over the map. Most were on the low side, but some were really, really high."

"Different batches?"

"Don't think so. All the buds looked the same."

"So, what's that mean?"

"At first, I thought it was the equipment, so I tested some of our bud. Results were accurate. I then tested yours. Same wild results. I'm guessing that at one time, the baggie held superior weed and some of that residue rubbed off onto the shit stuff."

"Hmm," was the only trenchant observation I could make. But in my mind, Johnny's results confirmed that recently-fired Benjamin had been switching out Pete's quality merchandise with crap.

I asked him how the industry pressures were affecting RMHH Enterprises.

"We're in kind of a sweet spot," he said. "I bet three-quarters of all the pot, legal or illegal, is grown east and northeast of here. No big surprise that it's near where 75% of the population is, in around Denver, Pueblo and Colorado Springs. That leaves us in a comfortable niche here where the big boys aren't that interested.

"We do have more field-grown here for the local market because of wide open spaces, but overall, it can't be more than 15%. It's mostly grown by old timers who do it cuz they've always grown it that way. And those are the growers being busted. Which is too bad because those geezers aren't a threat to the business," Johnny observed.

He went on to describe the lengths to which Stan went to hide his outdoor crops. From mid-September to when the snow flew, law enforcement sent up planes or helicopters (and now drones, Bellini had noted) because the weed plants stay green while the other vegetation around them turns light yellow or brown. Stan planted his pot among rows of corn and would harvest early before the corn died back.

"Smart man, your father."

"He sure was," Johnny said, obviously proud. "He'd sacrifice quality for safety. And the fact is, over more than forty years, he never got caught. And he was quick to switch to indoor growing when weed went legit. He had a head start."

I wanted to steer Johnny towards the present and talking about the family business from his perspective.

"Are you worried about RMHH's future?"

"Yeah, I am."

"What's bothering you the most?"

"The illegals. Dad was right. Let's face it: we're farmers and just like farmers everywhere we are subject to market forces. Over-supply, reduced demand, increased number of competitors. But the biggest difference between us and other farmers is they don't have the extra threat of a black market undercutting them all the time. There's no real black market for milk or corn."

"What can you do about it?"

"Basically, what I'm doing. Experimenting with different strains, different hybrids. It takes time but it's working. My testers—"

"—Testers?"

"Yeah. I don't smoke anymore, but I have two guys and a woman who try out the new products. They're very good on giving me detailed reactions. They're telling me that at least five of the new strains are killer. If they're right, we might get closer to selling at $400 an ounce, about double the current price for primo."

Johnny believed that the only way they would become really successful is if they went after the elite consumers. And the only way they could do that is to offer the absolute best. He cited Ben & Jerry's—just two guys who started out with an ice cream shop in Burlington fucking Vermont. They'd grown to almost a half a billion-dollar company by doing three things: goofy marketing, a commitment to keep quality up and refusing to back away from premium pricing.

"We have to pattern ourselves after them. I'm sure that'll work."

"Joe seems worried about employee theft."

"Pfft! He's overreacting. It's not a real problem. We have to record every hybrid seed, enter it on the state's METRC tracking system. The government brags about knowing where everything is from seed to final sale. We've got security cameras all over the store. Guy would have an easier time stealing from a bank or jewelry shop."

"Didn't Greg fire two staff for stealing?"

"Yeah, but I understand it was for real small quantities."

"What about folks around here sneaking into your place? Back in my day, we used to raid people growing in their backyard."

"They'd have to find us first."

"Oh, I'm sure people know about the growing that went on around here before legalization."

"Yeah, but that's a lotta hard work to get to the herb. Speaking from experience, stoners aren't crazy about hard work."

"What about sober criminals?"

Johnny showed me the security cameras inside and out, and the motion detectors.

"There's also a camera by the road and I lock the gate every night when I leave. That's a long way to hike in and an even longer hike out with garbage bags full of weed while you're being chased by our security officers" he said, rubbing the neck of Dax, their German shepherd. "Plus, most of the family lives here, so there's always someone around."

We continued our tour in the second white Quonset hut. Half its massive space was devoted to their drying and curing operation. That was divided off by a thick plastic barrier from the area used for the seedlings in rows of small pots sitting on table-height shelves. The height of the plants varied.

"My babies," Johnny said.

"So, these little guys are going to save the company?"

Johnny didn't answer as he was engrossed in examining the tallest of the up-and-coming crop for any sign of mold, whipping out his gardening shears to nip off a leaf or wandering stem.

"You seem to have a real flair for this job," I noted. "I'm guessing you picked up a lot while you were in Hawaii. Could you tell me about that?"

"If you can swing it, Hawaii is a great state for just fucking around. I know. That's what I did for almost six years. I did get pretty good at surfing. Bummer, but Colorado isn't famous for decent waves," he said, with a big grin.

"Make any money from it?"

"Nah, I wasn't good enough to turn pro or anything. You need a low centre of gravity, so 5-8, 5-9 is the ideal height, not 6–2."

"What did you do for money?"

"I got real good at growing and selling pot."

He went back to tending to his young crop.

"Dad and I used to do this," Johnny said out of nowhere. "Just walk around and chat."

"You miss him."

"A lot. Dad used to talk to me. More than to my brothers. Joe's all about the numbers and his family. Greg will say anything to anybody. So, dad would come out to the hothouse, see what I was doing, give me tips, and let me bounce ideas off him."

"And he spoke to you about the threats he was getting."

"Yeah, and they weren't exactly subtle about it. It wasn't just the late-night phone calls. He showed me the e-mails he got before he deleted them, because he didn't want mom all worried."

"Saying?"

"Shit like: "Stop talking or we'll stop you from talking.""

Or "Mind your business or we'll destroy yours. And you." Big bold type, all caps, a lot of exclamation points."

"Who's they?"

"Dunno. Untraceable ISPs. But there's a long list of people who were pissed at him. In the last few years, he called the cops on seven pop-up stores that were selling. One in Montrose, three in Colorado Springs, two in Pueblo, and one right here in Gunnison. They were easy wins for the police. They'd go in, ask to see the state license, and if they didn't have one—boom—they're out of business, their pot confiscated."

"That must've pleased the old man."

"You don't know dad. He was bullshit that the cops just stopped there. He wanted them to investigate who was supplying them. Guaranteed, they were illegal growers. And new stores would open up within a week."

"Anybody else he piss off?"

"Oh yeah. Dad would act as a mystery shopper. He'd browse legal stores, buy some products and then test them here. He identified two stores in Colorado Springs and one in Montrose that were selling the same strains we were for about 40% less. He was sure that they couldn't do that without buying cheaper illegal pot. So, he called the cops. No action. That's when Dad really turned detective."

"What'd he do?"

"He found the owners of those stores, all numbered companies. He dug a bit and found those companies owned other businesses. Each store also owned a self-storage company. He figured those storage companies did the growing in their units. So, he staked them out, saw some funny things going on, like traffic during the night and early morning."

"What happened?"

"He was able to convince the police who raided all three of them. They opened every storage locker and didn't find anything. Dad was still sure they were dirty, so he identified the three storage companies by name in the Growers Association and MIG newsletters. He also went on a few social media chat groups and called them out. He was becoming more and more convinced that the illegal business in this corner of the state was consolidating to the point that one or two outfits were running it all. So, he'd spout off about that wherever and whenever he could."

"What about the other two on his list?"

"One was a grow op, and one wasn't."

"So, your old man was one for five."

"In his mind, he was four for five."

"Beyond cool shirts and taste in movies, I also have some talent in rooting around corporations; Alexandra's even better at it. Would you happen to have a list of the grow ops that your dad was trying to out? I thought they'd be on your website."

"They're not? Greg must've pulled them off. He hates anything negative. But Dad blind copied me on his e-mails to the police and the industry associations. I'll dig them out. I think there were five that he couldn't make heads or tails of."

"Thanks. Can I ask why you don't live out here?" I said, changing the subject.

He paused.

"I will some day. But I've got a few debts to pay off before I can build."

"What kind of debts?"

"I don't think that's any of your business, so I'd rather not say."

"See, Johnny, I'd rather you did say, because it *is* my business. Look, your mom asked me to dig into all this, so I'm digging. Something here was the reason for your father's death. I need to find that reason and you need to trust me."

"Alright, alright. Charlize and I left Hawaii with a substantial amount of cash. Strictly speaking, most of it wasn't ours."

"How much?"

"About fifty thousand."

"How'd you pull that off?"

"I got involved with some people I shouldn't have. They ran a big but strictly local operation with lots of cash lying around."

"So, what happened?"

"They found me here; it wouldn't have been that hard. They told me they just wanted their money back plus interest. A lot of interest."

"How are you paying it back?"

"Slowly. Between what I make and what Charlize makes from her jewellery business, we send them something every month. We're almost clear."

"And if you just stop paying?"

"I have zero interest in finding out what happens. And, the fact is, I do owe them."

I instantly admired Johnny for that. Yes, he was obviously afraid, but as importantly, he knew he had fucked up and was trying to make good by paying the piper (although, truth be told, there just weren't that many pipers around anymore).

"Sounds like a rough business these days," I said. "And Greg getting robbed right here."

"Yeah, about that...."

"What about it?"

"Maybe you don't have the full picture."

"Can you fill me in?"

"It was about a year ago. Greg said that it happened in the late afternoon on the road between here and Montrose. He was making a delivery to a store there that we supply. Greg said a car forced him to the shoulder. When he stopped, two masked guys jumped him. He said they had guns and got him to open the trunk, made off with about 3K worth of pot."

"Cops find anything?"

"No. Not much to go on. No prints on anything. No tire tracks they could find. No good description of the bandits."

There was something in the way Johnny spoke, his tone

was quiet, almost halting. And his eyes were diverted, dancing around. That got my attention.

"Do you believe him, Johnny?" I asked.

"I want to. I mean, he's my brother. But..."

"But what?"

"It was kinda strange. Greg's a car nut, but all he said he told the cops was that their car was green and *maybe* a Chev. No plates. And with all those miles he drives, Greg's really good behind the wheel. And that vehicle of his is a tricked-out 429 Boss Mustang."

"I've seen it in the yard. Pretty nasty looking."

"Well, there's not much on the road that that muscle car couldn't outrun. So why did he stop in the first place? Didn't make sense to me. Then I got thinkin' about it. Not a scratch on the car, no dust either. And that's a busy road that time of day; nobody sees two guys in masks with guns? Plus, we always make deliveries in the morning and rarely for less that $5000 wholesale. And I usually go along with him in case the owner has questions."

"Doesn't add up, does it? *If* it wasn't a robbery, do you have a theory?"

"There's only one explanation. He stole it himself for personal use or to resell on the side."

"He's surrounded by weed. Why steal it?"

"Four or five years ago, when he was up in Denver, Greg was a real wild man. Stoned all the time. Mom and pops offered him a job out here, but on the condition that he'd clean up. He swore he was straight. And that he had stayed straight. So, there's no way could he ask me to set aside a little space for him in the hothouse. And no way he could be stealing from here either; cameras would've caught him."

"So, he could be selling?"

"Doubt it. He gets caught and it would be business suicide. The state would yank our license, shut us down *and* arrest Greg. I refuse to believe he'd risk everything. But he is using."

"You're sure?"

"I spent ten years as a stoner; I know the look. I also think that he ran out of the weed from the so-called robbery and began lifting it from the store, a bit at a time."

"Then he blamed those two employees."

"That was really shitty."

"You talk to Greg about all this?"

"No," he said.

"Or your mom?"

"No."

"Why not?"

"Short answer: I'm a chickenshit," he admitted. "I could see all the damage it would do."

There was a moment when Johnny seemed overwhelmed or regretful about revealing all he had to a complete stranger. He wasn't being a dick about Greg, but you could see he'd been carrying his suspicions around by himself for a year and now felt unburdened a bit by talking to me. And he was worried.

"You going to the cops with this?" he asked.

"No."

A look of profound relief passed over his face.

I admired his honesty and could see how he was pinned. In a strict sense, he had knowledge—or at least a strong suspicion—of a crime his brother had committed. And he had done nothing about it. If he was right, then at the very least, in addition to theft, Greg had illegally bullshitted the police and cost two people their jobs. Not inconsequential at all. Johnny had to wrestle with that versus completely wrecking the business, putting more people out of work, threatening his mother's security, and further enflaming the brotherly rivalries. And that's not even considering the weight of being responsible for destroying his father's legacy.

If you've never farmed or owned a small business (and I haven't), you can't imagine the appeal of having a son or daughter take over the family business. It's proof that the life you chose wasn't an insane fantasy if a child of yours wants to keep your dream alive. Johnny just couldn't imagine blowing it all up.

I walked away thinking that Johnny was smart and the most honest and engaging of the brothers. I liked him for more than the fact that he had great taste in movies and shirts. Bonus: He also had an obvious sense of humour. That sealed the deal for me; dumb people aren't funny.

CHAPTER 10

I was pleasantly surprised when, two days later, the PR lady from the Colorado Bureau of Investigation called back to tell me that my story had checked out. I was to meet a Detective Frank Bellini of the Illicit Marijuana Team within CBI's Special Investigations branch at their 'satellite office' in Montrose the following day.

Punctual as hell, I arrived at the cop shop and asked the sturdy desk sergeant for the department's Illicit Marijuana Unit and the office of Frank Bellini. She smiled and pointed to a man at a desk in the middle of the squad room as she dialled his extension.

You may have a view of police as being of only three types: the beat cops, impressive as hell in uniform, now with thick black bullet-proof vests, the detective class, all rumpled and weary, and the undercover kind, suitably scuzzy enough that they could pass for Ratso Rizzo's kinfolk.

I could see that Frank was none of the above as he approached. He put the plain in plain clothes. He wore everyday clothes, the same ones that I suspected he wore off-duty. Maybe fifty years old, he was perfectly medium in height and weight, normal looking face with sandy blonde hair threatening to turn grey. What stood out were his penetrating blue eyes, the trademark that all diligent cops had (I know, as I've been around a lot of them in recent years and I have a Toronto homicide investigator for a daughter who's had the same lively, probing gaze since she was a baby.)

When he reluctantly shook the hand I offered, his glare said: "I would rather burst my or—somebody else's—hemorrhoids than babysit you."

"Nice to meet you, Detective Bellini," I said. "I bet right now you're thinking that you'd rather burst your—or somebody else's—hemorrhoids than babysit me."

"That's about right," he said in a deep, gruff voice.

"Look, I know you'd rather be out investigating the growers instead of talking to me."

"Right again."

"When do you want to start?" I asked.

"How about right now? I booked off to do this."

"My, my, aren't you the keener?"

"No, I just want to get this fuckin' thing over with. But not here," he said looking around at the busy squad room and his lonely desk in the middle of it.

We left the station and walked a couple of blocks to the main street in Montrose. I couldn't resist busting his chops about the size of his department.

"Quite the empire you built your satellite office into."

"Fuck off. I'm based in Grand Junction and I'm only in Montrose maybe once or twice a month. Some PR genius thought calling it a satellite office would strike fear into the hearts of the locals and make us look bigger than we are."

We went to a diner he knew. As we walked in, I said I'd pay. He said no I wouldn't. He had a gun. He won.

After we sat down in a booth and ordered coffee, the only chit-chat I could think of was to talk about Steve's books, (both had been international bestsellers and both featured *moi*—coincidence? I choose to think not). He said he'd read them and that he really liked his most recent one, *Jackpot*. Apparently, he'd been personally involved in the aftermath of the great con job being perpetrated on tribal casinos. He had been pulled off his anti-weed beat and assigned to the raid and arrest detail picking up some of the baddies who were fleecing the casinos in that corner of the state.

As he stared at me, he went out of his way to indicate that he didn't much care for guy who uncovered the whole scheme.

That would be me.

"Guy was an arrogant asshole," he offered by way of a character study.

"And still am. Look, I know that pulling PR duty isn't why you signed on."

"Christ, you're on a streak. Right again."

"Trust me when I tell you that I don't live to piss you off or make your job harder," I said as our truly great coffee arrived. "I'm not interested in a bullshit "authentic" experience of a ride-along and I couldn't give a good goddamn about your background or what you do in your off-hours."

"You mean you're not going to ask, like everybody else does, how someone with the name Bellini wound up with blonde hair and blue eyes?"

"I care more about the Gross Domestic Product of Luxembourg."

"OK, so what *do* you want?"

"Information. *Real* information. Answers to some questions I have about what you're seeing, about how the illegal operations work, where you see the industry going, where you're winning, what's hindering you. That kind of stuff."

"So, not the kind of crap you're going to get from a PR department?"

"Exactly. I once made a darned good living shovelling shit like that. I don't want that."

I couldn't say for sure if my answer had satisfied him or not. I detected something that resembled a slight smile, (or maybe he was stifling a fart). I just didn't know if his expression meant "Good!" or "We'll see if you're telling the truth, asshole." Either way, I was further ahead than if he'd opened with a crisp "Get fucked. I'm outta here."

"Go," he said.

"First question: Why didn't you flat-out refuse to cooperate with me? I assume you didn't want to do this, and I also assume they couldn't make you."

"Yes and yes to your assumptions. I didn't tell them to fuck off for two good reasons. One: I figured I'd get brownie points from the brass and, brother, I could use some of them right now. There have been a few incidents that don't look so good on my record."

"Want to talk about them?"

"No," he said with a significant helping of definitiveness.

"Okey-dokey, then," I said, withering under his glare. "So, what's the second reason?"

"Our unit needs to get bigger. I figured some good press might loosen the purse strings in Denver."

"Why the need for money?"

"It's crazy but we've got twelve investigators for the whole state. And this ain't Rhode Island. We could keep twelve agents busy in the Denver area alone."

"That's it? Twelve?"

"Now, we often work with the DEA and the FBI, but usually that's only when they or we suspect out-of-state smuggling. It's federal then. Otherwise, we have to be "invited" by the state police or local cops who catch the cases to join their investigations already in progress. And guess what? Cops don't like to share. We're missing cases we never even hear about, some cases that could be connected to ones we got."

"It's not the small mom and pop growers you're after," I said. "This has to be organized crime. Am I full of shit or what?"

"You might be full of shit anyway, but you're not wrong about that. I spend most of my time on the storefronts, almost like a state inspector. But I want to go after the illegal growers in a big way. This isn't a bunch of stoners chipping in to start a grow op. This has become big business. And, yes, they're organized."

"Who are the players?"

"Take your pick. Mafia, biker gangs, regional crime outfits, even smart-ass college kids. A month ago, up north, we busted some guys from another state."

"That can't be unusual."

"Their home state was Sinaloa."

"Oh, shit. Cartels are figuring in?"

"Think about it. They've had a distribution system in the States for decades. They just have to supply it with product. What's easier: growing their inventory here or trying to get it across the border?"

"You worried about your safety?"

"Not yet. Mafia, bikers, college kids aren't going to kill cops. But the cartels, well, that's a different story. Back home, they don't think twice. I'd rather not find out what they'd do here. Lucky for me, but this corner of the state seems pretty quiet; the big bastards—the mob or biker gangs—aren't here yet. But they're coming."

"How would you know?"

"I'd know. I have to cover a lot of turf. I'm talking to a lot of people. You pick up rumours or rumblings, you piece them together and you get a picture."

"You have any big targets in mind?"

"A couple."

"Any chance you've got your eye on RMHH Enterprises?"

"Nah, they're OK. By the books, as far as I can tell. Shame about Stan Harding; he was a decent guy. Gave me some useful leads."

"Stan was a good friend of mine."

"You son of a bitch!" Bellini suddenly erupted. "They didn't tell me about that! You son of a bitch!"

"Whoa, what's the big deal?"

"I'd like to know about someone who I'm working with is the big deal."

"Why?"

"You got a dog in this fight. It's personal. Meaning you could compromise the work by getting all emotional, then going off and doing something really stupid."

"I won't. I'm just gathering info for a writer," I said. "But, yeah, I want these guys, like you do. That's it, that's all. OK?"

My explanation seemed to settle him down.

"Did you know Stan at all?" I asked.

"Not really. I know he was always upset over the growers. I could see his point. We busted two field grows from his tips but got really burned on another one. I gotta ask: Stan died in St. Petersburg, right? What are you doing in Colorado? Why aren't you in Florida?"

"Stan was murdered there because he was raising a stink about the illegal growers here," I said, as I watched a Bellini eyebrow shoot up. "And his killers travelled to Florida from Colorado. [Here his eyebrow elevated farther into Jack Nicholson territory] I believe that there's a big operation around here who put out the hit on him. They had him killed in Florida for a reason. If they'd done it here, it would have likely turned up the police heat, and they don't want that."

He looked surprised. So, without being asked, I went into a description of what I'd learned in Florida and along the way here to prove to him I wasn't just an old fart in a tin foil hat yelling at the clouds.

"You go to the cops here?"

"No. I would have been an out-of-state old fart in a tin foil hat yelling at the clouds. But Laura Harding did a few days ago right here in Montrose, after I told her what we had figured out. No response yet."

"I'll follow up. Let me check with them, but they're strictly local cops. This should go to the CBI either in Grand Junction or Colorado Springs."

"Thanks. And the spirit of full disclosure and co-operation," I added, "My wife and I are staying with Laura Harding. You have a beef with that?"

"That's no problem. I'll put a highway patrol car stationed at the gate."

"I don't need protection."

"Not for that. To bust you when you pull out onto the road too fucked up to drive."

"This may surprise you, Special Investigator Bellini, but I do not partake."

"You don't?" he asked skeptically.

"Oh, I see. The long hair, sketchy appearance. You just profiled me, didn't you?"

"No. I just figured you had to be on something to be that weird."

"I used to indulge...a lot...but that was back during the Jimmy Carter administration. I've got no fucking idea what's going on these days. That's why we're sitting here. Perhaps you could enlighten me."

"Going by your age, I figure you're out of date. This isn't *Smoky and the Bandit* running tractor-trailers filled with garbage bags of dope instead of beer. Let's start with some basic math. In Colorado, a pound of really good bud sells for about a thousand dollars, give or take. That same pound retails for about four thousand in Texas, higher in Florida. Where are you going to sell your product? You can pack a panel van with a ton of the stuff. So, you're looking at upwards of ten million bucks' worth per load. They could just sell it to a couple of wholesalers for about half that and be done with it or, given the money involved, hire and pay their own people on the ground in those states. Either way, it's worth a daytrip to Texas or three to Florida with a stop in New Orleans where it's even more expensive. A couple of vans doing a fifty runs a year, that's a cool half billion with a 'b', minus costs."

"Their costs must be enormous, but they wouldn't be doing if it wasn't profitable," I added. "I've heard they're getting nastier; and that means they've gotta be getting squeezed."

"Fuckin' right they are. Look, sooner or later, there's going to be national approval of cannabis for recreation, like Canada. They know that, so they're pushing to move as much product as they can right now while the prices are way up in the non-legal states."

"So, you think they're afraid that national legalization would put them out of business?"

"Not out of business but really reduced. It's legal here in Colorado, but we still have the big outlaw grow ops. Same as California and same in Canada, I understand, where it's legal everywhere."

"Simple question: If their business is dying, why would they stay in it?"

"Simple answer: Git while the gittin's good. Like I said, they're mostly in business to supply the other states. Texas and Florida have one sixth of the population of the whole damned country. Until national legalization comes—and realistically, that'll be years from now—there's a lot of money to be made. But a shakeout is going to happen and the ones that are left will brawl for less than half the money, like the cartels are doing down south. We know they're gobbling up smaller illegals. People are dying right now, and that murder rate will only go up as they're forced to fight over a tighter market."

During what turned out to be a lengthy conversation, I felt like a late-night talk show host with an interesting but long-winded guest. Other than a few smart-ass comments, I played the straight man, prompting Bellini to go on and on about the situation. I wasn't being polite; I needed to know this shit if I was to get anywhere with digging into Stan's murder. In the grand scheme, he was actually saving me time. Without him, I'd have to spend hours down Internet rabbit holes, with no guarantee I was getting the straight goods.

"We haven't even talked about the inter-state competition between Colorado and California," Bellini offered. "California's the wild west when it comes to illegal weed, especially Northern California. Big surprise there."

"What's so special about California?"

That's where what's called the Emerald Triangle is— three northern counties—that was *the* spot back in the 1960s when the hippies started up their communes. They grew a little pot as part of that lifestyle. The hippies got lucky by setting up in a favorable climate that produced good quality weed outdoors. Now coming on two generations later, the residents view it as their main industry. In some way, it supports almost everyone living there. Somewhere along the line, all that peace and love stuff changed into the belief that it was their *right* to grow and sell as much pot as they could. And they aren't above using guns to defend that right. Now, everybody's packing. Cops don't even think about going into those hills."

"So, they're free to expand their grow ops which produce tons of pot. And that means exporting to other states or taking over other operations."

"You got it. If they can't partner with you, they're just take it from you. What are you gonna do? Call the cops? If it hasn't happened already, I bet they'll want to seem legit by moving on the legal mom and pop shops, like RMHH. If they're big enough, they'll probably go after the bigger legal companies."

"Like the garbage collection companies that the mob ran in New York back in the day."

"Yup."

"Surely you have the technology to go after their fields."

"You really do know fuck-all about this, don't you? Yeah, we have a plane—single-engine Cessna that can't fly more than half the goddamn time because of the weather in this state. It's busy right now because late fall's the best time to look for illegal plots because the plants stay green while everything around doesn't. But the fact is, just about nobody tries to grow the good stuff outdoors. It's all inside where they can control everything. We only send the plane up to get the holdouts who insist on growing outdoors. Looks good in the press, but, really, it's not making that much of a dent."

"So thermal imaging."

"Thermal imaging can't see inside a building no matter what Hollywood tells you. It can only measure the heat of the outside walls. If it's an abandoned warehouse they've bought that we know is empty, but it's reading 70 degrees when it's minus 20 outside, then we got 'em."

Here, Bellini paused.

"I'm sounding like a damn PR department; I apologize," he said. "The truth is: We *used* to get them that way. Then they got smart. Like they always do. The big tip off with thermal is the orange and yellow ribbons around windows, doors, roof lines where the heat is escaping. These guys started buying their own infrared cameras—they cost a couple of hundred bucks—to check their buildings and then they'd close off and insulate the windows, then caulk the hell out of everything."

"Saves on their electrical bills too."

"Big time, when you've got R-50 in the walls and a hundred in the ceilings. Then they figured out, it's easier to either set up or take over existing warehouses—electrical or automotive suppliers, storage outfits, shippers and so on—

which you expect to be occupied and heated. We were getting them by just dropping in and pressing the real owners of the businesses."

"Smart. But you said you *were* getting them.'"

"It's costly and time-consuming for them to set it all up and you've got to use muscle to enforce the takeover which can be messy. And these guys want to fly under the radar. They hate messy. We think that they've pretty well stopped doing things that way."

"So, what are they doing now?"

"More and more, they're using private houses—the bigger the better. That's what we're trying to focus on."

"All this effort for single houses?"

"*Big* single houses."

"I can't believe this is such a huge deal."

"No mystery; it's just math again. Say the empty-nester of a homeowner has three extra bedrooms and a basement he or she doesn't use. They can get 75 plants to 80 plants a room, more in the basement. Let's say three hundred plants, each one yielding about a pound of buds for each harvest. Two good crops a year, so six hundred pounds in total. The bad guys'll pay just under a thousand dollars a pound for good quality. That's close to a half a million bucks a year to the homeowner. In cash and tax-free. Now imagine fifty or more houses in the same network."

"Doesn't all that humidity fuck up the house with mold?"

I asked, still trying to imagine rooms in fancy-shmancy houses filled with pot plants.

"I'll say it again: half a million bucks a year. You can do a lot of repair work for that."

"Hell of a nest egg when you do the math."

"Trust me, these are smart people. They do the math. That's how they got the big houses in the first place."

"You can't trace the cash?"

"These same smart people are taught how to launder it, if they don't already know how. They started out by putting it into cash businesses like laundromats or restaurants. We have a lot of nice restaurants in Colorado, lots of clean clothes too. But even that's changed, and they're moving the money offshore."

"BUT HOW CAN THEY AFFORD TO PAY THEM THAT MUCH? THAT'S almost the over-the-counter retail price in a legal storefront, isn't it?"

"It's worth it to them at first. They attract satisfied, *quiet* growers and they can afford it because they're getting four or five grand a pound in Texas or Florida. More in Louisiana. Over time, they pull a bait and switch, and start dropping their price. The homeowners have no choice but to put up with it."

"Wait, what does, say, a retired lawyer know about growing primo weed? It looks complicated," I said, remembering my chat with Johnny.

"It is. But he or she doesn't have to know anything. Their buyer sets them up. Everything—lights, plants, fans, drip hoses—then he regularly checks the crops, does the harvesting, drying, pruning, and packing. All the homeowner has to do keep the temperature steady and pay the power bills. And shut the fuck up."

"Can't you access power companies to find customers with big-ass electrical bills?"

"Yeah, but it ain't easy. We knock at the door and the homeowner we suspect takes you on a tour *outside*, pointing to the pool pump and heater, his outdoor lighting, and his A/C and furnace running 24/7 by season, saying he likes to be comfortable, and he can afford it. So, the cops have no grounds for a warrant and, legally, he doesn't have to let us in."

"How long has this been going on?"

"In the houses, we think at least five years. Probably longer."

"Fuck, sounds like you could shut half the illegal ops just by going door-to-door in Aspen."

"I wish. But in a way, you gotta give them credit because,

again, thermal imaging doesn't count for shit with an occupied house."

"What about using drones?" I suggested, as if I had just brilliantly arrived at an answer the cops hadn't thought of yet.

"We use them, but mostly to spot outdoor fields. Lot more effective and cheaper than flying our Cessna. But like I said, there's hardly any of the good strains being grown outside. For sure, not the stuff the big illegals are growing. Plus, it's a can of worms. You got FAA rules because they run all airspace, privacy laws, local by-laws. Oh, and these home-owners use a high-tech defense: they shut the curtains. What are you going to do? Have an operator take his drone and hover all day hoping to see the guy load some boxes or garbage bags in his car? Boxes and bags of what? You don't know. So then what? You're going to waste more manpower just to follow him to the landfill or church thrift store?"

"Well, how *do* you catch them?"

"Same way we catch most criminals. Someone rats them out. A witness—a guy with a beef with his neighbour—tells us they saw a room full of plants, then we can go in. Cops get the smaller grow ops just by visiting a house for an unrelated reason—a parole check or domestic complaint—and they stumble on the plants. But these are small one-offs because, usually, the mopes we get that way don't tend to own big houses. And even if that hobby grower was part of a network, we'll never know because the guy understands that blabbing to us would be injurious to his health."

"But you have gone into the big houses."

"Yeah, and often not much happens. Nab a rich guy and he ties us up in court. Chances are he walks or gets a fine that he writes off as a cost of doing business. And they *never* give up the name of the buyer."

"What about busting them during their out-of-state runs?"

"Again, we just get lucky. Pull a van over for speeding or some other traffic violation, then take a whiff or a look inside."

"Why don't drivers just take off with their millions worth of cargo and disappear?"

"I know of two occasions where the wheel men did just that. It didn't end well for them."

Bellini fell silent, as if his far-ranging description of the illegal biz had overwhelmed him.

"You know what really pisses me off?" he finally said.

"Besides nosy Canadians? What?"

"We're falling behind. Christ, our unit didn't get started until 2018, six years after legalization. I was one of the first agents at the IMT. Since that time, I've watched the illegal operations go crazy. Nobody seems to understand or admit how fuckin' big this is."

"I get it, trust me. Over the years, I've learned it doesn't matter what the commodity is—guns, drugs, human smuggling, bank fraud—big money means big criminal outfits."

"And big criminal outfits mean violence," Bellini continued. "Last couple of years, in Denver and Boulder, between us and the local cops, we've been able to nail three of these bastards for murder. But there's been more—at least a half dozen more we suspect. And that's not counting the broken thumbs and busted kneecaps. We're making a difference, but there's so much more we could be doing if we had more feet on the street, more co-operation from local cops, and less bullshit from the courts."

At this point, Bellini's expression had changed to one of anger from his evidently normal grim and pissed-off look.

"Ever think of giving up?" I asked.

"Nah," he said, taking a deep breath to arrest any threat of hyperventilating. "I'm not built that way."

"Are you winning?"

"We're not losing. We are taking some of the players off the board."

"But new ones step up in their place."

"Hey, thanks for the pep talk. No, really. I mean it."

"My pleasure."

"Frankly, part of my frustration is watching these operations get bigger and bigger. We can't pin down who's buying from who."

He looked out the window then back at me.

"So that's where we are," he said. "For better or worse."

Bellini looked at his watch.

"Anything else?" he asked.

"No, Detective Bellini, I think we're about done for now," I said, as I flipped through the notes I'd taken.

"That's the best fucking news I heard all day."

"Unless there's something else you want to add," I said.

I had a hand on the tabletop as I was getting up to leave. He suddenly grabbed my wrist and not playfully either.

"Yeah, there *is* something else," he said, his eyes fixed on me. "There are some dangerous people out there. You have to understand that. And you better tell me where you're going information-gathering and who you're talking to. OK?"

"Well, in that case...," I said and sat down again.

I then laid out my buffoonish attempt to penetrate the world of street dealing weed. Bellini sat back and took my description in. Towards the end of my sad tale, I feared the detective would become a whiplash candidate such was his violent head shaking.

"This is what I'm talking about!" he said. "Peter Khrisorozvensky."

"Peter who?"

"Khrisorozvensky. We call him P.K. Locally, he's a big deal. He's not a very nice man."

"How bad is this P.K.?"

"Officially, he has had two minor possession convictions a few years ago. The $500 fines weren't much of a deterrent. We suspect that he's moved on to bigger things and that he got smarter. He doesn't ever carry. We staged several stop and frisks and got nothing except a big fucking grin on his face and a police harassment lawsuit that the bastard won."

"So, his minions complete the deal, like the one did in my case. Any idea how many of them he runs?"

"Not really. But quite a few. We know he travels to all the towns around here. A state cop I trust pulled him over on his way to Durango. He was just visiting "friends," he claimed. Cop searched the car. She found diddly-squat. And her stop was part of the evidence in his harassment suit."

"Someone else handles the distribution."

"Yup. I'm guessing P.K. makes the rounds to keep his street level dealers under control. Like I said, he's a bad man. More than a few unexplained injuries have shown up in local hospitals."

"But surely, he has to take shipments of larger loads to break up and sell."

"Yeah, we surveilled him for a while, even got a search warrant for his house. This was before the lawsuit. He's smart; I'll give him that. His house was clean; we'd tail him to what we hoped was a drop site, but he seemed to know we were following him. He led us nowhere."

It dawned on me.

"We're meeting here," I said. "For another reason, besides the coffee's better than at the station: You suspect a leak."

My normally chatty guest went silent.

"I don't know who the mole is—and maybe there isn't

one," he finally said. "But it's just uncanny how P.K. has stayed ahead of us. And then we got the word to lay off him. CBI honchos told us that another lawsuit would really undermine the Illicit Marijuana Team."

"Must really piss you off that he operates a few blocks from here."

"You don't know the half of it."

"Did you try to find the cop who's spilling the beans?"

"It's not exactly easy to run a one-man investigation into the people sitting around you who are supposed to be on the same team. So, I just don't take a chance anymore. Damn, the coffee's good here."

Then he got serious. Real serious.

"If you tell anybody—and I mean *anybody*—about this, I can promise you the end of this police co-operation and an obstruction of justice charge. Understand?"

"Got it. Thanks for all the info."

"Thanks for asking mostly not dumb questions. Stay in touch," he said, and he meant that too.

On my drive back to Gunnison, I considered Detective Frank Bellini. He was a decent guy, as most cops are, fiercely dedicated to his job but getting worn down by the restraints put on him that prevented him from doing that job. Scarce resources against wealthy criminals isn't ever a fair fight. Especially when there was the possibility of an inside guy ratting him out to the baddies.

I was pleased that, setting aside his shitty demeanour, he

seemed to trust me. Maybe I was kidding the hell out of myself by believing that, but the fact was, he had given me a ton of information and a clearer understanding of what he—and now I—were up against.

I thought about our chat on the economics of illegal grow ops and the rising use of violence as an intimidation tactic. With the larger outfits now having have their own Vice-president of Murders & Acquisitions, it was only going to get rougher. You simply cannot run operations of this size without an element of fear. Its willing participants can justify what they're doing. Pot is legal so what's the big deal, they say. Or they may not even think about the morality of it at all as long as big moo-la keeps rolling in. But in some dark corner of their mind, maybe late at night as they stare at the ceiling, they become aware of the implied threat of not doing things their way. Not the fines or possible jail time, but the physical fear of them or their families being hurt or worse if they stepped out of line.

Take the *real* pirates of the Caribbean; most of them hated combat, and with good reason. After all their swashes had been buckled, they knew they were likely outgunned and outmanned and were sailing inferior vessels. Their success came from the dread that would wash over a Spanish merchant ship whenever they'd see a ship approach flying some variation of the Jolly Roger. More often than not, they'd surrender without a fight, immediately after changing their soiled pantaloons. For sure, the buccaneers could and did commit terrible acts. But then they'd ensure that stories of their barbarity would seep out across the Caribbean, become embellished and exaggerated, as they always are. Not a lot of fact-checking outfits back then to stem the tide of the buccaneers' alleged atrocities being amplified and made more horrific.

These modern-day operations in Colorado and every other big criminal enterprise anywhere works that way. They're not constantly, routinely savage, but you just *knew* they could be.

I gave Alex a summary of my newly found larnin' (excepting the possibility of a spy in the house of law) and ended it with a question:

"Tell me, babe, who would you rather tangle with—mobsters, a Mexican cartel or a bike gang?"

"We have a choice?"

"Probably not."

CHAPTER 11

W ithin days of us arriving, we had settled into an almost rigid routine with the mistress of the house. All three us were early risers. Guess which one was a lazy fuck for at least the first hour. Right you are. Laura did some kind of meditation/yoga thing in her room while Alex marched off to her river walk. I would grab another coffee and sit on the front porch catching the sunrise and wishing I had a smoke.

We'd then convene in the kitchen. Laura and Alexandra got along famously, kind of a big sister-little sister act. You could see it in their chatty joint effort of making breakfast. I was assigned clean-up duty (which is the only kind of low-skill task that I can be trusted with). By eight o'clock, Laura would disappear to her studio and stay disappeared for four hours as she worked on her arts and crafty projects.

She was no fanciful painter, creating whenever the mood happened to strike her. She would block off most of the mornings and then chunks of time in the late evening to dedicate to her art. Working mainly in water colours, she would research her subjects—First Ladies, state birds, state flowers, Indian tribes—to produce series of paintings with accompanying descriptions and/or histories that she'd post on Face Book. She also had a few showings at art galleries in the area and it was her colourful work that adorned their Ponderosa-like home's walls.

Upon her emergence from the studio, her mood was always sunnier. Instinctively, she had gained some measure of peace through the always-therapeutic act of creating things. She was healing.

She would stay beaming as she tended to her twin grand-kids, after driving up to the main gate to meet them getting off the school bus. She went 'off-duty' at four when Cynthia, the girls' mom, got home from work. Then she'd head into the kitchen with Alex. Both loved to cook. Both loved it even more when I wasn't anywhere within sight. Remember when Les Nesman in *WKRP* would mark a "door" to his cubicle with masking tape on the carpet? The ladies may as well have put tape across the hallway floor and posted a sign saying: "Stay the fuck out of our kitchen, you useless tit!"

After an invariably swell meal and after I'd completed my scullery duties, we'd settle down in either the back porch or the great room, depending on the weather, and drink. Not excessively as I do understand that alcohol in sufficient quantities can be depressing, and Laura had a lot to be depressed about. So, we'd try to keep the conversation light. We did that by asking a bunch of powder puff questions like: "What's the RMHH stand for?"

"We wanted the name Rocky Mountain High for the business. Seemed like a natural. It turned out that another company already had the name—and right beside us in Montrose. So, we went with RMHH for Rocky Mountain Harding High, more as a private joke."

One evening, we asked her about the 'pop, pop, pop' sounds of what I thought was distant gunfire.

"Deer and elk hunting season just opened. The other side of the highway is federal land. They're allowed in there, but they usually don't come down to the river."

"*Usually*?" Alex asked with some measure of alarm in her voice.

"It's rare. But I suggest you wear some bright-coloured clothing just to be safe."

We also got her talking about the days of yore before legalization. She remembered those times fondly, as we often do whenever we look back and either can't recall or choose to forget any unpleasantness in our past.

Stan and she came back from Mexico to their two hundred acres with great tans and bags full of seeds hidden in their VW van. They worked hard in those early years, applying the agricultural lessons learned down south while building some place to live other than their van down by the river. And they played hard, as word—discretely—got out and their ranch slowly became a community hub for artists of every kind within a fifty-mile radius who were always eager to get high. We're not talking about a disciplined group of budding Renaissance masters here, but rather artisans skilled or semi-skilled in producing artifacts of the day in the late 1970s: stained glass, pottery, macrame, silk screening, elaborate candles and soaps, batik and tie-dyed anything.

This eclectic mix of artisans all got along, Laura told us, and every evening the guitars would come out and the tribe would make and/or enjoy music. She made it sound that their place was where the deer and the antelope played and hardly any discouraging words were ever heard. It was fanciful and fun to think of their ragged company as a band of outlaws – say, the Hole in the Wall Gang—but in many ways, they were. She seemed wistful for those times but still proud of the business it had become.

"I know it may not look like much, but Stan figured we were the largest legal grow op in at least a two-hundred-mile radius. Just like we were back in the day."

"I couldn't help but notice that Gunnison is smack dab in the middle of nowhere," I said. "Three hours to Grand Junction, same to Pueblo or Colorado Springs, three and half hours to Denver, four to Durango."

"Why do you think we picked Gunnison?" she chuckled.

"No people means no police. Forty years later, there still isn't a big police presence around here."

For once, I didn't say the quiet part out loud. But I was thinking: I bet the bad guys know that too.

ONE SUCH EVENING, ALEX AND I DETERMINED IT WAS THE right time for a more focused interview.

"Can I get a look at the business's books?" Alex asked.

"I don't have the latest ones, but I'll make sure Joe has a copy for you. Why do you want them?"

"We want to get a better picture of how a business like yours operates," I said. "We need to examine all the angles."

"You do know our financials are audited; they have to be," Laura pointed out.

"By whom?" Alex asked. "You guys are CPAs, right?"

"*Were* CPAs. That was long time ago. Colorado CPAs have to renew every odd-numbered year. We didn't keep up our license. And besides, we'd never be allowed to sign off on our own audits. Joe is a CPA, but he can't sign off either."

"So who does?"

"A fellow named Jeremy Brown. Joe used to be his partner in Harding and Brown in town."

"So now it's just 'And Brown'. Like 'And the Pips' after Gladys Knight left," I noted.

"Eight years ago, Joe left there to join our business here," Laura continued, wisely ignoring me. "But they've stayed good friends."

"What do you think of Jeremy?"

"I...like him...," Laura said, hesitating just a bit.

"But..."

"He's so different from Joe. He's, I don't know, a lot flashier."

A bowl of vanilla ice cream on a white counter against a beige wall would be flashier than Joe, I thought.

"The way he dresses and talks. It's like he sees himself as a big player. In Gunnison of all places. That's what I'm trying to say," Laura said.

DETECTIVE BELLINI CALLED TO TELL ME THAT HE'D LOOKED into the investigative progress since Laura reported her suspicions to the Montrose cops. He delivered less than stellar news. Apparently, Laura's official statement about Stan's murder had kinda drifted down their to-do list.

"It doesn't really surprise me, because they're local cops doing local things," Bellini said. "So, I gave the tip to the CBI in Pueblo. They got back to me and said they'd called the St. Petersburg police who told them there was nothing in their investigation indicating a Colorado connection beyond the victim's residence. Officially, it was an unsolved case, but they have concluded that it was a local drug deal with a tourist gone bad."

"They're wrong," I said. "It started here. I just know it."

"Oh, well then, you just *knowing* something is good enough for me."

"For fuck's sake, Frank. Look at what we've already found out," I said, oozing exasperation.

"What can I tell you?" Bellini said. "They're going to need more evidence to change their minds."

CHAPTER 12

When you're retired, it usually means you're old (or senior or elderly or a gummer, geezer or old fart; pick your least or most offensive term). You start losing track of things. Like your car keys. Like why you went into a room. Or days of the week (although I had already regressed past that to being incapable of definitively naming the month I was in. Or, sometimes, even the year.

For about six months of the year, NFL Sunday is my placeholder, so I knew it was Sunday morning as I sat on Laura's front porch, drinking coffee and baggin' morning rays when I spotted Greg rolling his car out of the garage next door. It's kinda hard to miss a bright orange vintage Mustang. The burbling motor of the beast rumbled in Greg's driveway. He loudly gunned the engine a couple of times. Those revs are a siren call to all males and some females of a certain age within hearing distance, inviting them to come check it out. So, I walked over to check it out.

Verily I say unto you, I am the anti-Christ to car guys. I couldn't care less what I drive, and I have absolutely no idea what makes a car work or even how to keep one clean. But Greg obviously did, as I met him coming out of his garage with buckets, various rags, sponges, and an array of spray bottles.

"Time for her once-a-week bath," he announced, setting down his cleaning paraphernalia. "But take a look at this first!"

He popped the hood, and we stood side-by-side marvelling at the big engine idling away. I, of course, had no idea what I was looking at and the commentary from Greg didn't clarify things. Here's what I heard: "375 horsepower...429 cubic inches...Quick Fuel carburetor, Weiand intake manifold, and a PerTronix distributor, with an FSR racing radiator,aluminum heads...0-60 in 6.8 seconds...4-speed manual Hurst shifter...9000 rpm red line."

Here's what I understood: "inches," "seconds," and "red."

"Only five hundred made," he said emphatically as he slammed the hood closed.

I figured I should contribute to the conversation.

"Cool," I said, not knowing if it was or wasn't.

As he unspooled the hose, I decided to switch to a non-automotive subject.

"Do you mind me asking why you live here and not in town near the store?" I asked.

"I've got to be close to Johnny and what he's coming up with. No choice but to stay current. Today's consumers—the younger ones anyway—are always looking for the next big thing, and then, right away, the next big thing after that."

"The way they descend on trendy restaurants like locusts and then move on."

"Exactly! Plus, I do love it out here. And so does Elena. Smell that air!" he said and, as if to demonstrate how to do that, he took in a deep, deep breath.

A word about that air: Yes, it was clean and fresh but, because that air was about a mile and a half higher than sea-level, there wasn't much of it. I got dizzy the first time I had a big toke of it.

"So, you're here trying to find out what happened to dad?" he asked out of nowhere.

"Your mom told you."

"Yup. Anything I can do to help, you let me know."

"Now that you mention it. I need the names of the two store workers you let go for stealing."

"Why?"

"We're looking for anybody that had a grudge against you, your father or the company in general."

"They couldn't possibly have been involved," he insisted.

"Maybe not directly, but who knows who they talked to or maybe encouraged to get even."

"One was Dawn Van something or other. And honestly, I can't remember the other one's full name. Brittany, I think. Sorry. They weren't with us for very long."

"Alright...oh, there's something else bothering me. Alexandra said you weren't particularly keen to talk about your robbery."

"She's right. I'm not. It wasn't pleasant."

"I understand, but we have an idea about who might've been behind it."

"You do?" Greg asked with a hint of surprise in his voice. "Who?"

"I'd rather not say right now because we don't have anything conclusive. That's why I need you to think back. Anything, anything at all that you can remember about the bandits."

"Like I told the cops, they wore masks. Honestly, I don't remember much else."

"Yeah, but height, colour of their eyes or hair, left-handed or righties when they held the guns, anything about their voices, an odd phrase they used, anything stick out about their clothes."

Greg looked to be in the act of remembering before he answered.

"One was average height, wore camo pants, grey hoodie. He did the talking—and that wasn't much. He ordered me out of the car, said "Trunk now!" and then after he had the weed, he told me to sit there for a half an hour. The other guy was taller and skinny, jeans and a plain black t-shirt, he had a blue ball cap pulled down tight. He didn't say anything. Both right-handed."

"Anything on the ball cap?"

"Uh...a small crest, white and red, not a pro team or anything."

"Thanks, Greg. You've been really helpful."

"If I think of anything else, I'll let you know," he offered.

I left him spraying his tires with something that made them factory-black again. Our brief chat bugged me because, in my experience, anyone who feels it's important to use the word 'honestly'—twice in a short conversation—usually isn't. Yet he didn't flinch from my questions, immediately supplied answers, and maintained eye contact throughout, while appearing to be totally co-operative. But I could not accept that he didn't instantly remember the full names of the two store workers he whacked, after being with them for weeks or months. Nor could I buy his earnest but vague descriptions of his robbers.

Conclusion: Greg had a swell car. He was also a terrifically good liar, which, I guess, is a real asset if you're a 'tell 'em what they want to hear' salesman.

I RETURNED TO LAURA'S HOUSE JUST AS SHE AND ALEX WERE heading out on a shopping excursion to Colorado Springs. I did the math: three hours to get there, three hours back, lunch then raids on selected stores. I had the day to myself and myself determined that watching "big men fall down go boom" as my toddler of a daughter had once described football, was the only acceptable way to fill that day.

I readied myself for seven hours of NFL on Laura's big screen. Stations found, remote in hand to switch back and forth, and a line-up of frosty Banquets in the fridge. Good to go. I didn't count on an hour's nap happening; but in my defence, it was either the Titans-Browns or the Broncos and Saints, for Christ's sake, and Laura had a great sleepin' couch.

It was dark and I was refreshed and well into the Sunday night game when the womenfolk returned. They went to bed early because they're also early risers who are real busy during the day doing things while I'm busy pacing myself— for what I've never found out. I was wide awake, and the house was dead silent. Sadly, the game (Giants-Falcons) was boring as fuck, so I forced myself to turn it off.

I figured Alex needed some reading material. We hadn't yet picked up the financials from Joe, so I thought I'd trot over to his place and get them.

I knocked on Joe's door well after nine, when I figured his kids would be in bed. He seemed irked and he seemed semi-drunk when he opened the door. Perfect, I thought, as he led me to his office; he just might accidentally tell me something useful. He plunked himself down in his chair and picked up a large glass of red wine. He didn't offer me any which was surefire hint that he wanted me the fuck gone. That was just as well, as I have avoided red wine since my university days when I had more than a few tangles with it, always ending up on the losing end as judged by the massive, whanging headaches the next day.

"Now," he said as soon as I sat down. "Tell me what you want."

"For starters, the most recent financial statements for RMHH Enterprises."

"I can't think of a reason you need to see them."

"That's OK, you don't need a reason; you just have to hand them over," I said, getting immediately pissed off at his resistance.

"Why?"

"Alright, you win. I'll give you two reasons: First, they're public information and second, and best of all, your mother and the majority shareholder in the company told you to."

After pausing, he slid a slim binder across the desk.

"Anything else?" he more or less demanded, as he poured himself another glass of wine.

"Yeah, there is. I'm dying to know why you're being such a dick?"

"I'm sorry, but you being here is a constant reminder to

mom of Florida and Dad's death. She needs some peace and quiet so she can heal and try to move on."

"Fair enough. But she did invite us, and she did tell us she enjoys us hanging around."

"My mother's very polite."

I reckoned a change in subject was needed before I lost my shit on him.

"Alexandra told me you were concerned about the business if Johnny and Greg didn't up their game."

Joe took another huge swig of wine. I could see he was getting amped up.

"I am. I just record things, but I can see where we're falling down. They have to grow better product and sell more effectively. If dad was around, they wouldn't get away with their excuses. They won't listen to me, and Mom babies them."

"How so?"

"Greg's a Class 'A' bullshitter. He can wriggle out of anything, all the while convincing you that he's a marketing genius and that he's working flat-out."

"He isn't?"

"He spends more time with that damn car than he does working sales leads."

"And Johnny?"

"Johnny the Master Grower this and Johnny the Master Grower that! It's sickening. And what he does isn't even that hard. But mom always takes his side; just like when we were kids. The guy's spent most of his life as a fuck-up. Mom and dad rescued his ass, paid his tuition, paid for rehab, gave him the best lot to build on while I got the worst one. Him—a supposed adult—and they had to save him."

"Look, Joe, I was an only child, so I don't claim to know the feelings of the eldest kid. But maybe you could try to understand that your parents realized Johnny needed saving, whereas you other two didn't. I bet you got the worst building site because they knew you'd do something with it. Think about it; it was compliment really."

My spur of the moment defence of his parents made him pause, but not stop.

"Think he won't fuck up again?" Joe said. "Think again."

I came away from his house more than a little surprised at the apparent depth of Joe's bitterness towards Greg and Johnny.

Tolstoy started off *Anna Karenina* with this: "Happy families are all alike; every unhappy family is unhappy in its own way." Maybe ol' Leon was right. I don't know. I've really got no idea about the dynamics of a family, mostly because I never had much of one. A saintly mother, a largely absent father and me, that was it. And now, I'm the only survivor.

But I do know that everybody's different (earth-shattering observation, huh?). Each member will be affected by whatever chemicals are in their brain mixed with different experiences, largely, it seemed, based on birth order. Toss in the fact that this particular family had three boys, all relatively close in age and residences, and it's not tough to see that they had no choice but to bring their jealousies and rivalries to the Sunday dinner table.

All that to say, that despite Laura's understandable desire —especially after the loss of its patriarch—to present the Harding clan as one big riotously joyous unit, they weren't. The more we talked to her sons the more abundantly clear it became that there were fissures, chasms perhaps, in the rock wall among the siblings.

The only serious question for me was: did it matter at all, and did it have any bearing on why Stan Harding was murdered?

THE NEXT MORNING, BEFORE ALEX'S MANDATORY (AND unaccompanied) walk, I filled her in on my Sunday discussions with the two boys, as well as the delightful result of the Raiders beating the shit out of Chicago. She didn't share my joy over the Raiders' victory but was intrigued by my conversations with Joe and Greg and by the financial statements I plopped down on the breakfast table.

As was her habit, Laura had already disappeared upstairs to her studio, but I whispered, nonetheless.

"Just maybe there something in there."

As promised, Johnny walked over the list of companies Stan had publicly called out. Five names, all with official-type designations like Sunrise PLC Inc. or 5786211 Pty Limited that revealed nothing about their business or their ownership.

Now why would an illegal pot business need legal incorporations, you ask? Well, if you'll just settle the fuck down, I'll tell you.

Regardless of its size, illegal pot operations are a cash-only biz. Nobody's paying with credit or debit cards, or by cheque or money order because those transactions are all traceable. For small local outfits, taking in cash is not an issue for them or their buyers, unless the sellers are suddenly overcome by a fit of conscience and report it on their 1040.

On the other hand, hard currency presents a real problem for the bigger criminal enterprises. When you have millions of dollars in fives, tens and twenties, their sheer volume alone is an issue. Back in the day, Pablo Escobar stashed mounds of cash in oil drums and buried them; he counted money by weight. But then, he discovered the wisdom of finding banks which were low in ethics and high in greed for more revenue. They'd take his gigantic deposits of small bills, no questions asked, and no authorities informed. Suddenly, the money's all clean and can get moved around in cyberspace as anonymous ones and zeroes to wherever they're wanted.

If Stan was right, the five names on his list were dummy corporations set up to arouse less suspicion over large e-transfers.

Got it? Good. Shameful admission: I had to have Alex use baby talk when explaining it to me.

After she had walked me through the mechanics of money laundering, Alexandra tore the list from my hand and went charging off like those a police dog after catching the scent of a kidnap victim.

CHAPTER 13

A car pulled up to house. I recognized its occupant.

"Release the hounds!" I yelled. Not that Laura's canine guardians needed or sought permission or encouragement to charge a stranger.

Steve wasn't exactly a nature lover. Toronto-born and -bred, he lived in a high-rise condo downtown, bordering on Lake Ontario. Except for his occasional trips to the Hovel at the lake where flora and fauna abound, the only birds he would routinely have seen were screeching seagulls and shit-bombing pigeons, the only animal, a toy poodle on parade and maybe an alley rat or two. Having three giant unleashed dogs galumphing towards him, their eyes full of business, would not be a comfort to him.

Steve was rooted in panic as the canine wave swept around him, until the dogs were called off by Laura.

"Welcome to Colorado," I said, just before our manly and manful hug.

"Excuse me, while I change my underwear," he answered.

Ever hospitable, Laura made a fuss about Steve having to stay in the big house, but Steve wouldn't budge. He had booked a motel near Gunnison so that he could write in peace.

"Added bonus," he said. "It means less time hanging around with Jake."

We had drinks on the back porch. There was a ton of conviviality going around, but the conversation was superficial.

I could see Steve getting antsy and knew he wanted to swing into full journalist mode. As a crime beat reporter for years, he'd conducted hundreds, thousands of interviews, dealing mostly with tough cops and bad guys. Empathy and gentleness were not his guiding principles.

"Let's get you settled in, my friend," I said. "I'd like to see where you're staying."

He agreed and said he'd drive me back.

Alex told me to bring my one and only sweatshirt. Instantly, I was reminded of how, when I was a kid, my mother would tell me to wear a sweater, no matter what the temperature was. So, I ignored my new wife.

Once in Steve's rental car, he turned on me.

"What the fuck was that?" he demanded. "Like you give a shit where I'm staying."

"Of course I don't. But I wanted to fill you in first before you started grilling a recently widowed friend of mine. And there's some stuff I'd rather she didn't hear that you need to know."

We bought a twelve-pack of Banquet, then pulled into Whispering Pines Cabins about a mile from the Harding compound. It was a conglomeration of maybe twenty small log cabins strung along or near the banks of the Gunnison River. Steve's joint was right on the river. Picturesque as hell.

We settled back in his varnished pine emporium—walls, furniture, countertops, kitchenette cupboards—all honey-coloured wood accented by varied kinds and colours of plaid.

After one sip of beer, he was on me.

"C'mon, what up? Whaddya got?"

I spent the next two hours turning over everything Alexandra and I had learned or suspected, beginning with Stan's murder and ending up with my dealings with Detective Bellini. Along the way, I laid out the potential size and dynamics of the illegal grow ops, the imminent arrival of big, nasty criminal organizations in that region of the state, and the efforts Stan had undertaken to expose them, efforts that, somehow, had led to his death. I also talked about the apparent friction of between Laura's sons, and their differing viewpoints on how things were going. I tossed in my belief that Laura seemed oblivious to that rivalry or even the health of her business.

Steve wrote furiously, filling pages and pages of his notebook. He'd stop for questions and clarifications; I answered what I could.

"Does this strike you as something big?" I asked.

"Seems to be," he said, without looking up from his notes. "I need to talk to all the people you dealt with. Especially that cop."

"Not a chance he'll do it. But I'll ask."

"And the sons."

"No."

"You do realize, I don't need your permission. Free speech and all that."

"Steve, I'm telling you: we're going to play it my way."

"Or what?"

"Or your estate is facing a hefty bill for shipping your body home. If they ever find it."

There actually was a moment, a nano-second really, when Steve looked worried, maybe because of our considerable height and weight difference. Or maybe it was because I'd killed a man and, to my knowledge, he hadn't.

"OK, OK, I'm not going to murder you," I said. "But you got to trust me. You haven't been involved in any live-action shit like this. You write about crimes after they've been committed."

"Stan's murder isn't on-going," he noted.

"But the cause is. Whatever our suspicions, we need proof. The same way you always confirm your sources before you publish. We haven't ruled anybody out and there are likely big operators that we haven't even touched yet. But if you show up on their doorstep for your fucking *J'accuse!* moment, they'll either panic and shut everything down and/or kill you. Before you know it, they're in the wind and we've got fuck-all. Oh, yeah, and you're dead."

I hereby acknowledge I was being a touch dramatic with my warning, but he needed to understand how dangerous this could all become for us.

"Jake, think I came all this way to sit around and stare at shiny logs? Not a chance. I want to do something!"

"Patience, my son. Meanwhile, with all I've just given you for a start, why don't you learn more about the business and start writing? Get some local colour in. Research the national scene. Compare and contrast with Canada. As a newbie to the subject, you know you have to do all that shit anyway, so do it here."

"Fine, but this isn't going to be a long fucking essay on growing weed in Colorado. The human story is right here somewhere. But sorry to say, you haven't even scratched the surface of the bigger drama. No one's going to give a shit about how one pot business is doing. Oh, and—stop the presses!—brothers don't always get along. But my audience will care about how and why your friend died. I thought you might too."

That stung. But he was right. Up until that moment, I'd been thrashing around in a small pond. By all indications, there was an ocean, or at the very least, a giant lake of bad stuff going on.

It was dark by the time we'd finished drinking and talking. He drove me back and, as Johnny had told me earlier (but I forgot), the gate was padlocked. Fuck. By the car's headlights, I couldn't see a gap in the surrounding high fence. To the sounds of Steve's laughter, I squeezed my bulkitude through two of the bars in the 20-foot-long barrier and started walking.

It had turned cold, and the wind—at my back, mercifully—was still cutting. Clearly, my Hawaiian shirt wasn't up to the thermal challenge. Oh, and it was pitch black. Not Hollywood backlit blue dark where everybody can see where they're going, but blindfolded black, that required me to scrape my flip-flops just to hear the sound of the driveway gravel under me.

I don't own one of those Big Brother devices that you strap to your wrist and that tells you how far you've travelled, your heart rate, who's going to win the Super Bowl this season, and what time it is in Prague. However, I do like to get my daily steps in. But my target is under twenty, not the five hundred or so that lay between me and the house.

My shivering and pissed-off self was greeted by a roaring fire and Laura's profuse apologies for not telling Johnny I was out and coming back.

Alex was waiting for me too—with a cruel, cruel grin on her face. She had my sweatshirt draped over her arm.

The witch.

STEVE SHOWED UP THE NEXT MORNING BUT WASN'T GREETED BY a menacing canine chorus as the furry guardians had clearly decided he was now one of the family. Steve waved off Mama Laura's offer to feed him and instead wanted a tour of the operation. I walked over with him and told him he ought to be ready to take notes, lots of notes. I left after an introduction to Johnny who seemed keen to educate a stranger on the ins and outs of his domain.

Steve returned to the main house two hours later.

"Fuck, that dude's into it," he said. "Guy seems to know his stuff."

"No shit. He say anything about the family business?" I wanted to know.

"He sorta clammed up when I asked. Said it was doing just fine."

"What's next for you?"

"For sure, not wasting my time talking to you. I've got a book to write!"

After Johnny had exposed him to the complexities of growing pot in the 2020s with the actual product under his nose as a show and tell, I could see that Steve's mind was now racing a mile a minute (sorry, you metric freaks, but a mind racing a kilometre a minute just sounds stupid) over a whole new industry that hadn't been on his radar. I recognized that look he wore. It's the same furiously distracted look I know I have when I'm imagining characters, picturing scenes and, searching for ways to plausibly connect them to some kind of action that, ultimately, has a point. The whole effort is frantic and joyous. Steve was shaping the thing in his brain, imagining the skeleton of the thing. The three cherries of his internal slot machine had tumbled into a row.

So off he went, warning me to not bother him.

While I was illuminating Steve and plunging myself into blackness the night before, Alex was ploughing into the labyrinth that can be corporate ownership if owners do not want to be identified. For private companies, there a lot of ways to stay private, but sooner or later—if you know where to look—names of officers or board members and addresses pop up in their filings or registrations.

I had told her about Stan spending hours outside these businesses. After he figured that a particular parcel of land or a business he'd been watching could very well be a grow op, he'd head to the county land ownership registries or municipal tax records to find the owners. But that was it. He was stymied because one company was owned by an offshore company that was owned by another company, then another. The trail grew fainter and fainter.

Alexandra had a keener nose for this kind of hunt, the

result of years of reading footnotes on company filings. She eventually wound up in a cyberspace that I'd played around in a couple of years ago: The State of Delaware's corporate registration database. Delaware was widely known to be the most secretive state and as a result, had more companies incorporated there than they had people living within its borders. Alex eventually found three of the companies on Stan's list, each one owning a storage business and—would you look at that—a legal pot storefront.

All six businesses had owners who had owners who had owners with the same Delaware post office box number. I knew that registering companies also had to list a physical address, unlike the various Caribbean tax havens. Alexandra found that all six had the same street address. In Vancouver, British Columbia of all places. All of them listed a T. Whelan as President, Owner or CEO and Chairman; no other officers or board members were listed. The most puzzling part of Alex's discovery were the footnotes saying that all six corporations had voluntarily become inactive within the last month.

"Any idea what the fuck all this means?" I asked.

"A bit. Mostly conjecture. It's obviously an organized attempt to cover up the ownership. But why go to all this effort for small straightforward businesses like self-storage or a one-off cannabis store?"

"And why the 'Inactive' listings for them after Stan had stirred the pot of pot?"

"Something's just not right about these companies. They're trying to hide something."

"Cops raided them, didn't find a thing," I pointed out.

"Maybe they were tipped off," Alex offered.

"No way you tear down a big grow op on short notice. Think about moving hundreds, maybe thousands of plants and pots, all the lights, truckloads of soil, piping and all the other gear, and then spotlessly cleaning everything up. You have the address of the storage company in Montrose? I want to check them out."

"I called them and got a recording saying that "Due to unforeseen business circumstances, George's Store-All was ceasing operations immediately." They said that all customers had until the end of the month to re-locate their items in storage, oh, and they apologized for the inconvenience."

"Well damn. OK, let's pay a visit to the stores that Stan said were growing their hybrids. Maybe we'll find something," I said.

"Let's not bother," Alex said. "I called them all. Their phones were disconnected. Looks like they're shut down too. Hate to say it, Jake, but it looks like a dead end."

"It can't be. We're forgetting something real important here. Stan *had* to be on the right track. It scared them and they killed him."

On a hunch, I called Bellini who, as he always did, made clear his annoyance about my peskiness.

"You won't believe this," he said, "But I was just sitting here right this minute hoping I'd get a call from an irritating Canadian."

"Happy to make your dreams come true," I said. "Now, could you tell me about how a tip from Stan Harding burned you?"

"Not my proudest moment. Everything Stan told me made sense, so we moved on it. About two months ago. Two of us and ten local cops hit George's Store-all in Montrose at 6 AM. I had convinced Colorado Springs and Denver to raid the other two places on Stan's list at the same time. We went in with SWAT and dogs, the whole bit. I dragged George outta bed and he opened every storage unit as we looked for this huge grow op."

"And you found shit."

"We found shit times three. Nothing but people's junk."

"Any idea how Stan could be so wrong?"

"No. And I'm trying to blot that day out of my mind. Put it this way, I got passed over for a hero biscuit."

CHAPTER 14

"Guess what I found?" Alexandra asked me after one of her down by the river walks.

"Oh, don't tell me! True enlightenment? A cure for the heartbreak of psoriasis? A lost Stones' record?"

"Arsehole. We're going for a walk. I'll show you."

We had settled into married life—after all, it'd been close to two months!—to such an extent that she now blithely ignored my "Awww, mom, do I hafta?" face when the subject of physical exertion was raised.

So, with my beer in hand, we went walking. West, past Joe's place, along the riverbank obstacle course. After what seemed like an eternity, she then cut inland, along a faint path, leading me through a maze of, first, scrub brush and the prerequisite boulders, then a thick, tangled mini-forest of pine, spruce, whatever the fuck, until we came to an open space.

Unmissable in that clearing was a plot of land, maybe fifty feet by fifty, hosting a decidedly non-native shrub. Eight to ten-foot marijuana plants, their green leaves fluttering in the breeze, their branches laden with large buds.

It took me close to half a second to see these pot plants weren't growing wild. The fact that they were planted in neat rows was definitely a tip-off. As were the three wooden platforms holding up big rain barrels with plastic hoses snaking along the ground throughout the stand of dope. A netting of light-gauge chicken wire on posts was laid on top with the crowns of the plants assigned a square to poke through, I assumed to prevent their heads from snapping off in the wind. On top of the horizontal fencing was a gauzy net with a desert camouflage motif, of the sort you'd normally see draped over artillery in use for a foreign war.

"A secret pot garden on a pot farm," I mused. "That's gotta be a first. I wonder exactly how many plan—"

"—One hundred and ninety-five," Alex quickly answered.

"You counted them all?"

"Not hard. Fourteen rows with fourteen plants each—one died."

"Any idea whose handiwork this is?"

"Yup."

"Well, don't keep me in suspense, woman! I'm bettin' it's Greg's."

"Bzzzt! Wrong! It's Joe's."

"What!? How do you know that?"

"You know how you mock me for walking all the time?"

"Yeah. Highlight of my day."

"Unlike you, Joe walks almost every day."

"So?"

"About a week ago, I noticed his regular strolls along the riverbank, always mid-morning. Yesterday, I followed him. He led me here."

"And now the big question: Why the fuck is he doing this? Let's just assume he's not smoking—what?—about two hundred pounds of this stuff a year."

The answer was obvious.

"He's selling it."

"But to whom?" I wondered.

"If he's supplying the company store, it'd probably show up in the books somehow."

"I don't think he could've borrowed seeds from their indoor operation. Johnny told me they have to record each one."

"Surely a few hundred missing from a batch of thousands wouldn't be missed."

"But how could he inject it into audited statements?"

"Maybe he just calls it something different—like revenue

from consulting services. What's the chance of a state auditor in Denver chasing little RMHH in the middle of nowhere?"

It was no real surprise that Joe's fear of detection would be at the low Defcon-5. Bellini was pretty clear that they didn't have enough bodies to chase all the leads.

"Joe's a math guy. I bet he's calculated the statistical odds of being audited down to the last decimal," I said.

"I should go and talk to him."

"Not just yet, OK?" I said. "Let's keep this in our back pockets for now."

ALEX DID HAVE OTHER PEOPLE TO TALK TO, STARTING WITH Johnny's long-time girlfriend, Charlize Ackerman. On the pretext of buying some sparkly things, Alex arranged to visit Crystaline Designs to check out Charlize's jewellery creations. Crystaline Designs headquarters were located in the one-bedroom apartment she shared with Johnny.

Alex did, in fact, return with several sparklies—a necklace, earrings, several bracelets and a ring—all finely worked silver, uniquely designed and encrusted with polished jade or amethyst gemstones. What she didn't bring back was much in the way of new information.

"She had a vague, airy way of talking," Alex reported.

"Not to be bitchy, she sounded like she was heavily medicated."

"Well, that's bitchy."

"You weren't there. I picked this bracelet which led her to dreamily lecture me on jade's mystical properties. I'm sure you already knew that jade reflects the heart chakra, and will give me feelings of love, empathy, and high self-regard while taking me to a higher plane where I'll be linked through my similarly higher self to the unity of the world."

"I thought that's what your pinot grigio was for."

"Wait. Then came the amethyst talk. Apparently, through this ring, I now have greater intuition and psychic abilities. What's more, my chakra is balanced, and I will soon become serene and calm, free of stress, anxiety and anger."

"I'm all for anything that helps you chill the fuck out, girl."

"Actually, I was thinking of imprinting the side of your head with this ring."

"Whoa! What happened to serene and calm?"

"That might remove my stress."

"Besides thoughts of elderly abuse, did you learn anything that might be helpful?"

"Not really. Apparently, she's got a thriving business in buying and selling crystalline quartz. She collects the rocks on hikes. Charlize doesn't like to come out here because of Laura's 'negative energy' towards her. She was disappointed that they wouldn't be moving out to the main house for the winter as she'd already told some people. She misses Hawaii where she 'communed with similar souls' not found in small-town Colorado. She then got some negative energy of her own going, railing against vaccines, the weather control base in Alaska, and I forget what else, maybe our mistreatment of the aliens who watch over us."

"Conclusion?"

"A strange one, for sure, but harmless, uninvolved in all this dope business. And she makes great jewelry."

Alex felt that she was on a roll and so decided to seek out the remaining two women connected to the Harding boys. Division of labour: I had a nap.

The brain fog of waking up had started to burn off when Alexandra came back with the results of her brief chats with Elena and Cynthia.

Elena was up first. She worked from home, running a court transcription service, turning taped testimony into word docs. When her knocking wasn't answered, Alex went around back and startled Greg's wife who sitting was sitting at her desk, headphones on and typing away like a demon. She motioned Alex inside and they had a quick cup of coffee together.

Alex then crossed the compound to Cynthia and Joe's place where she found Cynthia watching her outrageously cute kids as they horsed around on an outdoor playset.

Alex summarized her impressions of the conversations.

"Both seem to be delightful women, friendly and polite.

Neither had any strong views about the weed business, I suspect because they're busier than hell with their own lives and careers. Here's the difference. With Elena, it was "Greg this and Greg that and Greg says." With Cynthia, it was "Joe needs to do this, and Joe needs to do that, and I told Joe that he should." She wasn't being nasty, but she definitely is used to being in control. I imagine it comes from running a classroom efficiently. I also bet that she's trying to offer solutions because Joe gripes more than Greg."

"Net-net, nothing sticks out?

"Nope."

As promised, I called Detective Bellini to ask him if him if he'd agree to be interviewed by Steve.

"No," Mr. Terse said.

"Are you sure?"

"Yes."

"Why not?"

"My agreement with my bosses is that I deal with you. That's it."

"You'll like him better than me."

"Probably. But maybe not. I'll stick with the devil I know."

"Awww, Frank, I'm getting all misty-eyed, ya big lug."

He hung up.

I messaged Steve to tell him a chat with Bellini wasn't going to happen.

He wrote back: *We'll see.*

I had to smile. I knew Steve wouldn't take 'no' for an answer. But I also knew he hadn't experienced a Bellini 'no.' This should be good, I thought.

CHAPTER 15

A couple of days later, Alex returned from her morning walk. She was limping badly, and her left ankle was bandaged up.

What the hell happened, babe" I asked as I ushered her over to a chair and slid an ottoman under her legs. "Wait. Do you need ice on that? Or heat? I can never remember which. Like, is it feed a cold and star—"

"—Ice, please."

I retrieved a dish towel packed with frozen cubes and wrapped it around Alexandra's ankle.

"Now where was I?" I said. "Oh yeah: What the hell happened, babe?"

"I usually walk west past Joe's place because it's wilder and more interesting. But this time I headed east along the river, past Greg's and then all those estates. There are a lot more rocks to climb over. It was maybe ten or eleven houses away—a great big Tudor-style place owned by a guy named Singletary. My foot slipped, got stuck in a crevice and I twisted it. Hurt like a bastard."

"And that's when you magically realized that the home-owner's name was Singletary?"

"Arsehole. I'm getting to that. Listen; this is important. This man was sitting on a lawn chair watching the river when I cried out. He came running. He helped me up to his patio, sat me down and went into the house to get me a tensor bandage."

"Sounds like a champion Good Samaritan."

"Yes, but here's the important part: he left the sliding glass door open when he went inside. That's when it hit me."

"What hit you?"

"The incredibly strong smell of marijuana."

"Maybe he had just sparked up a doobie."

"Not possible because a) he was outside on the lawn and b) no way one joint stinks that badly."

"Your conclusion, Watson?"

"Well, Shlepprock, I think this could be one of those grow houses you told me about."

"Why don't I pay Mr. Singletary a visit to find out for sure?"

"I want to come along."

"Not a good idea, babe. Things might get a little rough. And if the situation calls for fleeing, you can't exactly run away, can you? Plus, to be on the safe side, maybe there shouldn't be any witnesses."

"What the hell are you planning?"

"Nothing too specific just yet, but these fucksticks are part of the problem that got Stan killed. I know I'm going to have a hard time being all neighbourly."

I stopped on my way out the door to ask an obvious question.

"Is this guy anybody I should be worried about?"

"Doubt it. He's older than you. Even shorter, balder, and dumpier than you, if you can imagine."

I set off east along the river, passing some truly huge barns that were a mixture of architectural styles. A couple of modern houses sporting the new trend of being a gloomy dark grey with black trim along the windows, soffits, and doors to brighten things up (in total, looking as if a Goth had come into money), an ersatz Italian villa so over-designed with pointless arches and complicated roofs that Renaissance builders would have been horrified, a fake French mini-chateau with manicured symmetrical plantings, and of course, the more local style of log cabins on steroids or Frank Lloyd Wright knock-offs.

The more I walked—or rather, stumbled—among the rocks, the madder I got. By the time I found the understated Tudor-style McMansion, I was fucking pissed. I had decided to adopt the role of a mean, pushy bastard in my upcoming confrontation. Yup, full assault mode was the way to go. I climbed the riverbank and marched across the lawn towards the man sitting in the Adirondack chair and reading.

"Mr. Singletary!" I barked. "You and I have some business to discuss!"

"Wha-who are you?!" he asked with a look that was both surprised and irked by this insolent trespasser heading towards him.

As he rose from his chair, I could see that Alex had been dead on in her description of him. Mid- to upper sixties. Florid, round face topped by a feeble attempt at a wispy grey comb-over. Maybe five-nine, overweight and kinda doughy. This was not a man who had anything to do with physical labour, maybe in his entire life. But this was also a man who could afford workers to do that physical labour around his meticulously kept lawn and gardens.

"What do you want?" he demanded. "I don't know you! I'm calling the police!"

"Great idea! Tell them to meet us inside."

That stopped him. He lost his attempt to gain control over our tete-a-tete and confirmed that there no fucking way he wanted cops inside his home. I jammed a hand under his armpit and began leading that armpit towards the house. The rest of him followed as he recognized that resistance was futile.

"We can talk right here on the patio," he said quickly as we crossed over from grass to flagstone beside the sparkling pool.

"No, I'd like a little privacy," I said, as I tightened my grip and steered him through the patio doors.

Alex had been right too about the overpowering smell of weed as soon as the door opened. It was as bad as the stench caused by the audience of potheads I was in when I watched *2001: A Space Odyssey* as a teenager in a second-run art house theatre. The dope smoke was so thick the screen was barely visible. I gave up studying the movie and got high instead, as the joints were freely passed around. A solid-gone film classic, I decided, although I couldn't tell you why, but the whizzing light tunnel was really swell.

I sorta spun Singletary around as I released my hold, and he wound up against the granite-topped island in his designer kitchen.

I was briefly distracted, glancing at his kitchen that featured a giant gas stove with enough cooking elements to service a jam-packed banquet hall. That's when he inched open a drawer in the island and began to draw out that great equalizer, a handgun. I didn't have enough time to appreciate the prevalence of American gun culture. But there was a second available when I was able to pounce on him, slamming the drawer closed on the firearm and his soft, pink hand.

While he was busy screaming in pain, I took the black gun and heaved it outside onto the lawn. Singletary quietened down but looked defiant.

"What was I supposed to do?" he said, still holding the

injured hand. "A big stranger abducts me, forces me into my home for God knows what reason."

"And what was I supposed to do? Let you shoot me to prove that "good guy with a gun," stand your ground bullshit? And besides, you're the fucking criminal in all this."

"What are you talking about?"

I gave a couple of exaggerated whiffs of air.

"Do you have any idea," I asked, "what kind of damage this dope business—even your part in this business—is doing?"

"Marijuana is legal. So, I grow a few more plants than what's legal, so what?"

"So what?!" I almost shouted. "People are getting hurt!"

"I don't know about any of that."

"Well, I do! A good friend of mine here was stabbed to death in Florida, likely by the same sons of bitches who hired you."

"You mean Stan from downriver? I understood that was a robbery."

"It wasn't!"

I had to restrain myself. He was standing there, leaning against his gleaming granite countertop, not exactly smug, more like confident in his self-justified actions. He could look around his tight, little universe and command or make sense of everything in it. But like most people, when faced with a harsh world colliding with their bubble, he might see its foundations were not particularly solid. Because most people aren't complete dicks, I figured he just needed a tiny nudge towards doing the right thing.

I moved closer.

"The knife that killed Stan," I began, "went in about *here*," (I pushed hard at his ample belly with a fist), "then he brought it up like *this*, until it was inside his rib cage." (I almost lifted him off his feet with that fist tucked under his rib cage), "Then he gave it a sharp *twist*," I said, grinding his solar plexus, "so that it *ripped* his heart apart."

He was staring at me dumbfounded.

"Are you with me so far?" I asked, my face almost pressed against his. "And just so's you know, he didn't die instantly, so imagine the agony he was in as he bled out. All within fifty feet of his wife."

"I...I had no idea."

"Now you do."

I relaxed my hold. Singletary was shaking. I didn't know if it was because of my indictable assault on him or the realization that there were indirect but serious consequences to his actions.

"And now," I continued, "you have to decide if you're going to help me bring these bastards down or not. But, Mr. Singletary, I need you to think real hard before you answer," I added to go along with my menacing glower.

"What do you want me to do?"

"First, you're going to talk to me. And you're going to tell me the truth," I said as I backed off. "And you're going to wrap your pea-brain around the fact that this source of extra income has just dried up."

"I can't quit!" he pleaded. "They won't let me! Last year, I told them I wanted out and was going to sell the house. They told me that was a bad idea. A really bad idea. They reminded me that my two grandkids seemed happy to visit me here and wouldn't it be just terrible to see them hurt."

"Alright, alright. Act normal and keep doing what you're doing until after the next harvest while I figure out how to get at them. But first, get comfortable while we finish our chat."

Singletary and I sat at the kitchen table. I softened up my bullshit tough guy act, so he relaxed a bit. I almost felt sorry for the guy. One minute, his world is spinning along in greased grooves, the next, it all comes crashing down as his freedom, his physical health, and his money-making scheme were seriously threatened. And all because Alexandra twisted her ankle.

I said: I *almost* felt sorry for the guy.

"First off, tell me how you got involved."

"It was three and a half, almost four years ago," he began. "I had just retired from the bank. I was at a party in Pueblo, and I got to talking with a man I knew from another bank. He had just retired too. He wasn't a close friend or anything, but we were in the same business. Anyway, it wasn't long into our chat when he started telling me about the four-bedroom oceanfront condo he'd just bought in Corpus Christi and the cabin cruiser to go along with it. I knew he didn't have a very senior position at the bank, so I made some off-hand comment wondering how he could afford those things while I was just scraping by. That's when his voice dropped, and he told me he was renting out his house in Pueblo. I thought it was Airbnb or something like that. He corrected me, saying that he was renting rooms for an "agricultural enterprise." He made it sound like not that big a deal."

"He give you details?"

"Yes. He ran though the numbers, ending up with a very attractive bottom line. It sounded like a no-lose proposition. I admitted I was interested. Hell, back then, I had three kids in college at 40K a year each, and a big empty house, you understand. Why wouldn't I be interested?"

"Where was your wife in all this?"

"Somewhere in the south of France, I think, presumably having a grand time with her divorce money."

"So how did you make the deal?"

"After I told this banker I was keen, he said to expect a call."

"Any idea why this guy would even tell you all this?"

"Up front, he admitted they'd pay him a bonus for referring me."

"So, the call came?"

"No, this young man just showed up. Short fellow, early twenties, smartly dressed, driving a high-end Audi. Pleasant and well-spoken as all get out. It may sound ridiculous to you, but there wasn't any sense of illegality or danger as he more or less repeated the terms and assured me I had no need to be involved with setting up or operating the...the business. We even shook hands, like I used to do hundreds of times for business loans."

"Sign anything?"

"No. But almost as an afterthought, he said that his *company* required "utmost discretion" and then he asked me if I knew what that meant. His tone changed with that question. He was dead serious. Here's a man, a kid really, presenting a condition to someone twice his age, but I knew —I felt—that my silence was non-negotiable. I asked about the referral bonus that brought me in. He said I had a six-month probationary period. *If* everything worked out, he'd *groom* me for that."

"What's that amount to?"

"Fifty thousand."

"Did you qualify?"

"Yes. Twice. A neighbour along this road and a friend outside Denver."

"Did he have any other conditions?"

"Quite a few actually, but no deal breakers. I had to ensure all utility bills were paid on time, I had to monitor the pre-set room temperatures once a week. Oh, and I couldn't have anyone in the house for a two-month period when the plants were flowering."

"Why not?"

"That's when they stink so much that the carbon filters they installed don't work."

"I gather the little darlings are flowering now," I said, taking a snort of the pungent air for that unmistakable scent.

"Yes, unfortunately. I would guess that you're connected to the beautiful woman with the twisted ankle who was here earlier."

"You'd be right. I'll be sure to tell her. What's this kid's name?"

"Richie."

"Richie what?"

"No last name, just Richie."

"So, you sign on, then what?"

"A crew more or less moved in for several days. They took away all the furniture, put plastic on all the walls and ceilings in three bedrooms and the basement to reduce the mold, did a fair amount of plumbing and re-wiring, installed the lights, piping, fans, and air filters, and, finally, they set up row after row of these small plants."

"I'd like to see them," I said.

Singletary led me downstairs to the basement. The footprint of his house was huge, so the basement was correspondingly gigantic. The entire unfinished space was a thick forest of pot plants. In their straight rows, they looked like an army of seven-foot leafy alien invaders, which I suppose they kinda were.

The smell of weed was even more overpowering and, as

we stood there and beheld the foreign sight, the only sound was the hum of a fan system and the gentle burbling of the drip hoses feeding the big cash crop.

"What's this worth?" I asked.

"To me? About a hundred and fifty thousand for the basement. Well, it used to. They've been paying less and less."

"Let's get out of here," I said as I could no longer stand the stench. Some people claim to like the aroma as though it was some sort of bitter incense. I never much cared for it, certainly not in that volume.

Back upstairs, we adjourned to the patio. Our chit-chatting wasn't done; I wanted to get into the details of how the business actually worked, how he got paid and so on.

Singletary described the mechanics. Innocuous-looking white cargo vans would pull up. They were decorated with magnetic decals of national brand logos—Amazon, UPS and such—or local companies – insect exterminators, pool companies, plumbers.

That was another smart move on Richie's part, I thought. A fleet of service vans (or more likely, one or two vehicles with these interchangeable decals) driving around an upscale neighbourhood, servicing the needs of a wealthy and useless clientele. You'd see them on the street, or pulling into driveways and you wouldn't think anything of it. Who stops the bug guy? Or the cable guy (unless it's to yell at him)?

In this neck of the woods, there were lots of woods. Most

of these houses were invisible to their neighbours, their estates hidden by trees—pine, spruce, whatever the fuck—so you'd never see them loading small bundles of weed or unloading equipment.

Singletary went on to say that twice a year, at harvest time, a team of four or five young women would arrive to cut the plants down and suspend them from lines of thick strings anchored to the walls near the ceiling. They would adjust the room temperature down ten degrees and crank up the fans to circulate the air. Their final act would be turn off all the lights and warn Singletary to keep the rooms dark as the plants dried. Ten days later, they'd come back and turn his kitchen into a processing facility and his living room into a dormitory. With the consumer demand for all-bud all-the-time, they'd put in ten and twelve hours a day pruning and snipping away any trace of stem or leaf before tightly packing one-pound portions of pot in plastic bags after carefully weighing them.

"They must've been on some kind of quota system," Singletary observed, "because they worked quickly and were exhausted at the end of the day. They ate, watched a bit of TV, but mostly they slept on my couches and mattresses they'd brought."

Singletary had to feed them and then he would retreat to his master bedroom or outside as they worked away for three or four days. At the end of it, the place was as spic n' span clean as when they'd arrived.

Then the crew would go on to the next house. I figured it wasn't exactly seasonal work. The indoor-growing season wasn't dependent on the weather so a smart operator—which Richie seemed to be—would stagger the planting times, both to ensure a constant workforce and keep the product fresh.

Next came more vans to pick up all the wastage. That's a whole lot of compost material, I thought. I wondered what they did with it because burning that amount of thick stems, branches, and leaves would be a tip-off to anybody with a nose.

Finally, there was the settling up time. No bundles of cash ever crossed hands a la the Escobar years.

"Richie set me up as a company registered in the Caymans and then it was just a matter of e-transfers from one of his companies. Both of us had access to the account but I had a withdrawal limit. Richie told me he could make all the money vanish if I stepped out of line. He always paid when he said he would and everything just ticked over," Singletary explained.

"But you said the money was going down."

"Yes. Last year, I got about 20% less than when I started. A month ago, Richie drove out here to personally tell me they were reducing my pay by another 20%. He looked me dead in the eye and said business was tight and what was I going to do about it? He knew my answer: Nothing."

"Anything stand out about Richie?"

"He had another new Audi. It must easily be worth a hundred and fifty grand."

"Anything else?"

"Beyond the fact that he was extremely presentable, articulate, and self-assured—which I found highly unusual for a young person? No, not really. He was short."

"The new car. What colour?"

"Black."

"Happen to get a licence number?"

"No.... Wait, I did notice something. I was admiring his car, and I saw a blue triangle sticker on his windshield. I recognized it because my son had one. It was a parking pass for UCCS."

"UCCS?"

"University of Colorado – Colorado Springs."

Hmmm, I thought. Could he be a current student or had he graduated some time ago and just hadn't scraped off the sticker?

"What year was the car?"

"He said it was brand new."

Judging by the network of houses and workers he'd built, Richie would have been at this enterprise for quite some time before he found Singletary. Or maybe he had inherited the infrastructure.

"Are you going to the police?" Singletary asked.

"Not yet. Maybe never, as long you close everything down when I tell you to."

"Agreed. Listen: You can't let this get out. I think this Richie fellow may very well be dangerous."

"Piece of advice, Mr. Singletary: Don't worry about him. Worry about *me*," I said, bringing back my thug self to remind him of a clear, present, and nearby danger to his health. "And it's in your best interests to not tell him or anybody else about our little chat. You know that rule Richie has about silence being golden?"

"Yes."

"I've got the same rule," I added. "Understood?"

"Not a word. I swear."

"And I'll need the names of your neighbour and that friend in Denver. Oh, and the guy who recruited you."

"Is that really neces-"

"Yes, it is! I'm not fucking around, Mr. Singletary."

One last tough guy glare and I left with the names, stopping to pick up the gun I'd tossed onto the lawn. I heaved the deadly excuse for home safety into the middle of the river.

"I'll be defenceless!" Singletary protested.

"Just like you were when you had it," I yelled back.

Chockful of questions and comments from our little forced information session, I walked back along the river while staging a roundtable group discussion with myself.

"*Well, Jake, think Singletary will shut the fuck up and not go running to his employer?*"

"Ya know, Jake, I think he'll keep quiet. He looked

genuinely afraid of a more immediate threat right in his neighbourhood."

"So, what did you learn?"

"A whole lot about this large-scale part of the biz. And that Bellini had described it to a 'T'."

"Sum it up for me, Jake.

"Well, Jake, it looks like a smart college kid is using mansions to run a massive illegal grow op from his dorm room in Colorado Springs."

Think maybe he's not the head of this? Maybe he's the presentable, hands-on guy fronting for the nastier outfits Detective Bellini described. Mafia, perhaps, biker gangs or maybe even cartels."

"Maybe. But I don't think so. Yeah, there was the hint of violence, but nothing crude. The operation sounded way too slick and sophisticated."

"What's that tell you?"

"This Richie is incredibly fucking smart."

"Smart enough to not use his real name?"

"Thought of that."

Did it occur to you that because this Richie showed up four years ago that he probably graduated?

Singletary said the new Audi was this year's model. Why would he have a parking pass sticker on it if he'd already graduated?

"OK. So, where's that leave you?"

"Looking for an incredibly fucking smart kid who may or

may not be named Richie among thousands of smart kids at the University of Colorado in Colorado Springs."

"If he even goes there, and it's not just a trick to hide his identity."

"Oh, fuck off, will ya? I've gotta start somewhere!"

"Good luck, buddy."

CHAPTER 16

I duly reported to Alex when I got back to Laura's. She was still nursing her ankle but seemed to become more animated as I described my exchange with your friendly neighbourly criminal pot grower, even after I led with Singletary's comment on her beauty.

"I should've been there," she said. "I found him."

Gosh, have I mentioned how much I like these would've/could've/should've discussions? Unless you own a functioning time machine, they're at least as pointless as wishing you'd bought a winning lottery ticket after the numbers are published.

"We can head right back there," I said, with a dab of snark in my voice. "You know, try to re-enact my encounter. I mean, we can try, but it won't be the same because he's already met me."

"Arsehole," she said.

It struck me that, although she had used this term of endearment with me on hundreds of occasions, the tone was always playful. This time, if I didn't know better (and I usually don't), she meant it.

"I don't want to sound patronizing" I said in a patronizing way, "but just what the hell is going on with you?"

"It's becoming abundantly clear to me that you just expect the little woman to be at home darning socks."

"C'mon, Alex. Think you were the best person to go out on a drug-buying expedition trying to find people who were likely murderers? Or what about confronting that Singletary dude with the house full of dope? Oh, by the way, turns out he had a gun that I managed to get away from him before he shot me. Figure you were the person for that job, or that you'd able to run away if shit got real?"

"So wifey-poo stays in the cave while you do all the hunting and gathering?"

"Know how you always call me an old fart who's out of touch?"

"You *are* an out of touch, old fart."

"I'm trying to modernize."

"How so?"

"Try this: "Alexa...turn off"."

Have you ever had that moment when you say *exactly* the wrong thing? And you know it, even as the words are coming out of your mouth? I have them all the time so I'm quite good at recognizing them. This was just such a moment. Now, I'd seen Alexandra angry, mostly at someone else, but this, this looked like unbridled fury. Pity the poor bastard who caused this. Oh, wait, that was me. I braced myself for I don't know what.

But instead of going primeval on my ass, she took a few deep breaths and calmed herself. I was shocked as she grinned, then chuckled and then laughed out loud.

I joined her and, still laughing, we hugged like crazy, and I was reminded—yet again—of why I loved this woman so much.

"Now *that* was funny," she said as we broke the clinch. "Just don't use that line again."

Note to self: use that line again. But only as the last, last, last resort.

Show me a Rubicon and I'll take a power boat across it.

"Jake, I just want to help."

"I know, babe. And you have. Talking to all those people, finding Singletary and Joe's pasture of plenty. Now, that I think about it, you've accomplished a shit-ton more than I have."

"You somehow seem surprised."

"And, my favourite witch, what pisses me off is that you're going to do a lot more."

"How?"

"For starters, we—and I emphasize the 'we' part—are going back to school as soon as your ankle heals!"

CHAPTER 17

T he next morning, Alex tested her ankle. There was an occasional wince as she paced around but clearly her injury was getting better. She was hobbling less, and the swelling had subsided.

"Look like that goiter on your ankle is gone for now. But Dr. Jake says a bit more bedrest."

"No. It's fine," she insisted (and when Alex insists, I listen). "Let's take a drive to Colorado Springs."

"I don't know as you're up to strutting your stuff on campus, babe. Bound to be a lot of walking."

"Alright. I'll test it more around here. But first, I want to go through the company's books."

Off she went to do one of her favourite things: reading numbers in columns.

I hadn't seen or heard from Steve for a while, so I thought I'd pay him a visit. The cops call it a wellness check.

I knocked on the door of his cabin.

"Enter!"

His room was a complete disaster. Beer cans, Styrofoam clam shells with limp fries and ketchup blobs, pizza boxes. Any number of paper coffee cups, his clothes strewn hither and yon, random piles of paper and notebooks.

Steve was at his desk facing the large window overlooking the river. He was in a bath robe, hunched over his laptop. He was unshaven and bleary-eyed. Overall, he had the expression I know I wear when I'm coming off a writing jag. It's like being awakened from a trance. You can't quite focus or even speak coherently as you leave one universe and return to another.

"Whatja do? Scare away Housekeeping?" I asked, surveying the detritus.

'I think...they clean every week," he answered after pondering the question as if I had asked him for the square root of 12,748.

"You did all this in seven days?"

"Yeah...I guess," he said, looking around at the mess as if for the first time.

"Well, congratulations! I'm impressed."

"Jake, do you have any idea how big this business is? It's huge, not just here but everywhere."

"No shit? That's what I've been telling you."

"Like I take your word for anything."

"How's the writing going?"

"Great! I'm touching 40,000 words already. Spent a lotta time on research, talked to the FBI, ATF, RCMP, a couple of university-types. I added a lot to what Johnny told me about horticulture. Oh, and I contacted Detective Bellini."

""Contacted"?" I said. "Now that's a weaselly word. Lemme guess what it really means: you dialed, he answered, you identified yourself, he told you to get stuffed and hung up."

"No, smart-ass, he didn't tell me to get stuffed. His exact words were: "Why don't you go fuck yourself?""

"I'll talk to him again. But overall, you're pleased?"

"Yeah...I suppose. Except there's a huge chunk missing. The part you were allegedly working to uncover."

"Get out your notepad out, me boyo! I've got stories to tell."

"Coffee first!"

"How about some fresh air first?" I said, grabbing him and leading to the door.

I pushed him outside. He stood there stunned for a while, then took a few exaggerated breaths, performed a serviceable pirouette, and came back inside.

"Did you make the fucking coffee yet?" he asked.

Suitably java-fied, we sat at the small table, and I

recounted my misadventures over the last week. I decided to start with my interactions with Laura's sons, saving the high-light of the week which was my encounter with Singletary and his grow-mansion. When I'd finished the sibling stories, he flipped through his note pad.

"This is all very interesting," he said. "But I don't think I can use any of it."

"You kidding me? All that human drama! Your audience will eat it up."

"Let's see if I have this right: one son has an illegal grow op, another one steals thousands of dollars worth of pot from his own business, while the last one is being extorted by a Hawaiian drug lord after he stole tens of thousands of dollars in cash from him."

"Well, when you put it like that...."

"That's the *only* way to put it. Jake, you might not know this, but my publisher has a substantial legal department. No way in the fuckin' world are they going to allow me to accuse people of crimes when there haven't been any trials; Christ, they haven't even been arrested."

He was right of course. And the only way the legal process could begin was if I dropped a dime on all three brothers, something I wasn't prepared to do.

"I just don't see how the family angle could work," Steve said.

"Think harder, Homer. Talk to Laura about the history of RMHH Enterprises. For some reason, she seems to like you, so she'll probably spill about the good ol' hippie days of illegal pot growing. Compare and contrast with the giant, nasty business it's become."

"That might be good, but I'll have to interview the boys too."

"But only about the industry these days. And maybe their childhood memories; they grew up around all this weed. I'll pave the way, but you can't mention Greg's and Joe's lawbreaking to them. They don't know that I know. Johnny told me about his Hawaiian unpleasantness, but he won't want to see that in print."

"You got anything else? Because, after the family stuff, all you've given me is a pretty thin gruel."

I had barely started describing my little sit-down with Singletary when Steve interrupted.

"Bullying that guy, disarming him? You're painting yourself to be quite the tough guy in all this. That goes against established fact."

"I was *pretending* to be a tough guy, and I got lucky with the gun. Get that down."

I laid out the important part: exactly how this large weed operation works. All of which was as much of a surprise to him as it had been to me. That took time because there were so many moving parts and Steve, ever the fucking reporter, had detailed questions each step of the way. What I now took as a given was new to him, so I had to reimagine the whole process: A secret network of wealthy homeowners with an active recruitment drive, the logistics of installing the grow-op, the female pruning crew, how the harvesting and drying was done, the punctual offshore banking of likely millions of dollars. And the veiled threat of potential violence. At the centre of it all, a short, young, genius of a man with a high-end car who maybe attended UCCS.

"So did you identify the Mr. Little Big Man of this dope ring or not?" he asked.

"The hunt begins tomorrow in Colorado Springs."

"I want to go with you," Steve asserted.

I imagined breaking the news to Alex that Steve would be replacing her on our sortie to UCCS. Even somewhat crippled, Alex could run me down and disembowel me like a hungry cheetah hot on the heels of an elderly three-legged springbok (notwithstanding the fact that Mother Nature rarely allows three-legged springboks to become elderly).

"Sorry, dude, not yet. I'm saving you for the fourth quarter or third period or seventh inning. And besides, you're on a writing streak. If we learned anything from *Bull Durham*, it's this: you don't fuck with a streak."

He was all pouty for a bit, pointing out that he couldn't name Singletary for the same reason he wouldn't use the male Hardings' lawbreaking.

"All in good time, buddy," I said. "This shit's going to get resolved and, I'm betting, in a very public way. In the meantime, write the whole goddamn thing as if it's a done deal."

"Pure speculation."

"So, it's all not yet presented to you on a silver platter, the way I did for your first two books. I swear I'll wrap it up."

I left feeling uneasy for making what only can charitably be called a foolhardy vow to my friend.

I had no fucking idea how it was all going to play out.

CHAPTER 18

W hen I got back around noon, I quizzed Alex about the financial statements. She had spread out the pages and marked them up with questions and comments. I asked her about her opinion of them.

"I'm a little unclear on how they account for revenues and good will in this business, but overall, they seem clean."

"How's the biz looking?"

"Not good. Barely breaking even. The store's a real drag on income."

"So, what's next?" I asked.

"I want to interview the employees Greg fired."

"I told you; Greg didn't give me their full names."

"You may have failed, but I got them."

"How?"

"There was an addendum to the statements with

employee compensation, including those women. They also had photocopies of their severance cheques with the addresses where they were sent. Both are right here in Gunnison."

"Aren't you Miss Smarty Trousers?"

After Alex left to find the fired employees, I thought maybe I could save us a lot of time by using the Internet and phone in looking for Richie. Just maybe we'd get lucky.

But first, I wanted to get current on my reading. I normally spend a surprisingly long time reading about everything that catches my attention at that moment. It's a surprise, to me anyway, when I look at the clock and see how many minutes and hours I've pissed down the Internet rabbit hole. On-line newspapers and magazines, a couple I even subscribe to, the rest until I get booted out after my monthly maximum number of articles. News, politics, movies, sports, weather in the Kawarthas and Indian Rocks Beach, the lot. I pride myself on keeping current, although I have absolutely no idea why.

I'd even chip in my own views of op-eds in the *Globe and Mail* and *NYT* and that takes even more time because I'd rather not sound like a blithering illiterate idiot. I don't read any differing opinions about anything I've posted because why would I? Whoever is disagreeing with me is obviously wrong.

Hours went by pointlessly getting up-to-date. Hours that I could've spent trying to catch a college-aged drug lord.

I finally decided to do a little research, like I always do before heading into any kind of unfamiliar situation. And I do mean a *little* research, just enough to convince myself that I'm a goddamned expert. I do this not only because I'm terminally lazy, but because I fucking hate surprises.

So, let's find out about out about our hunting ground in Colorado Springs, shall we?

As I knew from previous misadventures, university websites are a font of information, so I started there.

The campus was a ribbon of buildings stretched out along Austin Bluffs Parkway in the city's north end. From the photos, the university was the same innocuous mishmash of architectural styles that all your newer universities feature because all of them grow and none of them have the coin to try to duplicate the centuries-old expertise of the stone masons when they were building near-religious cathedrals in Europe.

By American standards, UCCS was a smallish institution, just over ten thousand enrolled students (no way to determine how many were ditching classes to shoot pool, eat pizza and get drunk and/or high, all on their parents' dime).

Originally a high-class sanitorium in the early 1900s, it earned a widespread reputation for housing elite inmates suffering, presumably, from consumption, the vapours, ague, and the scrumpox. It officially became a campus of the University of Colorado in 1974.

That's about as far as I got by the time Alex returned.

"How'd the ankle hold up, babe?"

"Just fine."

She went on to describe her interviews with Donna Van Houte and Bethany Chalmers.

Barely out of her teens, Bethany lived in Gunnison with her mother who pointed Alex to her daughter's workplace, a family diner just off Tomichi Avenue, the town's main street. Alex waited until she went on break and the two sat down. Apparently, Bethany was young and pretty with curly blonde hair and an effervescent smile. She sounded as American pie as all get out, especially in the blue and white gingham dress uniform the restaurant had outfitted her in.

"As soon as I brought up Bud-inski's and Greg, she broke down in tears," Alex said. "She worked her way through several napkins and seemed completely devastated. She swore she had never stolen anything in her entire life and just couldn't bear the thought of being branded a thief."

Donna Van Houte was a different story. Alexandra found her at home. Alex said she was short, pretty with curly black hair, and wore black jeans and a black singlet. What immediately stood out was the fact she was heavily tattooed.

"She looked like she should be in punk rock band," Alex said. "She had the attitude too. When I explained why I was there, she damn near exploded. Even you would be impressed with the angry obscenities she directed at Greg. She ranted about not needing to steal from the store, but mostly about what an asshole Greg was for firing her. She was also pissed that she had to defend herself to Shar, the girl who got her the job."

"Conclusion, Watson?"

"I believe both of them, Sheerluck. I think that they were telling the truth. Bethany immediately cried when I raised the accusation. When I brought it up with Donna, the way she blew up right away; I was afraid she'd break something. In either case, I just don't think you can manufacture that kind of instant emotion."

"Sounds about right. Now. There are a couple of details I need to go over with you. Did Donna say anything else about this Shar, such as her real name, because nobody calls their kid Shar?"

"No. Maybe I misheard and it's really Cher. Or maybe it's short for Sharon."

"Or Charlize," I suggested.

"Johnny's girlfriend. Of course!"

"Can you describe her tattoos?"

"A bunch of different symbols, some Chinese characters. There was a snake slithering down one arm—"

"—And a black panther on the other arm, clawing at her neck?"

"How the hell did you know that?" Alex asked, verging on being dumbfounded.

"Cuz I'm fucking smart. I saw her in Montrose. She's the girlfriend of the dope dealer who ripped me off."

"So, what's it mean?"

"I don't know. Maybe nothing. Small towns, everybody knows everybody, close associations in the weed business."

Alex had contributed mightily to our storehouse of information while I had accomplished pretty much fuck-all. I told her about my meagre efforts at doing some long-distance sleuthing.

"Why don't you forget all that historical crap and start with whomever issues the parking passes?" Alex suggested.

I had my doubts but agreed to give it a shot. First, I came up with—modestly—a great excuse to talk to the Parking Guy: "You see, sir/madam, someone from UCCS, driving a black, late model Audi with a blue parking pass sticker, had been involved in bending my fender. He had fucked off from the scene, but I caught a glimpse of his sticker and now I just need the bastard's name for the goddamn insurance claim." (or words to that effect). Multiple phone calls and transfers later, I finally got the "fuck off and die" instruction I was expecting.

It is my experience that there are two types of people in the administration of anything. The pleasant kind who will at least go through the motions and, sometimes, actually help you. And the not so pleasant kind who will tell you they are either a) completely buried in work, without so much as two minutes to squeeze into their day to answer your question or b) they were entrusted with fiercely protecting precious private information that, were it to fall into the wrong hands, would lead to the utter collapse of Western civilization.

Guess which one I got?

Ms. Bromly/Trombly/Tweezly (she introduced herself quickly) educated me—at length—on the liability issues to the school and to her personally should she reveal the name of the reckless driver rampaging though the streets of Colorado Springs. She added, finally, that even if there were no downside, she couldn't possibly find the time to tap her keyboard a couple of times because she was buried by the avalanche of new parking pass requests for the next semester, didn't I know and don't I understand.

"So now what?" Alex asked after I had finished cursing.

"Well, we still need to find the son of a bitch. Time for a road trip!"

Next morning, on our three-hour drive through mostly hilly grassland and sage brush plain (again with officially verifiable mountains in the distance!) Alex and I cobbled together a darn good plan to infiltrate the university. We decided we needed cover stories, some bullshit but plausible personae that would allow us to forage for Richie without casting immediate suspicion. This was after we discarded the idea of going through the 10,000-name student directory (If we could even get our hands on one). We also abandoned the task of stopping all the male students to ask their first name. Nor did we think going to the Registrar's Office and wondering: "Excuse me, but does anybody named Richie go here?" would work.

"Let's focus on which faculties we think this "Richie" might belong to. From Singletary's description, the obvious choice is the School of Business."

"Too stereotypical perhaps?" Alex wondered.

"Maybe, but more likely than, say, pegging him as a post-grad philosophy student with a minor in medieval Christian monasticism."

"Agreed."

"Plus, if you had bothered to study the university's parking map, you'd know that there are blue sticker parking lots on either side of the school of business."

"So, we find an expensive Audi and wait for him?"

"Maybe, but maybe there are a few Audis, maybe he doesn't have classes today or maybe he's assigned one of three other Blue parking lots farther away that I'm sure you didn't know about either. We'd miss him. We need a name first."

We eventually agreed that we'd pose as recruiters searching for candidates to fill different high-paying jobs. We'd do that by asking professors to name their top students.

Alex is a terrible liar, so it made sense for her to use her honest-ta-god real identity as Chairman of Greenvest, origi-nally a one-woman ethical investment boutique that, through hard work and a dazzling brain, she had grown into a multi-multi-million-dollar national concern with upwards of a hundred analysts and brokers.

"Alex, do you really think you could pass yourself off as someone who knows the slightest thing about finance or running a business?"

"I could give it a shot, arsehole. Who are you going to be? An eccentric expert in college parking lots?"

"Close, witch. UCCS brags about its Business Innovation. They even offer a bachelor's degree in it, separate from a regular ol' Business degree. I'm going to be the president of an AI start-up looking for a new VP of Finance. I'll stress our new company's need for young, aggressive self-starters with business smarts and I'll dangle the possibility of getting in on the ground floor with the resulting stock options worth millions."

"Good story; I'd even buy it. Except, what the hell do you know about how AI actually works?"

"The same as everybody else: Absolutely nothing."

"Now, how do we get around the college's ban on campus recruiters?" she asked.

"What?"

"They can't have recruiters crawling around campus all the time. It's distracting. So, they allow them in during a Recruitment Week or a career fair. Companies come, set up booths or tables and do their headhunting."

"Like Amsterdam hookers?"

"A little more complicated than that. So how are you going to handle that?"

"I'll start with my famous "Please, please, please with a cherry on top" gambit. I'll say...I'll say that I heard great things about the UCCS School of Innovation and that I was from Palo Alto, but in the area on...on a hiking trip, so I thought I'd stop by."

"You think anybody's gonna buy your hiking trip bullshit, once they get a load of your old man chicken legs?"

"Witch, again! I'll just explain that I'm new to the sport or lifestyle choice or whatever you people call that utter waste of time walking uphill. Now what excuse are you going to use?"

"Yes, I could use good people at my company, but I'm also here as a favour to a friend. She asked me to check up on her nephew who goes here. But, silly me, I forgot his name. A Richard or Richie somebody. Really bright boy, but his aunt is worried."

"Geez, that's good, I said. "I think we're ready."

"Lock and Load," Alex said.

"What the fuck did you just say?"

"Isn't that what all you macho types say before a mission?"

"I was going to say: "Let's find him." But lock and load? Now you're scaring me. You aren't carrying a gun or anything, are you? Tell me you aren't planning to shoot him on sight."

"Can I say: Let's do this?"

"Absolutely not!"

"OK, then. Let's do this!"

AT THE BACK OF THE CAMPUS WAS A SORT OF A RING ROAD. ON one side, a row of buildings and parking lots; on the other, empty hilly land full of scrub brush that ran for a great distance. The road was called Mountain Lion Way, presumably to encourage hiking through that aforementioned hilly scrub brush.

One of the buildings along that road was the School of Business. We entered Dwire Hall that also housed the School of Business Innovation. The interior of it was the same, I assumed, as all the other newer faculty buildings. It had that institutional feel, with ridiculously high-ceilinged atriums, lots of pot lighting, lots of glass, lounging couches, and concrete pillars.

We agreed to meet back at the car in two hours and split up.

I was done first so I hung out at the car, doing what I always did those days: craving a cigarette.

"I found him!" Alex announced as she walked up to the car.

"No, *I* found him," I said. "But you go first."

"Our man is named Richard McGrath. Who do you think you found?"

"Our survey said: Richard McGrath! Ding! Ding! Ding! We have a winner!"

We recapped our interview subjects. Each of us spoke to four professors whom we trapped in their offices. After we spilled our exceedingly excellent cover stories that were not questioned, we asked them to name their most outstanding student. Seven of them immediately came up with one guy who was intellectually superior—by far—to the rest of his classmates. While they heaped praise on his academic achievement, they all noted his quirkiness, best summed up by one's description of him as "an odd duck, intelligent as heck, with a snazzy car."

One prof refused to answer. Alex told me that he was a nervous young guy who said he was uncomfortable with ranking his students.

Just to prove that both of us can be pretty fucking dumb, we established that neither of us had asked for a physical description. So, all we had to go on was that he was short.

"The teachers haven't changed a bit," Alex remarked. "Talking to them made me feel like I was right back at Vasser."

"Reminds me, and you'll appreciate this—"

"—Why do I highly doubt that?"

"No, no, listen: back in high school, me and a buddy would sit around stoned and think of punchy slogans for

American universities to increase enrolments. Like: 'Yale Won't Fail', 'Harvard Beats All', 'Stanford and Your Son', 'Smile at Colgate.'"

"So?"

"I came up with 'Yessir, Vassar!'. Catchy, huh?"

"It was a 99% female school when I went there, ya big moron."

"I know, but "Yes, Madam Vassar" kinda sucked."

"Seriously, now what?"

"Beer."

"Really?"

"We need a good long, frank, open, and candid, oh, and earnest discussion with him. We can't just confront him on the fly in a hallway or a classroom. Let's get something to eat, maybe have a drink, and find out where he lives. Then we catch him around dinner time."

Near the university, we found a casual, diner-type eatery where you'd expect the most adventuresome dish to be a club sandwich with real turkey instead of mock chicken slices. Mid-afternoon and the joint was less than half-full. To start off, I ordered an ever-reliable Banquet beer while Alex agonized over the extensive wine list of two white wine choices before settling on a cheeky Chateau de Plonk chardonnay, with the highly regarded vintage of last Tuesday.

"I think we should start with the university residences," I said.

"C'mon. With the money you told me this guy must be pulling down, do you really think he lives in a crappy dorm room?"

"Think about it. We know this guy is real smart. Why wouldn't he pretend to be an ordinary, unobtrusive university student? It's the perfect cover while he hoards cargo loads of cash. In fact, I wouldn't be surprised if he's got degrees from all sorts of universities. Remember, this dope operation was set up years ago."

'And if he's not in a residence?"

"Alright. Division of labour: I'll work the residences; you've got the city. Go!"

"Let's do this!" my cheeky new bride said again.

So, there we were, dueling laptops, ignoring each other, tap-tap-tapping and scrolling away at our devices, all the while fitting in with all the Millennials or Gen fucking K, or whatever they're called these days, sitting at tables around us doing exactly the same thing.

We raided every database we could think of, searched address books and list compilations.

Finally, I said: "Bingo!"

"Bingo for me too!" the ever-competitive Alex said.

"There's an R. McGrath in residence here. So there!" I said.

"And I've got one in the southwestern part of town. So there!"

"One of them's gotta be our guy. Odds are pretty slim that

there are two R. McGraths in this small city who routinely hire assassins."

"Who faces whom?"

"Another division of labour. Why don't you check out Southwest Richie and I'll handle Richie Rez? Make sense?"

"Okay."

"Any idea what your approach might be?" I asked.

"I'll turn on my feminine charm," Alex said, getting in a few practice eyelash battings.

"For Christ sakes Alex, *if* you find him, he's gonna see that you're old enough to be—"

"—Don't you *dare* say I'm old enough to be his mother!"

"Oh c'mon, Alexandra. That's not fair. That didn't cross my mind. I'm hurt that you'd even think that of me."

"What were you going to say then?"

"That you're old enough to be his grandmother."

"You flaming, *flaming* arsehole!"

"But funny."

"But funny," she admitted. "What's your award-winning approach going to be?"

"I'm going to lean on him, rattle him. Like my dealing with that dope house owner Singletary, there might be some monkey shines, maybe a little roughhousing. Chances are, he doesn't have a hit man as a roomie."

"Maybe he does keep some muscle around him to protect the operation."

"Maybe."

"Besides, I think the tough guy act is the wrong way to go about it," she said. "Clearly, he's a businessman. There's nothing ideological about what he's doing. He's after the money. Present him with a business deal."

That made a ton o' good sense to me.

"I've got it!" I said after think-think-thinking (oh bother) for a bit. "I'm the US rep of a cartel interested in expanding into Colorado by buying his business. There'd be enough menace implied that he'd listen and that he'd also not have me killed on the spot."

"That's pretty good."

"Pretty good? It's fucking brilliant! The masterstroke of a goddamned genius."

"You gonna clean up?" she asked, eyeing my habitual scruffiness.

"Nah. I'm supposed to be a secret mobster. If I show up in a black suit and tie, white shirt, and with shades on, I'll just be a walking cliché to our bright boy. But I promise I'll pretend to be articulate."

"Like using bigger words and not saying fuck all the time?"

"Fuck yeah, like fucking that."

CHAPTER 19

U CCS's Alpine Village Apartments were not even close to being either alpine—that was outside Colorado Springs—or a village of adorable Swiss-type chalets, nestled in the hills. Rather, they were three modest, five-story brick high rises. I picked the building reserved for upper year and post-graduate students and loitered by its locked double doors until a couple of students were coming out. Smartly, I thought, they challenged me with a "Who are you?" as they opened the door a crack.

I explained that I was visiting my grandson and wanted to surprise him.

"Who's your grandson?" one asked, holding the door half-closed.

"Richard McGrath."

"Richie? Cool. He's...an interesting guy. I'm sure he and the big dude he lives with will be happy to see you."

"Tell me," I said. "Is he still driving that Audi?"

"Oh yeah. He loves that car. Actually, we all do."

"I'm glad he's pleased with my present."

"*You* gave that to him?" another asked, after giving my shabbiness the once over.

"Yes. I've been fortunate. Say, would you happen to know his apartment number?"

"Sure. 5B," the first one answered as she pushed through the door and held it for me as I went inside. Funny, but the perception of having money means you couldn't possibly be a serial killer.

The slow elevator ride to the fifth floor gave me enough time to produce the bullshit story I was about to spin while getting in character for my performance and prepping for the bodyguard I now knew I was about to meet.

I knocked. An incredibly large, fit man answered. I knew instantly I'd found the Richard McGrath that I was looking for, as very few college students employed humungous protective muscle. The guy looked like Dolph Lundgren in *Rocky IV* on steroids—OK, on more steroids.

Get your game face on, Jake.

"Richard?" I asked.

"No. How can I help you?" El Gigantico said tersely.

"I need to speak to Richard, please."

"He doesn't need to speak to you."

"Why don't we let Mr. McGrath decide? Would you please tell him that some Mexican investors are interested in having a discussion with him."

"Wait here," the behemoth instructed me and closed the door in my face. I stared at the wooden slab for about a minute until the fleshy slab returned. The colossus in a skin-tight golf shirt opened the door wide as my signal to enter. I was then treated to a muscular pat-down, the way pizza cooks treat a ball of dough.

In my experience, master criminals come in all shapes and sizes. I didn't know what to expect in this encounter. I knew he was short, but for some reason, the image that stuck in my head was of a small, bald man sitting on a throne-like high-backed chair wearing a smug expression while stroking a hairless cat. Curse you, Dr. Evil!

I was right about one thing: He looked small sitting on the couch. The reality was he appeared to be an unremark-able frat boy, enthralled by and energetically engaged in a Formula One racing video game projected on his giant TV. I stood there for a bit watching him feverishly working what looked like a child's plastic steering wheel while the sounds of roaring engines, shrieking brakes, and explosive collisions filled the living room.

Finally, the noise stopped, and the driver's view of the racetrack froze.

"Helps me relax," he said, in a reedy voice that was anything but relaxed after his fake experience.

All five feet four or five of him got off the couch. He looked like he was going to a job interview instead of like a college kid lounging around his dorm room. Short-sleeved madras shirt, beige slacks with a knife's edge crease, polished loafers—almost the perfect preppy/nerd look from the 1980s *sans* plastic pocket protector.

What stood out, however, were his eyes. Dark brown and bright, they darted constantly, not like a squirrel's which are twitchy as fuck and looking only for ways of escape, but as a sign that here was a brain constantly engaged, analysing, strategizing. I'd seen eyes like that before. They belonged to my former boss of the technology company that questionably employed me years earlier.

And that old boss of mine was the smartest human being I had ever met.

"And you are...?" Richie asked.

"Brock Tarrington."

"And what do you do, Mr. Tarrington?"

"I represent a large Mexican firm interested in exploring investment opportunities in Colorado," I said, eyeing the bodyguard who stood there, with his huge arms crossed, for all the world looking as though he were a young Mr. Clean.

"Let's go to my office, shall we," McGrath said, understanding the need for privacy.

He ushered me past his colossal defender and into a repurposed bedroom. It was almost empty. His "desk" was one of those eight-foot folding tables that they set up for church bazaars or that Buffalo Bills fans like to drunkenly throw themselves onto from as great a height as possible. Other than a PC with two big-screen monitors hooked up to it and at least eight cellphones neatly laid out in two rows, the desktop was empty, not a shred of paper.

"And what part of Mexico is this business headquartered?" McGrath asked as he sat down.

"Sinaloa."

That got his attention right quick.

"First, Mr. Tarrington," he said, "would you please share with me how you came to think I even had a business and, secondly, what your people believe this business is?"

"Certainly, Mr. McGrath. We have come to understand that you are operating a substantial and profitable marijuana growing business that is, shall we say, not precisely within the law."

"Again, I must ask: *how* did you discover my operation? I pride myself on discretion."

"That, sir, is proprietary information. Suffice to say, much of my employer's success relies on intelligence-gathering. And he has the resources to conduct an extensive search for high-quality, actionable intelligence."

"Alright. Now, how about we drop the formality horseshit, and get down to business, OK?"

"Fuckin'-A," I answered.

It was clear that McGrath and I shared the ability to use educated speech when we think it's needed but would rather speak plainly because we know that decorated language just dances around and dresses up what could and should be said with simple words. Saves time, doesn't allow misunderstanding. Plus, I fucking love swearing.

"What kind of an investment are we talking about?" he asked.

"One that gets us 100% ownership of your business."

That took him aback.

"If, as you said, we are, in fact, big and profitable," he said. "Why the fuck would I sell to you?"

"I believe—and my employer believes—that you don't want to do this for the rest of your life. Is that true?"

"Yes."

"But, you see, we do intend to be in this business for years, decades even."

"So?"

"So, it means that your operation becomes our entry point into a new and permanent area while, you, given that you want to make as much money as fast as possible, get to fuck off somewhere, to do what you want with the all the windfall cash you've snagged, a lot earlier than you imagined. Am I close?"

"You are."

"My employer further believes that you understand your business will soon be squeezed by outside forces—if it isn't already."

He nodded.

"You understand that my employer has the resources to defend against those outside forces while you do not."

"Here's the part where you tell me how much you're going to pay to get me out."

"That depends. We need to know—approximately, of course—the number of houses you are supervising and your annual gross revenue."

"Last fiscal year, just north of three hundred and eight million from sixty-two houses."

"Do you also work with storefronts—legal or not—in Colorado?"

"No. We had a few legal stores but they're just too much hassle for the return, so we shut them down. The illegals are always risky because they could close tomorrow."

"But you do operate a street level business here in Colorado, I believe."

"A strictly legacy division. It's how we started out. But it's not particularly profitable anymore. We're in the process shutting that down too, here and in Denver and Pueblo."

"—And Montrose too?" I added. I figured that dropping that small town's name into the proceedings might point Richie to Pete What's His Face as the likely tipster that brought me to him. The larger the vat of shit Pete was swimming around in the better I liked it.

"...yes, Montrose as well," he said. "They're more bother than they're worth. We agree on a wholesale price, advance the product, and set them loose. But this street operation always comes with more squabbles, more chance for leaks. And none of them are meaningful contributors to the bottom line anymore."

"What is that bottom line, net after expenses?"

"Ten and a half million."

"Hmm...In that case, our offer is two hundred million."

In our chat so far, McGrath wanted to appear in charge and non-plussed by anything. My bullshit number made him pause, so that his huge brain had a few moments to whir away a little faster as he imagined a whole new life that kind of moo-la would bring and so much sooner than he had planned.

"An interesting offer," he said, trying to play it cool. "I'll need some time to think about it as I had the figure of three hundred million in mind."

"Really?" I said, almost amused by the naked gall of this little puke.

"Yup."

"My employer isn't used to negotiating."

"Ask him. Maybe he'll make an exception."

"You have one week to think about selling to us."

"Or what?"

"Or we go elsewhere in the state. We know and you know there are other businesses like yours. So, we have a choice. You, on the other hand, don't, because there's nobody else stepping up that we can see."

"And what if I turn it down?"

"If we take over another business—and we will—you should also understand that my employer is known for his aggressive tactics with competitors," I said, reverting to my proper English language usage to add a touch of gravity meant to let him know I wasn't fucking around.

Our eyes met briefly and there was no doubt he got my message.

"Nice meeting with you, Richie," I said.

"A pleasure," McGrath said as he got up and extended his hand.

"Oh, let's save the handshakes for your acceptance of our offer."

"How do I reach you with an answer?" he asked.

"You don't. We'll be in touch. Please give me a number."

Phone number in hand, I walked through the living room past the gargantuan bodyguard who was keenly involved in his college major (a bachelor's degree in Being Large) with a minor in Glowering.

I was oddly exhilarated as I walked out of the non-alpine, non-village. It wasn't because I'd escaped injury at the hands of the man-mountain. Of course, he could punch me soft and toss my six-foot, two-hundred-pound frame around like a rag doll, but I, strangely, wasn't worried. Based on Laura's description, I knew he wasn't the hitman who had killed Stan, and I had the power of a two hundred million magical dollars in my dad cargo shorts. For the time I was up in

McGrath's apartment, I didn't just pretend to be a ruthless cartel negotiator; I *was* him.

And I was dealing with a little bastard who had the balls to counteroffer.

As planned, I went back to the restaurant near the campus to meet up with Alex. She wasn't there so I waited. And I waited. After a while and three coffees, I was worried the diner owner was going to change the WIFI password to getthefuckouttahere. I hadn't been terribly concerned for Alexandra's safety; I had found the highly criminal Richard McGrath we were looking for and, besides, my money'd be on her in a scrap.

To pass the time, after I'd read enough on-line, I people-watched because that's what folks do when they're alone in a restaurant (if they're not phone-watching instead). The place was filling up. In the main, it was a university crowd. Young and completely devoted to not talking to each other as they scrolled and scrolled away or thumb-typed into their phones. That made the presence of grown-up adults more pronounced. An old woman, her hands shaking, carefully picking the nuts off a muffin. A mom and dad whose two young children laughed and chattered while they all shared a pizza on a silver pedestal. Two middle-aged Black women in the midst of a roiling argument, straining to keep their voices down. An austere-looking man, after brusquely ordering a coffee to go, turning from the counter to survey the restaurant while he waited.

That's when I saw this scar running down his cheek. Like the old woman with the muffin, the pizza-eating family and the scrapping Black women, he caught me staring and for a nano-second our eyes locked. I looked away because you can't keep staring, for fuck's sakes.

Ding! Ding! Ding! My wee brain swung into action.

Jake, that guy fits Laura's description of Stan's killer!

OK, so now what, Jake?

Call the cops?

And say what? Besides, I don't have a cell phone, remember? And there was no way to find a discoverable payphone close by, so I'd have to negotiate with the restaurant staff to use their phone.

Fine. Ditch that idea. So, you have to follow him, Jake.

Follow him and do what, Jake?

Well, you know, confront him. Maybe put him in a headlock?

Seriously?

I'm bigger than him.

But at least twenty years older. And damn it, didn't you leave your huge hunting knife in your other cargo shorts?

Good point. I could bring along my coffee spoon, but it wouldn't even up the odds.

That's assuming he's the right guy. You do know there are other people with scars, don't you, Jake?

So, what am I supposed to do? Sit there like a useless lump?

For Christ's sake, you have no other option, Jake! Follow

him and see what happens. Maybe he'll lead you to a car with Arizona plates.

It's lengthy internal arguments like that that make me wholly unsuitable for a position as an air traffic controller. By the time I turned around, ol' Scarface was gone. I was up and after him when the waitress started screaming at me about trying to skip out on paying my bill for three goddamn coffees. Did I have cash to hastily throw on the counter? *Of course* I didn't. Was my debit card accepted? *Of course* it wasn't.

"I'm coming back!" I more or less yelled, pointing at my laptop. As shitty as it was, that device would come close to covering my bill.

By the time I made it outside, there was no sign of him. I had no fucking idea which way he headed, and I almost got hit by a truck as I stepped into the street to get a better view down the block in either direction. Nothing. There was no extended discussion about what to do next. I went back inside where, big surprise, I wasn't met with cheerful smiling faces from the wait staff.

I sat down at my shitty laptop to wait for Alex and to think about my encounter with Richie Wants to Be Rich. When the little guy admitted to the "legacy" street sellers in Colorado, he talked about advancing the product to them. It came to me. Stan was right and wrong. Those self-storage businesses were involved in the dope biz but not as growers. They were drop sites. Pete or the Colorado Springs, Denver, and Pueblo versions of Pete would be notified of a shipment by Richie and meet it, maybe with all their street level vendors, so the shipment could be divvied up and dispersed within a couple of hours. Boy, Bellini would be interested in that tidbit.

But something was bothering me. If Pete was being supplied by McGrath, why was he also buying quantity from Joe through Jeremy Brown? The answer fell into the No Honour Among Thieves basket: Pete was double-dealing, selling product from both, likely favouring Joe's crop that even after Jeremy's middle-manning fee was more profitable for him. That rascal, I thought. I also imagined McGrath's reaction if he were to find out from, say, an overweight, scruffy, old, Canadian birdie. I realized that I couldn't drop that dime as the hitman McGrath would bring down on Pete would also find extra work in carving up Jeremy and likely, Joe.

About an hour and a half after I'd first got to the diner, after envisioning McGrath's operation and while I was musing about whether or not I was doomed to spend the rest of my life stalking people with facial scars, Alex appeared.

We ordered drinks and I recreated my chance encounter with a potential murderer. Once I added in all the buffoonish elements of my attempted pursuit, it rendered the whole event nothing but farcical. Attempting to redeem myself— something that I just about never manage to do—I went on to describe my meeting with Richie.

After I'd finished, I asked about her mission to the R. McGrath of southwest Colorado Springs.

"Disappointing but wonderful," she said. "I never had a chance to use my fake story. *Robert* McGrath was an eighty-two-year-old senior living alone in an old-fashioned bungalow with old-fashioned décor—orange shag rug, dark panelling, Hummel figurines, the whole bit. He invited me in for tea and we had a delightful time chatting. I sat there and mostly listened because he really wanted to chat. He told me that that's what he had done every night for years with Alma, his wife. But she died six months earlier. She was gone but his need for the evening ritual continued. It was sad and sweet."

We decided that there wasn't much else we could do in Colorado Springs and voted to head back to Laura's.

"You know, Jake," Alex said as we drove into the sunset, "I could see us in that kind of picture that Robert McGrath had with his Alma. It's not that far away."

"Except for the orange shag rug and the dying part, it sounds delightful," I said, as I too had imagined the pair of us some years from now (but not that many) in full *On Golden Pond* mode, affectionately bickering over the details of twenty or so years together. All filled up with the comfort and grace of just being together.

"What are we going to do when the week's up?" Alex asked, breaking into my old fart reverie.

"Fuck knows," I replied. "But we've got a whole seven

days to come up with something. It's good to have a deadline. Makes you focus on the task at hand."

"Why not go to the cops? I mean, we did find him; that was the hard part."

"Yeah, I'll tell Frank, but I can't see what he can do about it. There's no proof of anything. Yeah, he had a bodyguard but a guy like that has probably had one since kindergarten."

"Let Bellini decide, OK?"

I agreed, but I wasn't looking forward to that phone call. At the outset, I had promised to keep him up to date on my escapades, lest I do "something really stupid." One could argue—and I bet Bellini would—that strongarming a stranger in his own house and then rooting out and confronting an overachieving drug lord who had people killed just might fall into that category. And then there was the dilemma of what, if anything, to tell him about Joe Harding's sideline as an illegal pot grower and his connection to Jeremy Brown who was middle-manning a lot of herb to Montrose Pete.

As I expected, we were a couple of excitable boys early on in our conversation that night after I outlined the events that had taken me to Richard McGrath's front door.

"Goddamn fucking amateurs!" he yelled. "Just what I was afraid of! You could've fucked up any investigation we had on the go!"

"Were you investigating Singletary? Did you even know about McGrath?"

255

"No," he allowed, then quickly came roaring back, "But you didn't know that!"

"You said yourself that you mostly make arrests based on tips. In case you can't recognize it, this is a goddamned tip!" I yelled back.

Round #1 over, we both calmed down.

Bellini obviously sensed that no wild geese were about to be chased; this was the real deal presented to him on a platter. He told me it would be a while for him to bring resources to bear to investigate McGrath. There'd be co-ordination with the FBI and the local cops, subpoenas, surveillance, wiretaps, and flat feet on the street that he had to organize. For sure, it'd take longer than the week deadline for when I was next slated to speak to McGrath.

"So, what do I do at the end of the week, while you're busy bureaucratically fucking around?" I asked.

"Don't overcomplicate this, Jake. You call him as planned and you just tell him 'No.' Sorry, but your boss in Mexico withdrew the offer. Another business deal that didn't happen. Everybody moves on. And you are out of it."

"Aw, I was kinda looking forward to running a cartel operation. You know I have the people skills. I think I'd be really good at it."

"Jake, I appreciate the info but, I'm dead serious. I repeat: You are out of it as of right now. Go back to Florida," Bellini said.

"You're chasing McGrath for the dope crimes. I want him for Stan Harding's murder."

"That might shake out during the investigation."

Right then, I shut up. I knew that "might shake out" wouldn't cut it. Alex and I had made a promise to Laura and that meant we had a job to finish. Plus—and you may have noticed this—your average mule is a highly medicated pushover compared to me.

"Jake?" Frank said to the dead air.

"Fine," I eventually answered. "But it's my turn to ask that you keep me informed."

"Deal."

And he hung up.

CHAPTER 20

W ith a week to kill before my next conversation with McGrath, I figured I it was time for a come-to-Jake meeting with Laura's sons. I convinced her to call—but not attend—a business meeting with her boys—at Joe's place.

"Lads, we need to talk," I began, surveying what was largely a hostile crowd.

"About what?" Joe demanded.

"About some goings on around here that I find disturbing."

"Such as?" Greg asked.

"Wellll, for instance, Greg, I'm pretty sure you faked that stick-up on the highway, and also you've been the one lifting product from the store, not Bethany and Donna, the women you fired."

"That's bullshit!"

"Afraid not. We talked to both of them."

"You did? They're lying!"

"No, they're not. And you should be goddamn thankful they don't know the ins and outs of a wrongful dismissal lawsuit. And you should also be thankful I haven't called the police because cops really, *really* hate being lied to."

"That's a felony, you dumb meathead," Joe chipped in.

"Johnny. Let's have a chat about Charlize."

"What about her?" Johnny asked, instantly defensive.

"You told her about your uncle's death in St. Petersburg and your parents travelling earlier than usual to Indian Rocks, leaving the main house empty for the winter."

"Of course I did. I wanted to move in while Mom and Dad were in Florida, so I discussed getting out of our shit-hole for a while with her. But I swore her to secrecy."

"She didn't take her promise very seriously. Do you know Donna Van Houte?"

"Yeah, she's a pretty good friend of Charlize's. Charlize got her the job at the store."

"Know who she's dating?"

"No. I think some guy from Montrose."

"Not just some guy. Your old friend, Pete, who, I'm pretty sure, works for the big illegal ring that hired the hitman who murdered your father."

"You asshole!" Joe said, as Johnny just sat looking stunned that such a small detail had resulted in enormous harm being done to a man he loved.

"Joe, hang on a minute," I said. "Listen up, boys: I personally couldn't give a shit if you steal the place blind or if you
let slip some info that put the killer in the same place as your
dad. But I'm betting your mom wouldn't be as casual about
hearing any of this."

Their look said it all.

"You won't tell her, willya?" Greg asked nervously, as if he
were a kid hoping to keep a secret from his parents. Which I
guess he was.

Joe had a look of smug contempt that I wanted to slap off
his owlish face.

"Now, Joe," I said. "Let's talk about your hobbies,
shall we?"

"Hobbies?"

"Yeah, like walking – I guess that's more of an interest.
You like to walk."

"I do. Mostly along the river. It clears my head."

"But you also like walking inland too, don't you?"

Joe didn't answer. Instead, he wore an expression of
silent dread because he knew exactly where this was
going.

"Let's take this off-line," I said. If I had dropped his pot
growing and selling bombshell, I had every expectation that
his brothers would've beaten the shit out of him. And I
wanted him alive.

I told Greg and Johnny I needed to talk to Joe alone about
some accounting things. They left after I answered a few

questions from them with non-answers about what else Alex and I had discovered.

"I understand you like gardening too," I said to Joe when we were alone.

"I enjoy helping Cynthia with the flowers and plants."

"Cut the shit, Joe. We found your little grow op."

Joe was visibly surprised and took some time to re-calibrate his defense.

"It's fully legal with our medical certificates!" he protested.

"Oh, for fuck's sake," I said. "If it's so law abiding, please explain the camouflage netting. And if it's all above board, maybe you can also explain why you haven't told your brothers or your mother, because I'm pretty sure you haven't?"

"Mom and Dad did the same thing for years," he said, trying to establish precedent.

"That was then; this is now. You know that."

"What are you going to do about it?" he asked.

"I haven't decided yet. So many options."

"You could just forget the whole thing."

"Yeah, that's not on the table."

"So, what now?"

"Depends on how co-operative you are. How long have you been doing this?"

"This'll be my third year. I'm stopping for good as soon as the harvest is over, next week or so. I swear."

"I couldn't give a good goddamn about your future plans. I want to know what you've done with your harvests in the past. You can't add it to the farm's inventory; it's all tracked from seeds."

"I can add some. I do the reporting. Look, I'm helping out the business. And believe me, it needs help."

"You're helping yourself out too. What's the total you're bringing in? I'm thinkin' about 200K a year."

"Closer to 100, 110."

Joe then went into an overly long description about how he injected about fifty thousand dollars into the business annually by upping their sales figures and other revenue items from time to time, betting the government wouldn't bother doing a line-by-line audit.

"I believe that's known as money laundering," I said when he'd finished. "Oh, and let's not forget you put about the fifty thou a year in your jeans. Somehow, I don't think you've been in a big hurry to tell the IRS all about that."

"It's a lot of work to take care of the plants, you know! And I have to fix all the paperwork so it passes the smell test. I'm entitled to something; it's only fair."

"What do you do with all this 'fair' cash?"

"No cash, e-transfer to an offshore account."

"I want to know the name of your buyer."

"I'd rather not say."

"Joe, Joe, Joe, Joe, Joe. Time to follow the bouncing ball. Now, maybe you're protecting a friend or maybe you're afraid of the buyer or maybe it's both. I couldn't give a rat's ass. I need a name to get closer to finding the guy who killed your father. You'd like that, wouldn't you? Or I could turn over what I've got to the cops...and your mother. Why, I could do that as early as tomorrow morning. Whaddya say?"

"That's blackmail!"

"Or extortion. I get the two confused. The name, Joe. Now."

"Jeremy Brown," he almost whispered.

"Your ex-partner?"

"Yes."

"Who approached whom about getting into the criminal cannabis market?"

"Jeremy came to me. He signed off on the books, so he knew the business was really starting to slide."

"And who does he sell it to?"

"No idea."

"I call bullshit."

"No, I swear. I don't know!"

I was getting tired of this little dance. Joe was one of those guys who, from the jump, knew they were doing illegal things but who had put in the time to not only get comfortable with it, but also to conjure up the logic to justify their misdeeds.

"Tell you what, Joe. My next play is to go have a chat with Mr. Brown. Now before I do that, I need your word that you won't call to warn him. To help with your answer, I want you to think about, off the top of my head, illegal cultivation, money laundering, fraud, and tax evasion, because those'll be the fucking charges you go down on. And just maybe, when it all shakes out, accessory to murder."

"I understand. You have my word."

Our eyes locked. I have some talent as a bullshit detector. Joe had started out our little chat as a confident, self-exonerating asshole. But at that moment, I was looking into the eyes of a man who was smart enough to fully comprehend his situation and, best of all, who was scared shitless about how quickly it could deteriorate.

Not being a member of the Colorado Bar Association, I knew I had pulled the list of Joe's alleged crimes out of my ass. But they sounded plausible. Whatever the final tally of charges might be, it was clear to him that he'd be in for a world of hurt.

My last words to him were: "To ease your mind a bit, I'm not telling anybody about your grow op...for now. But if I were you, I'd figure out a way to do the right thing and let your mother in on your secret agriculture before you shut it down."

I didn't want to give him a lot of time to reconsider his forced silence. The temptation to warn his friend would have been pretty strong.

"Hey, babe," I said to Alex immediately after my chat with Joe. "Wanna take a walk on the wild side in downtown Gunnison?"

As a matter of fact, I do. I've got some grocery shopping to do to replace all we've eaten, and you drank."

"We can do that together. After we pay a visit to Jeremy Brown."

In the drive to Gunnison, I filled Alex in on my discussion with Joe. She was as perplexed as me over what to do with the information on Joe's book-cooking and his illegal commercial efforts.

GUNNISON IS A SMALL AND PRETTY TOWN, LIKE THOUSANDS OF other ones across the continent. As you approach it, you see a few newer housing developments, then some big box stores, a couple of fast-food joints, maybe a car dealership or two, and then you hit the older part of town, the section with all the local businesses lined up on either side of the one wide main street. The commercial properties downtown were low, bricked affairs, none of which would've required elevators and all of which had been restored and neatly re-painted.

Whenever you see an unbroken string of storefronts, you can be sure there's a back alley and parking spaces servicing them. We found the rear entrance to Jeremy Brown Financial Services and eased into a parking space alongside a big black Escalade. I imagined Mr. Brown could charge people to watch him try to park his land-boat as he navigated the narrow alleyway.

"Looks like ol' Jeremy's doing OK for himself."

As planned, Alexandra did most of the talking, first with the receptionist and then with Jeremy who had ushered us into his office. Jeremy was a big man but in shape, late 30s, stylishly dressed and groomed, and wearing a blindingly white shirt with the sleeves neatly, I want to say professionally, rolled up. He was deeply tanned and wreathed in the powerful scent of cologne. His short, curly blonde hair could easily have been a permed dye job.

I just watched and nodded as Alexandra spun a pretty good yarn about our upcoming move to Gunnison from Kansas and our need for an accountant to handle the bookkeeping for our new coffeehouse. The whole time, Jeremy had the look of someone who was utterly bored shitless.

"Are we keeping you from something?" I finally asked.

"No, not at all," he insisted.

"Oh, because I got the distinct impression you were distracted. Maybe this will help you focus: we'd also like to discuss the illegal weed you're buying from Joe."

That got his attention right quick and, going by his stunned expression, Joe had wisely kept his promise of not warning him. Brown got up quickly and closed the office door.

"What are you talking about?"

"Oh, I think you know. But to be specific, I'd like an idea

of what you do with about two hundred pounds of high-grade pot every year. You don't strike me as someone who bops outside on lunch hours to deal weed on the fucking street."

"OK, I sell it to some other storefronts."

"Illegal storefronts?"

"I don't ask."

"How can you make money buying from Joe at the going wholesale rate for good illegal pot when the price is about the same as the retail cost in the stores?"

"The deal with Joe is for heavily discounted product. There. Happy?"

"I'm not even marginally amused, Jer ol' buddy. In fact, I'm getting pissed off that you start out by lying to me."

Jeremy went to full pivot.

"You think I can make decent money doing the books for antique stores, small farmers, and plumbers?"

This piece of rhetorical questioning tripped off his tongue way too quickly. My bet: he had practiced this self-justification, maybe in front of a mirror.

"Jeremy, I'm not interested in a discussion about the profitability of a business like yours in a small town and, trust me when I tell you this: I don't give a good goddamn what you consider "decent" money. I just need the name of your buyer."

My demand was met with a mixture of fear and defiance. And silence.

"Okey-dokey then," I said. "Let me suggest a name. Pretend we're playing Clue. Here's my guess: Pete Somebody-or-other on a Montrose street corner with a big bag of cash."

By his nervous silence, Jeremy confirmed both my suspicion and bolstered Montrose Pete's claim that he alone had cornered the market for illegal dope in that corner of the state.

"There's no need to go to the police, is there?" Jeremy said.

"I haven't decided. That's a lot of weed, not to mention a fairly obvious conflict of interest."

"Maybe we can come to some sort of an arrangement."

"The only arrangement I want is for you to get out of the pot trade now and shut the fuck up about this little business meeting of ours."

"Done."

We left and were almost at the grocery store when Alex asked if I believed Jeremy.

"Not for a second," I said. "He folded too easily. Gimme a minute."

I wheeled the car around and drove back to the alley behind Brown's business. And there he was, standing outside nervously smoking a cigarette. I rolled down the window.

I said: "Here's another piece of info to help you honour your promise to me. Joe is scared shitless that I'm going to hold a little information session with law enforcement. If I decide to do that, do you really think he'll take the fall alone, with no mention who his buyer is? See, my money says no."

And we left.

I was starting to get nervous about the growing number of people who knew we were nosing around and who understood we'd found a bunch of crimes being committed. Something had spooked Pete, the street dealer in Montrose. Then there was both Joe and Greg, and the pot-house owner Singletary, and now Jeremy Brown. All of them had a lot to lose if I opened my big yap. Never mind jail time, Pete would attract some ugly attention from his overlord, Joe and/or Greg would destroy RMHH Enterprises, Jeremy would lose his business, his Escalade and his dope-selling sideline and Singletary would face years of legal troubles and public shaming.

Any one of them could drop a dime on me to people far more dangerous than they were.

Fact: I've never had so many people in so short a time, ask/plead with me not to go to the police over their obvious misdeeds. But really, what were the odds that every one of them trusted me when I said that I wouldn't immediately rat them out? Probably the same odds that they all absolutely believed that I wouldn't be a continual threat to them in the future.

A couple of days later—and just to prove to all you doubters that I'm not completely inflexible and annoyingly intransigent about some things like, oh, I don't know, physical exercise—I volunteered (yes, volunteered!) to accompany Alexandra on one of her morning walks along the river.

She declined my offer, citing the high probability that any joy she might have experienced would be pissed upon by my frequent bitching. I swore I'd keep my moaning to myself, and she relented.

We headed west, past Joe's place and, despite all the clambering over rocks (I'm not a big fan of any type of clambering), I was actually enjoying myself. The air was autumn crisp, the sun shone brightly, and the river was pretty as all get out. Even though my sure-footed bride was springing like a mountain goat ahead of me while I moved like an elderly sea tortoise over the uneven terrain, I thought I might like to do this again.

I was on the verge of telling her exactly that when the shot rang out.

CHAPTER 21

I t was a loud report instantly followed by the whine the bullet made as it ricocheted off the big rock between us. And sudden pain in my left thigh, not agony, more like a stinging shock.

I reached forward, grabbed Alexandra by the arm and yanked her back and around the boulder that was about the size of sub-sub-compact car.

The bullet had struck the big rock between us with piece of the stone shrapnel hitting the ever-trailing me right in the middle of my thigh. That led me to guess the general origin of the shot: downstream and across the river from somewhere in the bushes growing up the riverbank. For sure, it came from a rifle and not a handgun. Over the past several years, I have gained altogether too much familiarity with the sound each one makes.

JOHN OWENS

Alexandra saw the blood starting to soak through my sweatpants. Not a massive wound; a spot a little smaller than the size of an English muffin.

"You're shot!"

"Nah, a piece of rock must've chipped off. Bullet would've really fucked me up. 'Tis just a flesh wound." [Sidebar: Can any of you non-Monty Python fans think of something better to say at that moment? No? I didn't think so].

"Are we safe here?" Alexa asked.

"Temporarily."

We crouched there for several minutes until I thought we were alone. There didn't seem to be anyone around. The beating of our hearts was the only sound and our nostrils were filled by the acrid smell from the split rock.

With no further gun play, we made the decision to get the fuck out of there. If the shot was intentional, better for us to get gone, rather than wait around for the shooter to move and find a better angle.

Staying low, we scampered—wait, I've never scampered anywhere in my life—Alex scampered and I stumbled quickly back the way we'd came.

Back at the house, Alex immediately filled Laura in on the gunplay who then noticed the bloodspot on my leg. I told her a piece of rock had done that.

"Drop your drawers, young man," Laura instructed.

"OK, but if you ask me to cough for you, I'm outta here."

I pulled down my pants and she examined the wound,

determining that the stone shard was still embedded but that she could get it out. She disappeared to get a first-aid kid while I stood around trying to look nonchalant with my sweatpants around my ankles.

"Ya know, you're lucky Laura's here," Alex said, "I was going to vote for amputation."

"Witch."

Laura fished the stone out with a pair of tweezers while I was being a brave little soldier. A bit more blood flowed which Laura dabbed away before applying bandage and tape.

Dr. Laura cautioned us to watch for signs of infection.

"That's when I'll push for amputation," my witchy new wife said.

Borrowing a pair of binoculars from Laura, I scanned the far riverbank from the back porch. No sign of anybody. I turned to Alex with the all-clear and couldn't resist being a smart-ass.

"See? I told you walking was dangerous."

I say stupid stuff like the preceding because I have the odd habit of making jokes—mostly poor ones—when shit gets real, when threats and dangers abound.

But I had serious questions—again, with the questions. Was it a hunting accident? If it wasn't, was that a deliberate miss or just a shitty shot? Purposeful bad guy or careless hunter? A lively debate ensued. Be it resolved that the shooting was accidental. Laura took the affirmative side, arguing that it was likely a moron of a shit-faced hunter.

Her summation: "This time of year, the hills are crawling with drunk yahoos, and you weren't wearing...ahem...any bright colours as was previously advised."

I was firmly on Team Pre-meditated Murder Attempt, noting that most game hunters used powerful scopes that magnified their targets and there was no goddamn way in the world either of us looked like an elk close up.

Alexandra wisely stayed neutral, pointing out that we had fuck-all in the way of solid evidence one way or the other.

With nobody to adjudicate, the debate was declared a tie. However, by mutual agreement, Alex was to curtail her river walks until further notice, and everybody vowed to stay closer to home and be more watchful.

"Maybe we should prepare," Laura volunteered. "I know Stan had a gun."

The inventory of our defensive arsenal showed meagre results. Stan kept an elderly-looking single shot Winchester 30/30. Laura found a box with seven cartridges.

"He got it for the bears and mountain lions when we were living in the van," she explained.

"And Greg has a gun," Alex piped up.

Our next topic up for discussion was whether or not to call the police.

All three of us were on the same side. We guessed the

there would be fuck-all in the way of evidence to find. The bullet would've been smashed beyond recognition. Maybe a good ballistics guy could find the calibre and the exact angle of the shot by looking at the damaged rock, but so what? At the other end, they might discover some trampled grass, bent branches. But unless the shooter dropped his wallet with his ID at the scene, we'd learn nothing more, while the police presence would attract attention.

And as far as the possible identity of the shitty marksman who took a potshot at Alex and/or me, I looked at my hierarchy of suspects—every case has one. Line them up, Jake. Who's the most likely to take arms against the source of their sea of troubles?

Even I know that all suspects aren't created equal. Obviously, Stan's contract killer would be at the top of the Most Likely to Take My Life list, but he was anonymous. In descending order of probability after him, I ranked Pete Whatever, Jeremy "The Apparently Acquiescent" Brown, Joe and Singletary's hired man in a tie, then Greg, with Johnny trailing the pack as I couldn't immediately discern any kind of motive he might have. The others had every incentive, both financial and in the interests of remaining at large, to put a stop to our nosing around.

Physically, any one of Joe, Greg, Jeremy Brown, Singletary, and Pete What's His Face could have done the sniping. While I couldn't see the pudgy Singletary wading across the river and trundling up the slope, he did have enough money to find someone who gladly would. And speaking of contract killers, what about the one already on McGrath's payroll? Maybe he was multi-talented, with proficiency in distance shooting on his resume, as well as his close-up work experience with a big ass knife.

But here's the thing, I thought. The shooter could've been waiting for hours for Alex or both of us to be down by the river where they attempted to shoot us dead. How did the gunperson (how 2020s of me, right?) pick his/her shooting site? How did he or she even know that we—well, Alex— took regular walks along the river? And how had he or she known when Alex went walking? Obviously, whoever pulled the trigger had to have been given some inside knowledge about our routines. Otherwise, the shitty sniper would've had to randomly pick a spot to set up and then could've been waiting hours or even days for one or both of us took a riverside stroll.

Wait, whoa, Jake. The shooter would've known *Alexandra's* routine. This was only my second time doing the early morning river walk. Which meant that *she* was the target. If the tipped-off gunman wanted me, he would've set up *in front* of the house scoping me out as I had my morning coffee.

As a start, I thought that maybe Bellini could narrow down the shooter's name. I needed some information that I could only get from him. But I knew I wouldn't get that info unless I told him why I wanted it.

"So, how's my favourite dope agent today?" I asked after he picked up.

"My day *was* going just fine. What do you want now?"

"That hurts, Frank. I wanted to drop a little FYI on you."

"What?" demanded the man with even less patience than me.

"Just wanted to let you know that somebody took a shot at us."

"What?!"

"Yesterday. Alex and I were walking along the river."

"Anybody hurt?"

"Naw."

Bellini wanted to know if we'd called the local police and got downright exercised when I told we hadn't.

"Look, for all we know it might've been a shit-faced hunter," I said. "I presume you have them here."

"Any way you cut it, Jake, it's still a crime. You're supposed to report crimes to us."

"Let me go out on a limb here and suggest that that's what I'm doing right now. So, the question is: What are you going to do about it?"

"Give it to the local Montrose cops. They'll take statements, send a forensics team."

"Frank, they won't find shit. Maybe a crushed bullet that might identify the calibre, maybe some bent shrubbery and grass. And meanwhile, all the police activity might spook the bad guys to either step up their antics or disappear."

"Turns out, it's not your call. But I'll think about it."

"Think about this while you're at it: your mole within the station could use this info."

"...Yeah, and then there's that."

"Ya know, maybe there is something you can do. Can you check to see if a list of people I give you own guns?"

"Colorado doesn't have a firearm registry."

"Oh. OK, what about finding out who has or has had hunting permits?"

Bellini said he'd do that. He cautioned me that, because you didn't need a permit in Colorado to shoot at somebody, his search results wouldn't be conclusive. I gave him my roster of possible suspects. Joe, and Greg Harding, Pete Alphabets, Jeremy Brown and Mr. Singletary. I didn't bother with McGrath's name; that wasn't a guy who'd be keen to get all camo-ed up to disappear into the bush for days to cuss and spit and drink with the lads. I didn't have Todd the Giant's last name but doubted he would leave his master's side for a hunting expedition. And I couldn't attach a name to McGrath's hired killer.

I went back to wrasslin' with the facts behind the shooting.

Fact: Alex was the presumptive target.

Fact: The tipster who revealed her routine to the gunman could be one of only five people who would've seen her morning after morning: Joe and Cynthia, Greg and Elena and Johnny who was always early to work. Oh, and Laura.

Fact: Alex and not me had interviews with five of the six.

Fact: the tipster and gunman could have been one and the same person.

Fact: It's also entirely possible that the tipster could have innocently and inadvertently revealed Alex's routine to someone not so innocent.

Wild guess: Alexandra was targeted because of something she'd learned in her interviews or as a general warning for her and me to mind our own fucking business.

Aaaaargh!

I TOOK THE TIME TO REPORT TO STEVE ABOUT THE EXCEEDINGLY clever way we'd found McGrath in Colorado Springs. It was an odd sort of relief telling him about Richie. I'd given him a name to put on the record. Regardless of what happened, it was a black and white fact in the public, not just the police domain.

"When are the cops moving in?" he asked.

"Best guess: Sometime between now and the end of universe."

"You shitting me?"

"For fuck's sakes, you're not on deadline for tomorrow's paper. It'll happen."

"Well, you have started to get somewhere," he admitted.

"*We're* getting somewhere," I corrected him. "You're a reporter; go report on Richard McGrath instead of just hanging around moping and watching the leaves change colour. Track the fucker down on-line."

"I'm on it."

"Oh, by the by, somebody took a shot at Alexandra."

That changed his focus right quick as he really liked Alex. He was incensed and wanted details, none of which I had. And he didn't seem all that impressed by the dime-sized wound in my leg. That is, until he said good-bye and told me to take care. He meant it.

THINGS WERE HAPPENING. STEVE THE BLOODHOUND WAS NOW pointed in the right direction. So was Colorado law enforcement. Alex had people to talk to. And I...I was busy twiddling my goddamn thumbs. Normally, I love this kind of division of labour, but not at that moment. We were getting closer, hurtling towards some kind of resolution, and I didn't have a fucking thing on my To Do list.

I often have these internal struggles between my innate laziness and my innate impatience. Impatience won that day. What the hell, I thought. How about we nudge things along a bit? Time the beat the bushes. Beginning with Peter the Unpronounceable, after I had a brief consult with the Colorado Criminal Code.

As I drove to Montrose, I considered the fact that I have something of a talent for provoking people. Most of the time, I do it for sport. But sometimes, this talent for being mouthy and up in someone's grill comes in handy by causing nasty people to become unhinged to the point that they say or do things they hadn't meant to.

I don't know if Pete was being charged rent or not, but there he was, lazily smoking and leaning against the same red brick wall that was the background for our first two get-togethers. This time he was accompanied by a guy a little taller than me but even doughier than I am, who was also lounging against the wall.

"I thought I told you to fuck off," Pete said, butting out his cigarette as I approached. I couldn't see his eyes behind his mirrored shades, but his smarmy half-grin said it all.

"Ya know, Pete whatever the fuck your last name is, in some tiny way I admire your big-fish-in-a-small-pond swagger, but that's all it is. Remove this sack of shit beside you," I said, indicating his fellow lout. "And you're equal to or less than fuck-all."

None too surprisingly, the sack of shit wasn't exactly enamoured by my description of him. He angrily pushed off the wall and came at me. I truly believed that—horrors!—he meant to do me harm. Rather than let that happen, I took a step forward and stunned him with a quick left jab to the face followed by a heavy right hook to the side of his head. Backwards he went as he collapsed, smacking his noggin on the brick wall. Start the count; he was down and out.

Pete seized the opportunity to jump me from behind, but it wasn't a fair fight. Sure, he was younger and wiry but my additional forty or so pounds gave me a sumo-like advantage. I threw him against the wall, but he bounced back keen to extend the wrasslin,' so we grappled, first, standing up, but then soon rolling around on the sidewalk.

A small crowd gathered around our thrashing bodies. They weren't screaming "Fight! Fight!" the way they might've back in public school, but they seemed interested in seeing a good scrap. However, the scrappers were tiring, like fish flopping around on a dock. I had him in a headlock and he had his legs scissored around my thighs. At that point, we'd reached a stalemate and were just sort of wriggling around. The crowd parted to allow two cops into the fray. They separated us the way NHL referees break up a hockey fight, after waiting for the combatants to stop combatting.

As we were pulled apart, Pete threw a fist at me and missed. I returned the favour and didn't.

Jack snap, we were in handcuffs. I looked down and saw Pete's partner showing signs of reanimation as one cop was zip-tying his wrists. In that glance, I also saw Pete's sunglasses near me and, well, I just couldn't resist the hearing the sound of them crunching under my foot.

I determined to keep quiet while Pete was yelling his head off, detailing all the horrible things he was going to do to me, my family, and, I think, my neighbours and ancestors.

Another police car screeched to a halt. Pete and his dazed and confused buddy were loaded into that car while I was shepherded into the first one on the scene. Our little entourage left two officers gathering witness statements. It took us about a minute to cover the three blocks to the cop shop. I even thought, gosh, it's such a nice day; they could've frog-marched us there.

We were greeted inside the station by the same stout desk sergeant whom I had spoken to when I first met Frank. She opened the gate and led us to separate rooms where the beat cops on the scene took our statements.

I, of course, played the victim of this grievous assault. The big lad lunged at me and not because he wanted to shake my hand, officer. I was defending myself. That's when the second perpetrator jumped me and how was that fair? Two against one and me, a senior Canadian tourist at that. And now I'd have to live in fear as a result of the heinous threats. Yes, sir, Mr. Unpronounceable was known to me. I confess to attempting to purchase five ounces of a cannabis product from him two weeks ago for pain relief from my sciatica. No, sir, I was unaware that buying that amount is a petty offence, while selling it was a felony in this state. I plead ignorance, as I may have mentioned, just a Canadian senior who honestly thought it was legal everywhere in Colorado. Yes, I used a false name as they seemed unsavoury. No, sir, I don't have any of the product left. I used some and disposed of the rest as it was of extremely inferior quality. That was the reason I was in Montrose today, hoping the seller—my assailant— would address this quality issue, when the unprovoked assault took place. Yes, I made intemperate remarks in response to his, but surely that never justifies this sort of savage attack.

I had no idea how Pete and his poo-bag of a friend would spin their version of events, and it didn't really matter. They were in deeper shit than I was.

I figured I'd get a stern lecture, maybe a fine, and then be kicked to the curb. And that's what happened. A hundred bucks lighter for disturbing the peace, I drove back to Gunnison and was greeted by Alexandra who was alarmed at my dishevelled and dirty appearance that was far in excess of my normal seediness.

I told her what happened. Our relationship had deepened to the point that she wasn't astounded at the stunts I pulled. She shrugged her shoulders and only slightly shook her head.

"While you were out brawling in the streets, I had a thought. If the shot was deliberate, it was aimed at me. I'm the one with that routine."

"I had the same thought. Can you go over the conversations for anything that sticks out as something that somebody didn't want you to know?"

"I have. Nothing comes to mind."

"Then we have to assume it was a general warning to back off. It could have been me, but the only regular thing I do is have a coffee on the front step. The sniper couldn't have got any closer than the property line because of the cameras out there which means he'd have at least a six-hundred-yard shot. Doable for a pro; impossible for an amateur."

"But we're not backing off, are we?"

"I will, if you want."

"I don't want."

AFTER THAT, I PLANNED THE REST OF MY DAY. THAT PLANNING consisted of two tasks: hanging around drinking beer and waiting for Detective Frank Bellini to call and yell at me.

The call came during the early evening. As expected, it started out loud.

"What the fuck did you think you were doing?!" he thundered.

"Ruffling a few feathers."

"Do you have early-stage dementia? Did you forget what I told you?"

"Remind me."

Frank was damn near sputtering at this point. Remember I mentioned my talent for provoking people?

"These people are dangerous! And you were told not to do anything stupid! Especially not with P.K."

"First off, I'm not a cop, nor am I an agent of the police, so ol' P.K. can go fuck himself if he claims harassment. Second, I think Pete runs a bigger operation than you imagine and that he's part of an even bigger outfit, the outfit that ordered Stan Harding's death."

"Any idea what you think you accomplished?"

"I wanted to draw him out and I wanted to create a legal shitstorm for him."

"You did that. Harris Dittweiler, the guy you KOed, was carrying weight. There's no evidence against P.K., so it's he said/he said about the pot. But you probably knew that. However, eyewitnesses corroborated your story. Two said they saw Dittweiler menace you, the same two saw P.K. jump you, and at least six more heard the threats he made. And for that, he might get convicted of simple assault and could get up to a year in jail. Maybe a $2000 fine."

"You're welcome."

"Yeah, well, the local cops are pissed and that makes me pissed."

"You're always pissed."

"Did you really beat that guy up?"

"That sounds so harsh. I defended myself."

"But you knocked him out."

I told him about my years spent sparring at a local gym where I, literally, had a few lessons pounded into my head, one of which was not to retreat if you don't have to. Even though backing up is the natural, automatic reaction in the face of aggression, moving forward surprises the shit out of an attacker. And if you do land one, his momentum amplifies the pain.

TWO DAYS BEFORE I WAS SCHEDULED TO TALK TO MCGRATH again, I called Bellini for an update on the trap they allegedly were setting for him.

"Not much to tell you," Bellini said. "Like I said, the wheels are turning slowly. But Colorado Springs police are watching him."

"Watching him do what? Go to class? He does all his business on-line and on the phone."

"What can I tell you? Think I'm happy with the pace?" he said, more as a challenge than an apology that I had no grounds to expect.

I spent the next day pouting. My six days of relative inactivity (if you don't count getting shot at and being arrested for a street brawl) and then Bellini's nothingburger of an update were driving me nuts. Me. The guy who may very well be the personification of inactivity. I knew why I was restless too. Nothing was getting resolved. Even though we had identified the bad guy running the dope operation, no information had brought us any closer to the name of Stan's killer, and there was nothing I could do to hurry things along after my banishment by Bellini.

"Fuck this!" I announced out loud. However, I was alone at the time, sitting on a rock on the riverbank, safely behind a bigger rock, so my proclamation didn't have much of an impact.

I repeated an understated version of this to Alex, along with: "I need to do something."

"Trust the cops to find out," Alex said, trying to calm me down.

"When? After McGrath packs up the operation and fucks off? After that hitman kills again?"

"You can't fix everything, Jake."

"I can try to fix this."

"Quick question: you've read *Moby Dick*?"

"Yup. Most of it, anyway."

"So tell me: Do you think Melville meant for you to cheer for Ahab as he destroyed his ship and doomed his crew in his selfish quest for the white whale?"

"Geez, spoiler alert! Seriously, the only cost to me is my time."

"Don't be so sure."

"What's that mean?"

"It means it could also cost you your life. And it means I'm getting pretty tired of all this. We should've been gone a week ago."

"Of course! Then we could call McGrath from a Florida area code, or Boston, if we use your cell," I said, making a noteworthy bid to qualify for the Sarcastic Olympics.

The temperature in the room had been rising. Even as I completely understood Alex's reasonable position, I absolutely knew I would be unable to fold up my tent and go home. I did nothing to cool things down.

"If I call like I'm supposed to and tell Richie that the cartel is moving on from the deal, then it's the end of our connection to the only guy who knows who killed Stan. We put in all this work and time, and I'm supposed to just let it drop? Bullshit! I want another face-to-face with him."

The next morning, I was on the road. Alone.

CHAPTER 22

I felt a little guilty about not calling Steve. I knew he'd be keen to go but I couldn't think of way to introduce him into the proceedings. At 5-9, maybe 150, he couldn't exactly pass for my muscle brought to match McGrath's behemoth. He'd just be a driving buddy, without any meaningful role. And I'd have to listen to his pissing and moaning for the whole trip.

I called him from a payphone (after I eventually found one) when I got to Colorado Springs.

"Get anywhere with Richard McGrath?" I asked.

"Well, for starters, your wonderkid isn't much of a kid. He's 35."

"Get the fuck outta here!"

"Took a while to confirm it all. He's in his fifth year at UCCS. BA with Honours, almost finished his Masters. But I couldn't find anything on a Richard McGrath before his enrolment at UCCS that fit. That bugged me, so I kept digging and found that a *Trent* McGrath III—middle name Richard—graduated from another university two years before he came to Colorado."

"Where?"

"LLB from the University of British Columbia 2016 with a Specialty in international law. Called to the bar 2018. Established TRM Law Offices Inc. in Vancouver with a branch in Denver."

"This prick is Canadian?!"

"Nope. BC Bar Association publishes brief bios of their members. He was born in Mill Valley, California. Excelled throughout prep school, made early admission to the University of San Francisco in Pre-Law Studies, then graduated Summa Cum Laude, Dean's List, the whole bit. You should see his graduation photo. Guy looks like the lawyer version of Doogie Howser."

"Why would he go to the Great White North for a Law Degree?"

"Glad you asked. I was wondering that too. Then I remembered some stories about two Calgary lawyers caught laundering money for some sketchy American outfits."

"Wait a minute. His business is all cash. What's he do with millions in fives, tens and twenties?"

"Best bet: Richie the drug lord found a bank here that would take the bills on deposit, then he e-transfers money to

Trent the lawyer in Canada. It's put in trust and that makes it pretty much untouchable by law enforcement under lawyer-client privilege, especially because it's now in a foreign country. Then Trent the lawyer can do with it what he wants. A big plus as a lawyer: he knows how to set up all these shell companies and offshore accounts."

"Unbelievable. The lad's been planning this for a long time. Great work, bud! And all from the comfort of your shiny pine mausoleum."

"Oh, I ain't done. The second after he's busted, I'll be calling his parents, Thomas, an insurance exec and Candace, a stockbroker. Maybe they can shed some light on Richie's criminal leanings as a child. Then I'm on to my list of his classmates. I'm also trying to get a line on Todd the Bod. I'm gonna have so much fucking human drama, it'll make your head spin."

"I think Bellini could use all this info," I said. "Hey, I have an idea. Why don't you call him? Might soften him up some, when he sees you're so goddamn helpful."

I walked over to the UCSS residences feeling pretty gosh, darned pleased that there was an actual pro on the job. With almost forty years of sniffing around, it was second nature for Steve to logically, relentlessly dig and dig when he was hot on a trail. Any revelation along the way wasn't that big a deal for him. It was par for his journalistic course.

I knocked forcefully on the dorm door, having again sleazed my way into the building. No answer. I had no idea what schedule Richie and Captain Beefcake were on, so I had to loiter, which, luckily, is a specialty of mine.

Eventually, the elevator opened and out stepped the Hulk's big brother followed by the object of my disaffection.

"Mr. Tarrington, I was expecting a call," Richie said as His Humungousness opened the apartment door. "But I'm glad you came. Come in, come in. Can I get you anything?"

His instant hospitality unnerved me. We passed through the living room and seated ourselves in his office/spare bedroom.

"I took your offer to my employer," I said, getting down to business. "He surprised me by indicating his willingness to increase his bid to $250 million to buy you out, provided I'm allowed to see your more detailed financials."

"Two-fifty? Hmm. I'll need a little time to think about it."

"To be frank, what could you possibly have to think about? A week ago, we established a range. I just upped the bid by a lot, and now here's where you decide to become Richie Really Rich or not."

"That's not how I do business."

"You might want to pay more attention to how *we* do business."

"Believe me, I have."

"And?"

"And it just so happens that I did a little intelligence-gathering of my own, Mr. Tarrington. Or should I say Mr.

Lydon?" he said with a smug expression on his highly punch-able face.

Oh, fuck, I thought.

"I talked to a source I trust," McGrath continued. "And he talked to a source he trusts, and they both agreed that a big business from Sinaloa would never hire an American to represent them."

Self-preservation instantly became the order of the moment. Rather than point out that I was Canadian or try to bullshit my way out of this, I bolted from my chair and exited stage left to the living room just as he called out: "Todd!"

Mount Todd stood between me and the front door. Looked like I was in for a fight before the flight portion of this evening's performance.

The big lad seemed eager to earn his pay as he assumed the classic wrestler's pose, showing me he wanted to grapple. I wasn't real keen on that idea, knowing full well that if he got his hands on me, he'd choke me like a chicken or crush my ribs in a bear hug.

So, I adopted the standard boxing pose learned during my years of getting the piss pounded out of me at the very amateur level. We began circling each other, looking for an opening. Assessing the sheer size of the big bastard, I still didn't like my odds, so I abandoned the boxing stance, as well as any pretense of following Marquis of Queensbury rules. That's to say: I surprised him with a classic move known in my high school circles as "shooting the boots." And that's to say: I kicked him in the balls really hard just as he lunged at me. His momentum mightily contributed to the combo of pain and surprise on his face as it stopped him cold. It even stopped me for a nano-second. I know I thought —as every male on the planet would've thought—at that moment: "Geez, that's *gotta* hurt."

Down he went and out the door I went, deciding on the fly to skip the glacial elevator and hurtle my bulkitude down the stairs. I burst through the fire escape doors and dashed— well, trotted—actually, more like shuffled—towards the car because I was winded, and no one was following me. It'd be a while before Todd the Giant was running anywhere with his swollen gonads. Richie could've chased me, but it would have occurred to him that he didn't have any kind of plan once he caught up to my shambling old self. There was fuck-all he could do if he located me much beyond yelling "Tag! You're it!"

With Colorado Springs in my rearview mirror, I considered my next steps now that McGrath had unmasked me. First up was to prepare myself for the inevitably unpleasant reporting in to Frank. After that, I didn't have a fucking clue. Except, I imagined Richie, given his access to a professional killer and all, might really put some effort into finding me.

What really stumped me, of course, was how the fuck McGrath knew my real name. No one else outside the Harding clan, Bellini and my arresting officer knew who I really was. I tried to comfort myself with the fact that, on the law enforcement side of things, only Bellini knew I was staying with Laura.

It came to me. One other person knew for sure, and another one might have known my real identity and my whereabouts.

Arriving at the Harding compound, I went right over to Joe's. We went into his office, closed the door.

"Joe, I've got one question for you. Did you tell Jeremy Brown who I was and where I was staying after I asked you not to?"

"No!" he immediately answered.

I briefly studied his face, his unwavering eyes. He was telling the truth.

Inside the main house, Alexandra and I hugged it out and I reassured her that I was done with McGrath. She looked almost as relieved as I felt.

I then took Laura aside and quizzed her.

"Any chance you used my name when you first went to the Montrose police?"

"I had to, Jake. She insisted on knowing how I came to the information about Florida."

"She?"

"The desk sergeant who took my statement."

"Blonde woman with short hair, kinda stout?"

"Almost a buzz cut? Yes, that's the one."

"Did you tell her where I was staying?"

"No. It didn't come up. Did I do something wrong?"

"No, no, sweetie. You just did something very right."

BELLINI CALLED THAT EVENING, WANTING TO KNOW HOW MY conversation went with McGrath. He wasn't yelling at me which meant either that his Ambien had kicked in or the Colorado Springs police hadn't alerted them to the presence of a long-haired old geezer hanging around the UCCS residence.

Wanting to spare my new pal further upset, I didn't provide any detail of my encounter beyond saying, (without a word of a lie, I must point out): "I have now officially gotten the fuck out of the cartel business."

"Good. Now you can officially get the fuck out of my state."

"So, you don't want to know the name of the mole in the Montrose station?"

"You better not be yanking my chain."

"There's only one other cop, besides the lad who arrested me for street brawling and you, who knows my name. The desk sergeant on days."

"Sergeant Moseby?"

"If that's her name, yeah. I introduced myself to her just before I first met you. She had my name from Laura's statement, and she also saw me after I got into my dust-up with Pete."

"So she knows your name. So what?"

Fuck, I thought. There was a hoisting-type petard with my name on it. I had to 'fess up to meeting Richie.

"McGrath knew my name. I'm betting he got it from Pete who got it from Sgt. Moseby."

There was an agonizing pause. Agonizing in that I was waiting for Bellini to start probing for an in-depth account of my recent dealing with Richie.

But he didn't. Instead, he theorized how Moseby now made sense to him as the likely informer. Every weed operation he ran out of Montrose used Montrose cops as support. For surveillance, as foot soldiers on the raids of P.K.'s house and George's Store-All, for the stop and frisks, all of which had come up dry. Moseby wasn't just the desk sergeant sitting at the front counter all day. She was the duty officer who assigned the officers to the jobs and gave them the details of Bellini's operations.

"She has to be the reason Pete always seems to be one step ahead," Bellini concluded.

"In your spare time, dig into her past. Somewhere, there's something, bank records maybe, that connects her to Pete."

"Dagnabit, Mr. Lydon, I plumb didn't think 'bout doin' that. I shore do appreciate them thar tips on how to do my consarned job."

"Alright, alright, can I go now?"

"Yeah. Go. For Christ's sakes, go!" Frank said, losing his yokel voice. "And thanks."

Then Bellini, who was not exactly famous for long good-byes, hung up.

I called him right back as I'd forgotten to find out how things went with Steve.

"He supplied a lot of good info. You were right about him. He's a fuck of a lot nicer than you are and he—"

I quickly hung up on him. Jake the Kid strikes again!

ALEX AND I TALKED ABOUT IT AT LENGTH. I FELT BEATEN. I couldn't grasp a thread to pull that would lead us to Stan's killer. I hated to rely on what "might shake out" during Bellini's investigation. But there weren't any other possibilities open to us. Oh, and with my cover blown, McGrath and Todd would likely be real interested in finding out where I was. Answer: Just a two-and-a-half-hour drive away.

"I guess it's time to head back," I said.

"Not just yet. You—and I—need some cheering up."

"What did you have in mind, Mrs. Lydon?"

"Well, Mr. Simpson, since we got here, you've been bitching about not seeing any real mountains except in the distance. I'm taking you up close and personal."

The next morning, off we went. Laura stood on the porch and gave us detailed directions to the real Rockies.

"Just go north for a bit. Can't miss 'em."

Her advice wasn't needed as Alex had thoughtfully choregraphed our trip, because that's who she was.

Within an hour's drive, we were on the rise. I had flown over these Rockies numerous times decades ago on business trips to Vancouver or L.A. and I had driven across them several years earlier. The same feeling of ascending, always ascending returned. As well as the notion that, peak after peak, they were massive and endless.

We stopped at a scenic lookout by the side of the twisty road and approached the guardrail that wouldn't bar a toddler amped up on chocolate We wanted to get closer—well, Alex did—so we hopped the guardrail.

Because I can't sing at all, I resisted the urge to break into a rousing version of that "Hills are alive" tune. Instead, I chose to give voice to the only appropriate comment:

"Ri-co-la!" I shouted.

I was standing near the edge of a mountain ledge and looked down. All I could picture was indestructible Wile-E-Coyote—grasping his Acme anvil—disappearing to a dot before the "whump!" as he hit the bottom of the valley.

That night, we stayed at a condo rental in Snowmass Village which, for six months of the year, was a craven lie of a name for the town. The next day after a late breakfast, we walked around a bit, but there wasn't much to see beyond the infinite collection of ski resort condos that looked like the one we had just stayed in. But the weather had held, and it was a delight to be just joshing with my wife as we aimlessly strolled around.

Alex brought that leisurely walk to a screeching halt when she hurried us back to the car as, apparently, we had a lunch reservation not near there.

Back in the car we went and less than an hour later I saw a road sign for a town that I knew about. Woody Creek, the long-time and final resting spot of Hunter S. Thompson, the legendary and iconoclastic gonzo madman who put his stamp on journalism more profoundly than any writer in the last century. I was a big fan. How can you not be of someone who puts out a book called *Generation of Swine*?

The famous Woody Creek Tavern, where Dr. Hunter S. used to hang out, had all the makings of a perfectly wonderful dive bar which I was sure it once had been. Dark wooden walls, jumbled signage and eclectic decoration, Gonzo-abilia everywhere, and an overall pervasive sense of dilapidation. It still looked like a dive bar but really wasn't so much that anymore as it was a tourist attraction. Out-of-town gawkers stared at obvious locals as though they were human museum displays. Here's a simple rule of thumb if you want to distinguish between a faux version and the real thing: In a true dive bar, nobody's making reservations or taking pictures of their fucking food.

After eating, we sat in the car and Alex asked me if I

wanted to go to the nearby Owl Farm, Hunter's home. She insisted that there was an off chance we could talk the good doctor's widow into letting us in.

"C'mon, Jake. You can bullshit your way into any place."

"No, thanks."

She was obviously surprised by my answer.

"I'm sorry, babe. It just strikes me as ghoulish. Look, here's the kitchen table where Hunter stuck a .44 Magnum in his mouth. And over there is the stove range hood where the bullet lodged."

She looked disappointed.

"It's more than an accident you brought me here, isn't it?" I asked.

"Yes," she admitted.

"Betcha the phrase: "No fun anymore" rings a bell with you. He wrote that in his suicide note. You knew that. I'm also betting you're worried about me getting all dark about this murder case and staying that way. I won't. And, for Christ's sake, I'm not going to off myself."

I didn't know how convincing I was being, so I gave it another go.

"Alex, I've been depressed before, for years after Beth died. Life struck me as absolutely pointless. But I came out it. You led me out of it. Overall, life may very well still be pointless, but thanks to you, I don't care if it is or not."

WE STRUCK OFF NORTHWEST WHICH MEANT WE MISSED DRIVING to Aspen. I didn't mind as, by all accounts, we probably wouldn't have been able to find a parking spot anyway. All we'd be able to do was drive around for the privilege of seeing really expensive stores and restaurants and altogether too many BMWs and Teslas.

I assumed that, sooner or later we'd be forking to the left to circle back to Gunnison. Instead, we took a right and headed east through Vail and past Breckinridge. Rather than tell me where we were going or why, she chit-chatted about winter recreation.

"You know," she said, "we should come back here and do some skiing. You ever strap on the boards?"

"Once. First and last time. The hill was a sheet of ice and I was freezing. Instead of attempting those lazy 'S's down the slope, I decided to get that fucking exercise over with."

"Oh, no," she said, knowing exactly what happened next.

"Yup. I put my skis together, went into a crouch and aimed for the lodge. I shot down that hill, absolutely terrified as I picked up speed. I didn't fall, but I blew past all the picnic tables full of après-skiers by the lodge while busily pissing my pants, then managed to steer enough to whiz through an open gate and wound up halfway into the parking lot, brought to a stop by the bumper of a fucking Volvo."

She laughed. "But out here, the powder is so much fun," she insisted.

"Standing in that parking lot, I decided that, henceforth, on the nicest day of the summer, I wasn't going to run down a mountain. So there no way in hell I'd ever do it again in the dead of winter."

I still had no idea where we were going. The mystery was cleared up as we rolled into Denver and took the highway off-ramp for Empower Field at Mile High Stadium, home of the NFL Broncos. It came to me. It was Monday night, and the Broncs were playing.

As she turned the ignition off after we found a space in the ocean of parking lots, she said: "Football season is most definitely *not* over.""

I had to acknowledge her statement. Hunter S. had scrawled "Football season is over" as a final note to his wife (who, horrifically, was on the phone with him when he pulled the trigger).

UNLESS YOUR TEAM IS LOSING, IT'S ALMOST IMPOSSIBLE TO BE morose at an NFL game. I'd been to a couple in Buffalo and one in Pittsburgh and well remember the circus-like atmosphere. Game aside, around the stadium a collective craziness is pervasive. Acres of asphalt filled with tens of thousands of mostly over-refreshed fans, food booths, drink booths, bands playing (largely country music), more drink booths, tailgating, the smell of BBQ ribs in the air, every imaginable outfit sporting the team's colours, wonderful signs and funny T-shirts. The whole vibe is one of giddy and infectious unity.

Watching a game with 75,000 of my closest friends is not something I usually want to do. You miss too much of the actual game, which is the fucking point, after all. But I admit to being swept up, sitting in the delirium in the stands to such an extent that I was actually cheering on the Broncos, a team I normally didn't give a good goddamn about.

For all the strategizing and setting up, the game of football at that level doesn't have that much action—quick brutal plays of five or six seconds featuring smash-mouth violence with touches of balletic poetry. In a stadium, there are agonizingly long stretches in between plays that on TV are filled by ads for boner medicine or giant pick-up trucks (which are pretty well the same thing).

Throughout the four hours, I had a recurring thought that had nothing to do with football: I would love Alexandra forever. Not only because of the lengths and expense she went to in an effort to get me out of my funk, but the motive behind it. At its heart, it meant that much to her to have me happy.

But three days and two nights amid this athletic and mountainous grandeur were enough for both of us, although being in a big city for more than twenty minutes was, is and will always be instantly enough for me. Snow was threatened; Florida was calling. Time to head south.

On our return trip to Gunnison, Alexandra and I agreed that we couldn't keep secret from Laura the high crimes and misdemeanors of two thirds of her sons. The revelations would cause quite the mess, but Laura was highly capable of determining what to do about them. She had a fully operational moral compass as well as unusually large helpings of compassion and common sense.

When we got back to Laura's, we found her in a sombre mood. Not exactly the opportune time to snitch on her two law-breaking sons. But, turns out, we didn't have to drop a dime on one of them.

"Why so glum, chum?" I asked her.

"I had some unwanted family drama while you were gone."

"What happened?"

"Oh, it's not important."

"C'mon, Laura, what?"

Laura was a proud woman and old-school enough to shy away from publicly airing dirty private laundry. As well, like any mama bear, she was quick to defend her cubs—even though those cubs were in their goddamn thirties. So, it wasn't easy for her to explain that Elena had come to her just after we left, distraught over Greg's behaviour. She was certain that her husband was smoking weed again, that he'd been doing a lot of it and for a long time. As evidence, she produced a glass pipe, its bowl charred black with residue. She said she'd found it hidden away in the garage.

"I'm not completely blind, Jake," Laura said. "I didn't see him all that much and sometimes when I did, I thought he might've been high, but I accepted his denials, I guess because I wanted to. I've been around this business for a long time. I know the difference between routinely enjoying pot and becoming obsessed by it."

Rather than sit and stew about it, she confronted Greg with the pipe. Evidently, that led to quite the squabble.

"Greg was furious," Laura recounted. "He'd never spoken to me like that. He said he was a grown man, that it was legal, and that he was handling it."

"Laura," I said, as gently as I could. "All three of those things either are or could be true."

"Fine. But I reminded him of our deal. He said the deal was off and what was I going to do about it."

"How'd it end up?"

"Not well," she said. "I wanted to know where he got the weed. He wouldn't say. I pushed him, because it matters a lot to our business if he was buying illegally. He said he wasn't and also denied that Johnny was supplying him. I figured that he'd never buy from another legal store because he's known in town and it'd make him and our brand, as he calls it, a laughingstock."

"Doesn't leave a lot of options."

"No, it doesn't. He had to be stealing it from our own store then blaming it on his employees. Those poor girls! I hit the roof. And I'm still fuming."

"It's all fixable. Greg has to apologize to them, then offer, I dunno, some kind of cash compensation. See if that works. I can talk to him if you're on the outs."

"No," she said forcefully. "It's my job, my family."

"Did Joe say anything?"

"Joe? Why would he? He doesn't know about any of this."

That prick, I thought. I was about to open my giant piehole when I caught a sharp look from Alex, followed by a brief shake of her head.

When we were alone, Alex explained she didn't see the point of adding to her sadness just yet. We'd figure out a way to tell her, if Joe didn't man up.

As we were finishing packing up to leave, Bellini called again.

He sounded surprised when I answered.

"Why the hell are you still here?" he demanded. "I was calling to get a number for you in Florida."

"Do you have any idea how beautiful your state is? We're doing some sightseeing before we go back. But, I promise, no more trying to teach you your fucking job."

"It's the end of the road anyway. That's what I wanted to call you about."

"What happened?"

"Two nights ago, somebody carved up McGrath and the big guy he rooms with. Both dead. Real messy, I understand. The press jumped all over it. Two students knifed to death in a college dorm room, that's a big deal for that town, for any town."

CHAPTER 23

I was stunned.

"Fortunately, I guess," Frank continued. "That's put a real rush on our investigation into McGrath's weed business as being the likely reason he was killed."

"And....?"

"And we got access to his computer. The dummy had taped his complicated password to the underside of his table."

"And....?"

"Jackpot. Guy had detailed spreadsheets—sixty-two of them—on all his house grow ops. Names, addresses, directions, planting time, harvests, weight and grade of the dope. The whole shebang. He had another set of spreadsheets on all his deliveries to Texas, the Gulf States and Florida. And a third set on work scheduling for his crew, including contact info for their local sales, their organizations in Texas and Florida, installers, growers, pruners, and so on. And we also got our hands on his complete financial books: money in, money out, a balance sheet, for Christ's sake. And attached to that, details of his offshore accounts as well as all the businesses and First Western National Trust, the small bank where the cash was first being laundered."

"Congratulations, Frank! Sounds like you've got the whole kit and kaboodle," I said, not having a fucking clue what a kaboodle looked like.

"Not quite. Because of the out-of-state trafficking and the out-of-country cash movements, we've got the FBI and DEA crawling all over this. So, I have to step back."

"You must be thrilled." I said, trying to picture Bellini's face thrilled. I presumed it'd look about the same as his resting piss-face.

"Yes and no. They've got the horses to look deeper. But it bugs me that we couldn't figure out some things. Like, all the sets of spreadsheets had a weird annotation on some of the individual items."

"What's it say?"

"'ABC action' and a question mark in bold. It's on three of the houses. Four of the delivery people and two work crews also have it. Any ideas?"

A thought occurred to me.

"Was there anyone named Benjamin on the work crew sheets?"

"Lemme see...I've got the sheets here...Benjamin... Benjamin. Yup! Benjamin Carstairs. Right here. And 'ABC action' beside his name. But the question mark is missing. How did you know?"

"It appears the 'Action' was completed. I think you oughta tell the local cops they should be looking for a corpse named Benjamin Carstairs in or around Montrose. It seems as though McGrath's upping his homicide action on the disloyal. Poor, dumb Benjamin was switching out Pete's primo weed for crap. He must've got caught and Pete reported it to McGrath. Anybody named Singletary on the grow house sheets have an ABC?"

"Yup."

"Question mark?"

"Yup."

"That's the guy who spoke to me, somewhat against his will. Looks like McGrath may have caught wind of it. With McGrath dead, Mr. Singletary appears to have lucked out, if he's still alive. You might check."

"Ya know, that could be it. But what's 'ABC' mean?"

"No idea. Listen: Did you find any Arizona phone numbers?"

"Not yet, but we're still looking."

I tried to thank him for the update, but he'd already hung up.

I was dejected as hell as I got off the phone. True, McGrath had kept a detailed account of his weed operation, but he would have understood that there is a huge legal distance between dope growing and homicide. If I were McGrath, there wouldn't be a piece of paper or a banking trail that linked him to Murder Inc. Arizona-style. There would've been no witnessed face-to-face meetings either. All he needed to remember was one phone number.

It was also clear that Stan's death wasn't a one-off. [Longest sidebar yet: It seems to be universally true that once you've reached the top of the game in just about every field, you will do everything in your power to stay there. With authoritarian governments, that everything includes controlling the media, imprisoning or executing political opponents, supressing dissent, removing personal rights, and relying heavily on the military and secret police to walk loudly and carry a murderously big stick. In other words: Russia. Criminal enterprises follow much the same template, substituting hired thugs for the military and minus the media control.]

I went online to catch up on my news reading. Actually, just one story interested me: The UCCS twin murders. Colorado media as well as a couple of nationals went big on it. Almost all of them began with variations of "Two University of Colorado students, Richard McGrath, 35, and Todd Whelan, 26, were killed in their dorm rooms..."

Stop right there, before you read any further, I gotta

know right now: is that Todd Whelan, as in the T. Whelan listed on all those corporate filings? Why, of course it is, I mean was.

Once again, police were tight-lipped with the media. Courtesy of Frank, I had more info than they told the press. It wasn't a state secret, so I filled Laura in on what had happened in Colorado Springs and how Stan was really responsible for signaling the trail that led to dismantling a huge illegal weed business.

I didn't expect the news to cheer her up and it didn't. The best I could say when she asked about the identity of Stan's murderer was that the police were now getting closer.

"Listen to Bellini," Alexandra said, watching my half-hearted efforts to pack up. "Now it's time for us to head back to Florida. We've been here almost a month and half, mooching off Laura, using her car. And she seems a lot better now."

Alex was right. Although nothing could repair the hole in Laura's life without Stan, she didn't seem constantly grim and depressed. Bit by bit, and despite the drama with Greg, she had returned to being warm and friendly, even laughing again.

Yes, we knew for certain that the snot-nosed middle-aged kid had put the contract out on Stan. But he was our only lead and, unfortunately, he was no longer talking. We had smacked right into a dead-end in identifying the hit man who had killed Stan and who was still out there, footloose and fancy free to keep murdering folks.

Simply put: There was no moral victory, and we didn't get a participation trophy for trying. Ultimately, I—we—had failed. And that pissed me off to no end.

"I guess so," I said to her. "I'll get on booking the flights."

"Not tempted to rent a car and drive back? Tons to see along the way. New Orleans, the Grand Canyon, Hoover Dam, Painted Desert."

"We will some day, darlin'," I said, "But, please, not this time. I'm more tempted to see a beach near, say, Indian Rocks. Let's go home."

"Four days tops. I promise," she persisted.

And I swear she batted them big baby blues at me. Whatever she did, I relented.

"A little stop in Las Vegas?" she then asked.

Now that was a bridge too far.

See, I set rules for myself. Lots of rules. Like: I have never and will never watch *The Sopranos* or any of the *Godfathers*, I don't care how good the writing and filmmaking are or how, thematically, the movies are, above else, a paean to the hallowed family. It's a family whose men deliberately do really shitty things for money while their wives, girlfriends, sisters, and mothers look the other way and go shopping. So, some of the violent thugs are slightly less shitty than others. So what?

Here's another inviolate dictate of mine: Ignore

anybody who says you've gotta see Las Vegas at least once. Turns out, no, you don't. I know what Vegas looks like. I don't think there's a fucking soul in North America—maybe even the world—who doesn't. Billions of flashing lights, giant choreographed fountains, gargantuan hotels, fake reproductions of engineering wonders from some place else, elaborate stage shows with inoffensive singers or really bendy circus performers, endless food and drink. Literally, bread and circuses (if you're counting all the garlic sticks at the overflowing buffets). All of it built on the celebration of the sad, failed pursuit of winning free money in opulent palaces improbably put up in a desert. In total: Garish spectacle —like my Hawaiian shirts—but on a grand scale.

I despise garish spectacles on a grand scale. They exist only to momentarily dazzle, full of sound and fury but signifying fuck-all beyond somebody's got a big budget (Please see every comic book movie, except the *Deadpools* which at least were funny). Asterix exceptions also for the Super Bowl and Rolling Stones concerts.

Does that make me a flaming hypocrite standing on indefensible moral and intellectual ground? Why, yes it does. So what? I can quote you a literary giant, Walt Whitman who said: "So I contradict myself. So what?" or I can return to Popeye, as I always do: "I yam what I yam." I can also argue 'til I'm blue in the face—and you're bored stupid—that NFL football and the Stones' music have substance while the gigantic Vegas bling thing does not, beyond technical wizardry.

Mercifully, I spared Alex the preceding diatribe and instead replied: "Definitely not! We'll go see your big hole in the ground but no fucking way I'm going to Vegas. And right now, you've got me questioning my judgement in marrying you."

We were able to rent a car in Gunnison with a drop-off in Tampa. Alex, bless her, insisted on an upgrade, so that two fairly large humans wouldn't feel contorted and cramped for four days. And I was blessed with Dee-troit metal in the form of a Chevy Equinox.

I paid a final visit to Steve, who was still beavering away on his book, as I had to fill him in on all the developments that had come fast and furious since my last info dump. He confessed to living in a pine-scented bubble and not having read or heard anything about the Colorado Springs murders as he pushed his book above 70,000 words. He was jotting notes like a madman while I described—second-hand—the dismantling of a huge criminal enterprise and the messy death of its head. I finished up with the tidbit that the T. Whelan who was listed on the corporate filings he'd uncovered was now resting in the Colorado Springs morgue.

"You might want to pass this along to your new bestest buddy, to ensure he makes the connection."

"I will. But this whole thing ain't tied up yet, is it?" Steve said.

"No, sir, it is not. There's still a murderer unaccounted for."

"Damn, that would complete this thing."

LAURA WAS SAD TO SEE US GO, ALTHOUGH I THOUGHT THERE had to be some relief for her coming from the removal of us two reminders of Stan in Florida. Not that she was accusatory, but it was also clear that she was disappointed we were leaving without having solved the reason we were there in the first place.

As we milled around the driveway, two of her sons were nowhere to be found, not that I expected a farewell parade from them. But Johnny came out to the car as we were loading the Equinox.

"Dad would be happy you shut those fuckers down," he said as we shook hands and did that brief bro hug.

I had a thought. Maybe Joe just needed a little nudge towards doing the right thing. I took Johnny aside and asked him if he ever walked his parents' considerable acreage.

"Sure," he answered. "When I was a kid, we'd play and explore all over the place. Haven't done that for years."

"Maybe you should take it up again," I said. "Try the section west of here, near the property boundary, about two hundred yards from the river. There's been some recent developments out there you might want to ask Joe about."

"If you're ever back in Colorado again-" he started to say but I cut him off.

"Colorado? Colorado's no good for me."

"Should I play some Tangerine Dream now?" he said, picking up on and laughing about my riff on Roy Scheider's key statement in *Sorcerer,* another great flick from days of yore.

And we left, with Laura happy/sad, Johnny amused/puzzled, and me convinced that Joe's baby brother—all six-foot two of him—might have some persuasive power over him.

I swear Laura's dogs had...well, hang dog expressions as we were leaving.

To my complete lack of surprise, Alexandra, had prepared a detailed itinerary. I mean, down to the minute. Seemed like our two-day drive up the Rockies was just a trial run. Like any good tour operator, she had calculated time and distance between stops, booked the hotels, and made some meal and tour reservations. A spontaneous bathroom break or extra-long lunch would fuck up her intricate plans. [Note to self: Jake, spend an inordinately long time in the can

and linger for hours over a decent carne asada.] [Another note to self: Christ, I'm a child.]

It soon became apparent that Alexandra, the witch, had tricked me, by relying on my shocking lack of knowledge about the American Southwest. The Grand Canyon was not "on the way" to Florida. It was a day's drive in the *other* direction. But I didn't mind at all because the jolt of mountain joy and live football I'd just experienced with my love was sustaining me. And Alex was a great road trip partner— despite her excessive enthusiasm for Van Morrison tunes. Although the craic was good.

For parts of first day travelling, I'd slip back to thinking about Richard McGrath's violent murder. I wasn't sorry he died; the guy had people killed because they threatened the way he chose to illegally make money. But I was sorry I didn't get answers to questions only he could've supplied, beyond the name and address of his paid assassin. Questions like: Had he really spent at least eight years scheming away? How much in total had he netted? Gotta be at least $30 million. Where was that money stashed? Likely offshore. How'd he hook up with bodyguard Todd and the hitman he apparently used frequently? No idea and it didn't really matter.

I was only guessing, but the truth could "shake out" during the police investigation. As I looked over at Alexandra, I realized my only job was to not give a good godamn if I ever learned the whole story or not.

No question at all, the Grand Canyon was awesome. And not the kind of "Awesome!" you get from a restaurant server when you successfully order a club sandwich and a beer. *Truly* awesome. You can also tack on the superlatives that are now used day-to-day for the most inconsequential things. 'Epic' and 'iconic' accurately fit the bill.

It was a variation on the theme of the recently visited Rockies that's difficult to explain. Both were gobsmackingly impressive, but there was something more compelling, darker somehow, about the Grand Canyon. To me, anyway. The only thing that sprang to mind was the difference between mountains *rising up* to astonish while the canyon *plunged down* to show the depths of the world.

Standing there, close to the edge, I thought the whole panorama had not been designed for people with low self-esteem. If you want to feel genuinely small, just a speck on the planet really, all you have to do is stand on the rim of the Grand Canyon and look around.

For fifty bucks you can stand on the Skywalk attraction jutting out over the canyon, and then *really* feel like fuck-all, while treating yourself to the additional image of the structure sheering off from the cliff and plunging you three-quarters of mile down to your squishy death on the canyon floor.

"A little better than Google Images?" Alex asked when we were back in the car.

"A little...alright, alright, a lot better."

I had to concede that a photo just couldn't capture the sweeping view of the endless sky and the huge, chiselled rock walls. It had been breathtaking.

You can't sustain moments like that but it's mandatory that you file them away in your memory, to resurrect when you're in one of your "po' po' pitiful me" moods or when you need to be reminded of all the wonder and beauty and majesty out there in our world.

Next up was the Hoover Dam. Now you're *really* talking. As I stood staring down at the massive, sloped wall, it occurred to me that somebody actually thought of that, then somebody did that. A hundred years ago. And they managed to pull it off with nothing like the technology we have today. Millions of tons of concrete, an equal amount of intrigue and politics, engineering heroes and triumph. What not to like? And the damn dam actually does something by providing water to millions of people living in four states and northern Mexico. The topper would've been if Harrison Ford had jumped off that dam in *The Fugitive* but, alas, no.

On the other hand, for all its grandeur, what'd the Grand Canyon ever do? It just sits there. A winding river slowly eating away rock for five or six billion years. If you wanted to film the erosion in time-lapse, you'd need anywhere from a bazillion to a gazillion feet of tape.

"You know, Vegas is about an hour away," Alexandra felt compelled to point out.

"Don't tell me, west again? Why don't we find a high spot around here, wait until dark and you can see all the fuckin' lights from here while they ruin an otherwise perfect desert night."

AS REPAYMENT FOR ALEX'S DIRECTIONAL TRICKERY, I DID INSIST on a bit of a side trip down to Houston for a meal at the original Pappasito's Cantina which I had visited a lifetime ago before it became a chain, and I became unemployed.

That city was and is the very definition of sprawling. It looked like someone had airlifted Toronto, hovered, and then and let it drop to smoosh out over its delta flatland. The restaurant was cavernous, the crowd boisterous, the food portions gigantic and wonderful, just as I remembered, while the prices (sigh) were not.

Then it was an easy half-day hop to the Big Easy. I had been to New Orleans with Beth pre-pre-pre-Katrina and stayed in the French Quarter. In another lifetime twenty-five years earlier, we stayed in the stereotypical four-story courtyard house/inn that was walled on two sides. Every morning, we felt like we were livin' large, as we were served fresh beignets and strong coffee at a wrought-iron bistro patio set in the tiled and leafy courtyard while we read *The Times Picayune.*

Courtesy of Alexandra's hotel-booking mania, I was travelling back to the Quarter. Alex and I went way upscale and stayed at the five-star Monteleone (which is French for very expensive) and made a few new memories.

While it had sustained wind damage from Katrina—long since repaired—the Quarter was unscathed by flooding during that terrible storm, meaning that all the buildings were as they were before the hurricane.

Bourbon Street was not as a garish as it had been in the mid-1980s. Not as many cheap T-shirt joints, for one thing. The strip clubs were still there but with muted facades and no hawkers were stationed out front loudly doing their "She shimmies, she shakes, she crawls on her belly like a reptile" spiel. It all looked darker but less trashy than I remembered, maybe a kind of post-Katrina sobering up, although most of the evening pedestrians were not close to being sober.

The antique stores off Bourbon had proliferated, some were all tidy with their old wares "carefully restored and curated" we were assured. [Sidebar: Another one of my rules: Unless you work in a museum or art gallery, you're not fucking allowed to pretentiously claim you *curate* anything]. Some other stores, as I remembered, housed a musty, dusty, jumbled mess of a bygone era with ancient proprietors of the same vintage as their random inventory who studiously ignored your existence—although truth be told, we weren't in the market for an ornate China hutch half the size of the Hovel and weighing more than our goddamned car.

Artists still sold their watercolours or on-the-spot caricatures around Jackson Square with St. Louis Cathedral as a backdrop. The Big Muddy still muddied along. The street hustlers still hustled; the oyster shuckers still shucked; the buskers still busked.

And music still poured out from the clubs.

Way back, before Cajun food became a huge thing across the continent for people other than Cajuns (who just called it food), Beth and I were warned away from its restaurant origin in Storyville, on the other side of Canal Street. A cop standing beside us told us he couldn't swear to our safety if we crossed the boulevard. Now, there's a goddamned 26-story Harrah's hotel and casino as well as a Waldorf Astoria, and a Hyatt Regency over there.

Thomas Wolfe was right but limited. True, you can't go home again. But you can't fucking go anywhere you've been before and not find it changed, just about never for the good (except Pittsburgh).

BACK ON THE ROAD, WE PICKED UP OUR PACE. WE MISSED Mississippi and Alabama because, eager to git on home, we never strayed off the Interstate's four or six lanes of asphalt except to hit a Denny's and a Holiday Inn. We caught occasional glimpses of big water and continual glimpses of Dunkin' billboards.

Rounding the corner of the Florida Panhandle and we were in the homestretch, if by homestretch you mean two hundred fifty fucking flat, boring miles on a state highway meandering through hundreds of thousands of small towns all with neo-fascistic speed limits.

WE'D BEEN GONE OVER SIX WEEKS. FUELED BY THE END OF Michael's employment and the early fall rain—and one near-hurricane-strength storm we missed—the plants in our yard had shifted into growth overdrive. The Hovel looked like a tiny, ramshackle Mayan temple engulfed by the Yucatan jungle. In our absence, the yard had obviously flooded again as it had floated the other half the goddamned red mulch onto the meandering river rock borders.

After we unpacked, my perpetually energetic bride went shopping. Road-weary, I just wanted to lounge around, largely because that's what I always want to do. I was fishing out a beer from the fridge, calculating that the last two would sustain me until Alex's return, when the phone rang. I caught only the area code as I picked up. 970. Colorado.

"Bellini, you old enema bag!" I said.

"Excuse me?" said a woman's voice.

"Oh...Laura. Sorry."

Undaunted, Laura continued: "Jake, I saw it! I saw the silver SUV with the Arizona license plate!"

CHAPTER 24

"Slow down, slow down," I said. "Tell me what happened."

"I was in Colorado Springs yesterday for some shopping. Went to the historic Old Town for a bite. These days, I look at every silver SUV. And I saw it! A big silver Hyundai with Arizona plates!"

"What did you do?"

"I waited. Almost three hours. No sign of the driver. But it's him. I know it's him!"

"Laura, listen to me: Where did you wait?"

"I parked right behind him. I didn't want to miss him."

[Longish sidebar: You know what kills me about movies? Two cops on a stakeout, waiting for hours in their car right across from a possible perp's house. The bad guy doesn't look out the window then think: "Gee, I wonder what those two lads parked out front have been doing for five and half hours?"]

"Laura, if it was the guy, you have to remember he's a pro. He's always careful. He likely spotted you sitting in the car, got suspicious, and skedaddled for a while."

"Oh."

"Was it at a meter? Or did the parking zone have a time limit?" I asked, reaching for the possibility the guy got a ticket which might yield some useful info.

"No and no."

"What, pray tell, was your plan if he had shown up?"

"...I guess I really didn't have one. Follow him, maybe."

"To Arizona?"

"But I have the licence plate! I just don't know what to do with it. I called Colorado Springs and Montrose police and told them that the plate might be connected to Stan's death. They listened, and said they'd do what they could. Jake, I'm sure they're going to ignore it."

"Laura. I really hate being a shit-heel here, but maybe not blame the police. There's gotta hundreds, maybe thousands of silver SUVs with Arizona plates."

After I had effectively killed her excitement, she sounded a lot more subdued as she gave me the plate number, reiterated that she was sure this was the one. And then repeated "Arizona."

Being just as useless as the police, I told her all I could promise was that I'd see if I could do anything.

Despite me being a wet blanket on Laura's justice dream, that Arizona vehicle on Colorado streets was now the only semi-decent lead we had.

And its presence got me thinking.

Where do hitmen and hitwomen live? (sorry, but hitperson just doesn't work) What do they do when they're not out there murdering? I mean, it's not a full-time job. They don't spend forty hours a week busily killing away. Do they have friends, social activities for their down time? I can't imagine there's enough of them for a club. Where would they meet? What kind of shop talk would they have?

All that to say: if the driver of that car was our guy, why wouldn't he live in Arizona? Especially if he loved golf and hated humidity.

It occurred to me that I did know someone who might be able to narrow down the possibilities for me.

"So how are you, ol' buddy, ol' pal?" I said after I dialled the number, and he picked up.

"Cut the crap. Whaddya want?" Bellini snarled in that fake gruff tone that he plays up.

"Sir, just reporting, sir, that, as instructed, sir, I'm back in Florida, sir."

"That's all?" he asked, his voice overloaded with skepticism.

"Ya know, now that you mention it, Frank, I wanted to ask you if you can look up license plates."

"Of course."

"...In Arizona."

"Yeah...it takes a bit longer. Why?"

I repeated Laura's tale about spotting the silver SUV.

"Jesus Christ, Jake, I'm not a homicide investigator. I don't work Arizona and your tip is a slim one. At best. There's gotta be thousands of silver SUVs with Arizona plates. *Maybe* I could get the local cops to interview him, but say what? "Care to account for yourself in Colorado this week? Ever been to Florida?" It doesn't work that way. Sorry, Jake; I can't see how I can help."

Disappointed, I gave him the plate number anyway.

"And besides, Jake, I was pretty clear about you not fucking around in this," he added.

"I assumed you were speaking on behalf of Colorado law enforcement. The way I understand it, you've got no goddamn jurisdiction in Arizona which is where I intend to do my fucking around."

Bellini went quiet.

I thanked him and hung up.

An hour later he called me back. It was a short, one-sided conversation.

"Look, I sorta owe you and Steve did come across some good new info," he said. "There's a 2019 Hyundai Palisade registered to a Robert Hoffner, 47 years old, of 2831 Yucca Drive, Tucson. Never been reported stolen. Not the plates either. Your friend, Hoffner, had two assault charges as a teenager, both dropped. But he did get three years for tax evasion. Got out in 2015. Clean record since. Nothing violent."

Then he hung up as I furiously scribbled down the address he'd given me.

I was excited to tell Alexandra as soon as she got home that, possibly, we now had the answer to the question who killed Stan Harding and where he could be found.

"I want to be happy with the news, Jake," she said after I told her. "But so what? You know somebody called Hoffner owns that car. And nothing else. I can't see what you can do with the info."

"Oh, yeah?"

"Yeah."

Alex was right—as per usual. Was Hoffner the driver in Colorado? If he was, did he have a legitimate reason to be in Colorado Springs? Business, visiting family or friends, wanting to see the goddamned leaves turn colour? Fuck knows. I retreated to the patio to think and sulk.

In mid-pout, I opened my e-mail to see a note from Bellini. No text, just an attachment. It was Hoffner's mug shot and driver's licence photo. Yippee! (I guess). We now knew what our 'who' looked like.

Dark wavy, longish hair, high forehead, narrow, squinty eyes that looked black, long narrow nose, thin lips, strong chin. All those details took a backseat to the prominent scar that ran down the side of his face, from just below his left eye almost to his jawline.

Not only did the photo match Laura's description of Stan's killer but I had seen that face before.

Just for a second. Where, Jake? Think. I was in Montrose —no, it was Colorado Springs. The first time. He came into the restaurant where I was waiting for Alex. One of those moments that sticks in your mind for some reason or other. In this case, the ugly gash on his face stood out. I took a half beat too long staring at his scar, the way we all would have, and he did the same staring at me. Then I looked away and took over a dozen beats debating with myself about what to do which had given him enough time to fuck off.

At that moment, I knew that no oddsmaker in the world would take the bet that Hoffner wasn't the paid assassin we were looking for. I described to Alex the inconvertible evidence identifying our guy.

"I don't really have a choice now, babe. I *have* to go to Tucson," I said to Alex. "Care to come?"

She most definitely did not care. As well, she most definitely did not care for the idea of me going.

"Aww, sweetie, both of us made the promise to Laura," I said. "You didn't hear the despair in her voice. I can't just quit."

"Sure you can. Let the police take over. And Jake, if you're right, he's a professional killer!"

"Bellini just admitted to me that he can't or won't do shit. Think about it. We know that somebody's gonna step up to replace McGrath and likely rebuild his organization. If the new guy was already working for him, maybe he has the same Arizona phone number. And McGrath has already identified me. We know, with Stan's death, that they can reach across the country to Florida. Think you or I will ever be truly safe here? Or Boston, or even the lake for that matter?"

She went quiet for a while, obviously considering the real threat to us. I wasn't bullshitting her, and I wasn't too pleased with the prospect of having to look over my shoulder for any length of time. At my age, it's a real pain in the neck (Nyuk, nyuk}.

"And besides," I said, "I have the element of surprise going for me."

"And nothing else."

"Harsh, but you're right. I need a plan!"

Her shoulders slumped in resignation. She turned and walked away.

It wasn't only my innate stubbornness that compelled me to go west, old man. After Stan died, Laura had asked for my help to find his killer. And we did help. To bring down a big illegal grow op that, as Bellini had conceded, would probably be replaced by another one. But Stan's killer wasn't behind bars yet, and that had been the point of this whole fucking exercise.

A brief word from me about me. I'm not given to self-analysis, largely because I've known self for most of my life. And—rightly or wrongly—I like self just fine. I'm at the age where I could not possibly care about how I look, what I think, say, or do. If I'm being truthful, I reached that age around my sixteenth birthday. And why am I so confident, nay, arrogant? No fucking idea. To find an answer, I'd have to do some self-analysis and I'm pretty sure that earlier in this very paragraph, I clearly established I don't do that sort of thing. Instead, I like to rely on a mantra from Messrs. Henley and Frey from the Eagles' underappreciated *Desperado* album:

You got to gamble on your story.

You got no guts, you get no glory.

I choose to conveniently ignore their next two lines:

And I'm betting my money on an ace in the hole.

Think I'm getting out of control.

To be fair, Jake, don't you want to correct your weaknesses? As it turns out, I'm not aware of any, and I'd like to keep it that way. Be forewarned: Should you elect to rhyme off my flaws, I'll stick my fingers in my ears then loudly and endlessly reproduce the opening bars of *Jumpin' Jack Flash*.

If pressed, I could come up with a list of my strengths. That inventory would include:

- Above average Internet search capability
- Sometimes amusing
- Walking encyclopedia of useless trivia
- Really good at smoking (past tense)
- Decent left jab

- OK-looking
- A flair for landscaping
- Factory-installed bullshit detector

There. That's about it.

No, wait. There is something else I've got going for me, a quality that's directly responsible for me getting involved in brawling with all manner of criminal enterprise during my alleged sunset years. I sometimes surprise myself with the things I say without consciously thinking about them. I'm not talking about the answers to trivia questions or recalling past memories that magically spring forth from the folds of your brain. I mean about *forward*-looking things—like anticipating questions and formulating darn good answers, imagining realistic scenarios, or coming up with all those bullshit identities I've used, often on the spot. I run on automatic, sort of like a human-sized Roomba mindlessly zigzagging around a living room, bumping into shit, but nevertheless cleaning things up.

I STARTED WORKING ON A PLAN. MAYBE IT WOULD TURN OUT TO be a bad plan—like most of my other ones. But it would be a plan.

First, I needed the lay of land. Where the hell is 2831 Yucca Drive, Tucson. AZ? Why, there it is, right smack dab in the middle of The Villages at La Paloma, the Google told me. The Google further let it be known that The Villages were right smack dab in the middle of the 27-hole La Paloma Golf and Country Club in the northern reaches of Tucson.

Bingo!

Why would you live in the middle of a big-ass golf course with fuck-all else around it if you didn't golf? You probably wouldn't.

So, our hitman probably liked to squeeze in a few relaxing rounds between gigs slaughtering humans. But judging by the Street View which showed a modest (to the point of self-deprecating) white flat-topped modern house, Hoffner wasn't one of your elite paid murderers, jet-setting around the world to wordlessly whack VIP targets for millions of dollars, all the while dressed exclusively in different tones of black and dark grey. Call him a low- to mid-level assassin. And a low- to mid-level independent contractor in any business is always on the lookout for new customers.

I was relying heavily on that corporate new revenue imperative as I started formulating my half-assed plan. Now I had to find a way into bumping into him, as I had quickly ruled out knocking at his front door and telling him I'm doing a survey of professional killers in the neighbour-hood. The two most likely places for a chance encounter:

At the clubhouse bar (appealing) or on the golf course (repelling).

Please don't hold it against me but I had actually played golf before. In the Bahamas where I taught high school for three years. In the early mornings of a scorching summer after all the tourists and snowbirds had flocked off, a gang of fellow teachers, mostly Brits, would descend on the empty local courses armed with three-quart jugs of gin and tonics and no intention of improving their game. I joined them five times, was asked to leave three, an achievement of which I was rather childishly proud. Long stories short: I had started out OK, but with each succeeding hole my frustration level grew alongside the number of strokes and my alcohol consumption. That fucking willful ball steadfastly refused to go where I wanted it to. Apparently my loud, obscenity-laden yells of frustration and my aggressive behaviour towards the course and my rented equipment made the nearby golfers and groundskeepers feel less than safe. I will concede that being piss-drunk by the fifth tee for all three shortened rounds may have been a factor in my expulsions.

A couple of more clicks and I discovered that the La Paloma Golf and Country Club was a private, members-only course. Chances were that, given the general air of snootiness drenching their website, any Tom, Dick, or Jake wouldn't even be allowed to step onto their hallowed grounds.

Un-bingo!

That's when I noticed a Westin Hotel on the map, also

smack-dab in the middle of the La Paloma Villages. Now why would the Westin folks put up a big hotel there if their guests couldn't golf? A couple of clicks and, turns out, they wouldn't. Golf packages were available.

Bingo again!

I booked a room at La Paloma, largely because it was about a mile away from Hoffner's place as the desert vulture flies, considerably longer with all the twisty streets of the development. I mean, I could walk there from the hotel—although I had no intention of doing so. But I could if I wanted to. I figured I was doing legitimate field research paid for by Steve for his next book, so I splurged on a one-bedroom suite.

The table was set. Now, all I had to do was manufacture a plausible reason for an accidental meeting. I knew that I couldn't be the one to bump into him. When I saw him in Colorado Springs, he had seen me, and I tend to stick out in a crowd. Kinda hard to explain coincidentally running into him again hundreds of miles away, on his home golf course no less; not even Dickens would accept that (Oh c'mon, Oliver Twist makes it to London and, right off the cricket bat, just happens to run into Fagin and the lads in a city of millions?).

Nope, I needed another body. A body who knew what had happened and who we were dealing with. I figured I could con Steve into being that other body.

But after that, my plan got a bit fuzzy.

CHAPTER 25

"There's nothing I can say to talk you out of this, is there?" Alex asked rhetorically, as I dusted off my trusty bowling bag and crammed it with rolled-up Hawaiian shirts and my diabetes meds.

"I'm sorry, babe. I gotta see this through. Please understand."

I think she did understand or, at the very least, I think I was able to convince myself that she understood on our near-silent drive to the airport. I then tried to imagine her eventually being proud of me for my stick-to-ed-ness and hunger for justice and my commitment to honouring a pledge. Couldn't do it. Couldn't get past the worried look in her eyes as we said goodbye.

It was a decent flight to Tucson. I say that because I was

asleep for most of it, and no little bastard was kicking the back of my seat.

I did have time to consider how concerned Alexandra had been about my going. And I felt shitty about it because I loved her like crazy and hated upsetting her. But this was one of those either/or situations. Either I went to Tucson, or I didn't. There was no middle ground, no room for a compromise. In the past, Alex was on the outside of my ill-conceived escapades and was—justifiably—pissed off at my dangerous misadventures. This time out, she was right in the thick of things; she knew about the kind of commitment it demanded and the intensity it produced when going after major league bad guys. Together, we had found some of them, but there was one more to get. I truly didn't think I had much of a choice. I needed to nail this guy.

Well, weren't you a cocky son of a bitch? Not really. I was nervous as fuck as the plane descended. How nervous? After being clean for four months, I bought a pack of cigarettes and a lighter in the airport.

Exiting the terminal to pick up my rental I was hit with a blast of heat and cornea-frying sunshine. I know people say, "Yeah, but it's a *dry* heat." I call bullshit. It's still friggin' hot. Especially when you're surrounded by white concrete as you smoke a dizzying butt before you make your way to the "proudly smoke-free" rented car for which they would proudly charge me 250 bucks if they caught a tobacco whiff. I wondered if they charged the same for farts.

With the rental's A/C fan set to jet engine speed, the car cooled down just as I pulled up to the hotel.

The Westin La Paloma was real nice, from its cavernous ornate lobby to the expansive suite I had reserved. Cheap bastard that I am, I wasn't used to booking nice hotels. Alex had insisted on the boutique hotel in St. Barts a year ago and the hoity-toity Monteleone in New Orleans just recently. For someone who had become used to weighing the seven-dollar difference between the Red Roof Inn and Super 8, this was true luxury.

First thing I did was call Steve. Well, second thing. First up, I sent an email to Bellini under the subject head *Still reporting from Florida, sir*. It read:

> *Just for shits and giggles, if I were you, I'd check to see if there were any knife murders in Colorado Springs on or about October 24th, near the Old Town section.*

OK, the second thing wasn't a call to Steve either. I mean, there was a mini bar.

"Bud-dee! How's she goin', eh?" I said in Canadian hoser-ese, after my first sip of a Banquet.

"She goin' good, eh?" Steve answered.

"Getting sick of staring at varnished pine yet?"

"Why? What's up?"

"I just thought you might like a change of scenery. Maybe you'd rather look at adobe and cactus for a while."

Pause.

"What the fuck are you talking about?" he finally asked.

"You've been pissing and moaning about sitting on the sidelines while I was having all the fun nearly dying. I want to make it up to you," I said to entice him.

"Oh, *do* go on."

He, of course, knew first-hand everything that had happened up to and including Laura telling him she was sure she'd found the silver SUV, but, he confirmed, he was unaware of her desperate phone call to me after Alexandra and I got back to Florida or the identity of the hitman. So, I laid out what Bellini had told me about Hoffner and his confessed powerlessness to do anything with my sketchy info. Hence, my need to take some action. Which had sent me to Tucson, hopefully with Steve as my partner.

"Why the fuck would I go to Tucson?"

"Linda Ronstadt's birthplace? You kidding me? But seriously, folk, because that's where the bad guy is, you silly gosling."

"Say I'm with you so far. What do we do when I get there?"

"Yeah, well...that bit's still in the planning stage."

"You're fucking kidding me, right?"

"You're smart; I'm smart. By my math, we'll be twice as smart together when we figure out the local conditions on the ground. I've made a start. Just let me know when you're getting in."

"We'll see."

"I'm at the Westin La Paloma, Room 306."

"I'll think about it."

"Oh, and make sure to bring your golf clothes."

"What?! I don't have any fucking gol—"

I had hung up. I was tempted to stay on the line so I could finish listening to what I suspected was going to be an imaginatively obscene rant, but I had already set the hook. I was almost convinced he'd be curious enough to get involved.

And so it was, Steve e-mailed me early the next morning:

OK, you win, arsehole. I'm on United 2173 tonight from Denver, arrives 7:25 PM. See you around 8.

Yay! The first piece of The Plan—such as it was.

CHAPTER 26

I almost missed another unread e-mail. This from Detective Bellini:

It read:

You were right. Victim was Albert Lee Roberston, 27 – local thug with a bunch of priors for either possession or violent assault. Got whacked in Colorado Springs on October 23rd. Murder weapon was a knife. Older mugshot attached.

When I opened the attachment, a blonde, long-haired, broad-shouldered nasty-looking piece of work stared out at me.

Hoffner's sidekick in St. Petersburg. Had to be.

I e-dug out the *Colorado Springs Gazette* article about the murder. It was a very short piece. Editors have a sliding scale to determine the number of lines they devote to a murder they're reporting. As soon as you see a phrase like "known drug dealer," you can be sure it's a short article. That phrase was in the headline and the second sentence.

As per usual, the police were not exactly forthcoming with details about the demise of Albert Lee Roberston, describing it as violent, yet refusing it call his expiration anything more than a "possible" homicide.

But somehow, a reporter from a local TV station had gained access to the crime scene, a shitty-looking ground floor apartment. His shaky phone camera panned the gruesome scene and clearly showed blood splashed everywhere.

Bellini had confirmed that a knife had been the murder weapon. And speaking of knife damage, did anybody spring to my mind as a killer who used a blade? I'm in town anyway, I thought, so I might as well ask Mr. Hoffner if I see him.

With Steve arriving in the late evening, I had the day to myself. To plan. To drink. To bag rays by the swimming pool.

Hotels have taken their cue from airlines in finding ways to gouge their allegedly all-important guests by charging for things you'd think would be part of the room price. I couldn't just wander down to the pool area like days long gone. No, sir. I had to first pay a "resort fee." It's only a matter of time before they start dinging you with "elevator usage fees" and "hallway admission surcharges." At the same time, not to be outdone, you can expect airlines to up their game by levying "seat provision fees." "I'm sorry, sir, but we were clear that your ticket only got you onboard the plane. Now, sir, would you like somewhere to sit? Oh, and did we mention the "pilot salary enhancement tax?""

My grumbling was soon eased by a 16-buck margarita at the pool bar and a bunch of $10-beer, all charged to the room that Steve was paying for. In the midst of all this rehydration (It was hot, goddamnit!), I put together—conceptually, of course—more detail to my wispy strategy.

Thanks to the dynamo hum of the drinks in that heat, I couldn't quite remember all the details of The Plan as I lounged in the Roman tub in my room. Nor did they spring back to mind as I gorged on the lovely dinner that room service brought to me while I assaulted the mini bar. Some specifics did return to the surface as I sat on the balcony, illegally smoking and legally watching a spectacular desert sunset.

As expected, Steve turned up just after eight.

"Expensive tastes, my friend," he said, gazing around the spacious living room. "This isn't like your cheap ass."

"It is when someone else is paying for it. In this case: you. I went with the suite because I figured we'd need the space to spread out. And just to show you what a goddamn prince I am, you get the bedroom; I'll take the couch."

"How thoughtful of you."

"Beer?" I asked, using the Canadian catchphrase signifying peace, love, and understanding.

We sank down into the plush couches.

"Let's start with the idea that none of this is gonna be

easy," I said. "You won't just walk up to him and ask: "Pssst. Hey buddy, you wouldn't happen to be a professional hitman, would you?" and he won't answer: "You're in luck, pal! That's exactly what I do for living.""

"Obviously."

"So, he's gonna want to vet you."

"Then I'm fucked. It'd take him about two seconds to find out that I'm a crime writer."

"That's why we need a new you. Ever come across a guy who tried to arrange a hitman for anybody but got caught?"

"Sure. A bunch."

"Any of them sorta look like you?"

There were five or six that he recalled. Two were females who wanted to bump off their spouses, so we disqualified them. One guy was looking to be rid of a business partner but, Steve said, he was a huge Swedish-looking guy, so he was ruled out. One was a young Asian lad who successfully reduced his immediate family size by one with the for-hire murder of an older brother who was in line to inherit a half a shit-ton when their aged father kicked.

"So, who's left?" I asked.

"There was a guy, about fifteen years ago. Lemme think."

He paused and pondered. Steve had been in a lot of courtrooms, seen a bunch of people trying to do bad things. He finally snapped back to the present.

"Brian Seton!' he announced. "He got arrested trying to

arrange a hit on his wife with an undercover cop. Got ten years."

"And you and he could be twins?"

"Not exactly. He was a little taller than me."

"Who isn't?"

"Arsehole. And younger."

"They say prison ages a man."

"But he did have dark hair, kinda curly like mine. About the same build."

Steve then flipped open his laptop and began e-digging around for any newspaper photos, either from the trial or since his release after he'd did his time. He came up with one shot of his arrest photo (when, let's face it, no one looks their best) and another one as he was being led in handcuffs from the court, his face half-obscured. Tack on fifteen years and Steve could almost pass for that guy. Check that: Steve would *have* to pass for that guy.

Mr. Internet also produced a few short stories over the last six years in the Toronto business press about Seton Builders being awarded contracts for semi-large construction projects. Ol' Brian had obviously gone straight and become successful. And then—ta-da!—a four-year old announcement (no photo) of the impending wedding between Brian Seton and Mary-Ellen Talbot. I presumed the original Mrs. Seton didn't want to stand by the man who wanted her dead.

"Perfect!" I said. "Looks like you've decided that married bliss with Mary-Ellen wasn't all you'd imagined."

"So now what?"

"Now you have to book a room as Brian Seton."

"Are you sure all this is really necessary?"

"He's gonna check you out. Guaranteed. When—not if—he calls the Westin and no one named Seton is registered, this little caper of ours is over before it starts. He's gone and we're shit out of luck."

"How do we know he isn't travelling to a job?"

"He's here. I called the course, said I was supposed to play with Mr. Hoffner tomorrow, but I couldn't remember our tee time. They told me Hoffner was off at 2:15, playing eighteen. We're booked for nine holes at two o'clock."

"Any reason for the timing?"

"We'll be done around four. He'll finish up around five-thirty. Gives us time to figure out the set-up at the clubhouse."

"What if he doesn't go to the clubhouse?"

"I bet he will. He's a member and members usually have to spend X number of dollars a month in the restaurant or bar."

"You really do think about all this shit."

"I've made enough bone-headed moves *not* to think about these things."

"Humour me. What if he does go straight home?"

"If he skips the clubhouse, we switch to Plan B."

"Which is?"

"I'd give worlds to know, because right now I don't have a

fucking clue. Now, if there are no more stupid questions, I'd say we're good to go."

"Dressed like this?"

"I'm now going to speak a sentence I thought I'd never say: Let's go shopping tomorrow morning!"

It was a subdued evening as, I think, we both contemplated the enormity of the day ahead of us. Steve, that great pricker of balloons, did his level best to prove that we were totally deranged in thinking Our Plan (share the blame, Jake) could work.

"Do you honestly think a contract killer will be trawling for new clients at his clubhouse bar?"

"I do, if the circumstance presents itself. Near as I can tell, our boy is strictly a low-rent assassin. Hoffner's in his late forties; his dream of playing in the bigs is over. Meanwhile, he has to sustain his lifestyle. It's 20K to join and play for one year at that club of his. Never mind mortgage, property taxes, homeowner fees, all of which I looked up. It's not like assassins have retirement plans and it's not like he's going to take a side job as a Walmart greeter."

"I can picture it: "Good afternoon, madam. Can I take a stab at helping you?""

""Oh, and you should know we've slashed our prices on hundreds of items." No, our boy needs customers."

"What if I miss him in the clubhouse or can't talk to him?"

"I've got the perfect answer for that: Don't."

Before I turned in, I checked my e-mail. Another note from Bellini.

It read:

Did some more digging. Hoffner was in the military. But for just over a year. High scores in hand-to-hand combat in basic training. Assigned to the army base in Manheim, Germany. In a bar, he got into a knife fight with a local. Got cut up but the other guy was really messed up. Hoffner was court-martialled and kicked out of the Army with a dishonorable discharge. You may be on the right track. I might be able to scare up some local police back-up.

I wrote him back:

Of course, I'm on the right fucking track! And I don't want no steenkin' badges; too risky. Could blow our cover and we've got one shot at this. But why don't you take a few vacation days and come on down to share in the glory?

I can't speak for Steve, but it was a restless night for me. I spent most it smoking on the balcony, staring at twinkly lights near us that disappeared into the vast desert blackness in the distance.

The next morning, I received Bellini's e-mail reply to my invitation:

That's a hard pass. Too much hassle getting clearance to operate in another jurisdiction. But good luck. And be careful!!!!!

All those fucking exclamation points got me jumpy.

Steve wanted to grab a coffee and muffin, his breakfast staple for the last forty years as a reporter.

"Oh, no, my friend. I've got my eye on the buffet. We're going to need the energy. And your budget can handle it. And speaking of, right after we eat, it's time to shop 'til I puke."

Stuffed, after working my way through a pile of bacon stacked like cordwood, we went to a nearby mall where Golfapalooza or some other such chain store was located. There, we wandered stupidly up and down the aisles like aliens, trying to make sense of earthly economics that justified selling a goddamned putter for four thousand goddamned dollars.

I wanted to go full John Daly with a bright orange and lime green outfit from his outrageously cool clothing line. Steve talked me out of it.

"For *once,* Jake, try to fit in."

We left the mall, with Steve a whole lot poorer, but the pair of us really snappy-looking.

We drove to the course and clumsily picked up our rental clubs—Steve discovered that he apparently hit right-handed —and the cart. I then gunned/braked/jerked our vehicle to the first tee where a thirty-something groundskeeper was keeping the grounds by trying to wash away big splotches of green bird shit.

As we approached, the much younger guy apparently decided that he had important thoughts worth sharing with us.

"Some of those fuckin' Canadian geese stay," he

commented. "But most just stop over on their way to and from Mexico. So, I only have to clean up this crap for a couple of months a year."

"Look, if it's any consolation, I will quite often use a bathroom," I offered.

"Canadian, huh? A lot more of you human ones spend the winter here," he continued. "By the by, after five years here, I can tell you, you people are the worst golfers in the world."

"*You people.*" Have I ever told you how much I hate that phrase? Nobody should say that to anybody, least of all to me who has enough trouble representing himself, let alone the entire Canadian snowbird population.

"You ain't seen nuthin' yet, sonny," I said bending over the tee for my first drive. I managed to slice off a big enough divot to sod a medium-sized yard while my ball soared a solid ten, maybe twelve yards.

The xenophobic groundskeeper watched me light up a butt then reposition the lawn. He turned and stalked away in disgust.

If possible, Steve was even a shittier golfer than me. Unlike me, he's physically fit, owing to his inexplicable fixation with running. But that whole hand-eye co-ordination thing eludes him whereas I'm pretty good at it, something I had to pick up quickly when I was amateur boxing, lest I be beaten up more badly than I was.

We abandoned that part of our charade half-way through

an even more disastrous second hole. It was a long course, and we were far enough away from anyone that we decided to play shadow golf instead. And we were damn good at it. Faking monstrous drives, following the flight of the imaginary ball, making a tricky invisible shot from the rough, celebrating a ball-less long-distance putt, marking our mythical scores.

We only "played" eight holes. Steve carded a 39, but the fucker cheated.

In the clubhouse barroom, we put the finishing touches on what was still being loosely described as Our Plan. The first step was to identify Hoffner and get close to him. Then Steve had to establish a casual camaraderie using golf—which is always a share-sies sort of topic among golfers. Online, I found a glossary of golf slang. Steve studied it so he wouldn't sound like a complete moron.

"Order four or five drinks, but find a way to ditch them," I said. "You should be clear-headed while appearing completely shit-faced."

"I can play that!"

I wished him good luck then skedaddled back to my room so I wouldn't be seen. I sat on the balcony, waiting nervously, smoking nervously, and staring at the Catalina Mountains which were a fuck of a lot closer than the alleged goddamned mountains I could see waaaay in the distance from Gunnison.

Two hours crawled by until I heard the door open.

Steve was pretty excited.

"I think I just hired a hitman!" he said.

"Details, man!" I demanded as I handed him a beer from the replenished mini bar.

Steve described moving to a stool at the bar after I left. He positioned himself between the beer taps and the spot favoured by the bartender named Chip and started ordering double gin and tonics.

"Did you drink them?" I asked.

"Fuck, no. A sip or two, then I'd get up and wander around with it. There are a couple of potted palms that must be swaying like crazy."

Steve told me how busy the place got as dinnertime neared and how he spotted Hoffner and his prominent scar coming towards the bar.

He then called up the recording he made on his phone while I tried to picture the scene at the bar. Steve on a barstool, hunched over, both hands cupping his glass. Hoffner close to him, maybe reaching across the bar for his order.

The recording started.

In the background you could hear the usual hubbub of a busy bar. Multiple muffled voices talking, laughing, the clink of glassware.

"Two Coors Light draught, Chip," a strong voice says above the noise.

"How ya doin,' bud?" Steve says, his slightly slurred

words a dead-on impersonation of himself when he's actually drunk.

"Good. You?" the voice says in that automatic way that implies he hoped Steve wouldn't answer because he really couldn't give a shit how he was doing.

"Will that be cash, sir?" another voice says.

"No, Chip, put it on my tab. I'll be back."

Steve stopped the recording to tell me that Hoffner took his two beer and left the bar area. [Sidebar: I didn't just forget to make beer a plural. In Canada, beer is a collective noun like deer. So how about you climb of my back, eh?] Steve told me he waited twenty-five minutes for Hoffner to come back for his second round. He pushed a button on his phone and re-started the tape.

"Boy, did that goat track beat the crap out of me today," Steve says on the recording.

"I thought the course was in great shape," Hoffner says defensively. "I'm a member here. Your first time?" Hoffner then rather haughtily asks, I assume because he wanted to make the class distinctions real clear. The opinion of a one-time player didn't count for shit with a member who'd shelled out thousands to belong.

"Yeah. Listen, buddy," Steve says, "I didn't mean to insult your course. It was fine. I just played like a fucking duffer. How'd you do out there today?"

"OK, I guess. You know, it's golf."

"Tell me about it. I was either on the beach or flying the

green. Even hit a couple of dribblers and chunks. I guess I've got a lot on my mind. That ever happen to you, you know, when you're thinking about other stuff, and it really screws up your game?"

"Sure."

There was a pause, as the conversation was dying off.

"That bitch!" Steve announces out of the blue. I could hear him slam his glass onto the bar.

"Excuse me?" Hoffner asks.

"Sorry...my beloved wife. She's ruining my life."

"It's none of my business, but why don't you just get divorced?"

"God, I wish I could. I got into a tax crunch a while back, so I put her name on most of my businesses, *before* we got married, which means, in Canada, she gets to legally keep everything she came into the marriage with. She could take it all, *plus* half of whatever's left over that I'm entitled to. And the vindictive hog will do it too. She's already told me that's her plan. Yup, she's about to take Brian Seton to the cleaners."

"Sounds as though it's not a good situation," Hoffner says, being politely non-committal.

"That's all I can think about these days. That's why I came down here. To clear my mind."

"Doesn't seem to be working."

"Nope, you are absolutely right," Steve continues. "She needs to be gone.... Permanently."

There's a pause.

"You don't mean, like, permanently *permanently*," Hoffner says.

"Fuckin' right I do. Like, permanently not living.... Shit, listen to me, will ya? I'll shut up now. Sorry."

Another pause.

"Are you serious?" Hoffner whispers.

"I'm as serious as the cancer I hope she gets."

"I might know somebody who knows somebody else who might be able to help you," Hoffner says, his voice at near inaudible levels.

"Really?"

"I'll make a couple of calls. Be at this address tonight at ten."

"You're not a cop or anything, are you?" Steve asks.

"Do you think a cop's salary gets you a membership here? So, are you interested or not?"

"I am. Thanks, pal. I mean that. Hey, I don't even know your name. I'm Brian Seton and you are...?"

"Just be at this address tonight at ten."

End of recording.

"So whaddya think?" Steve asked.

"The guy's obviously an evil degenerate; I mean, ordering Coor Light draught? Jesus. But besides that, I'd say we're in! Good job, buddy!" I said, clapping him on the back. "And good job on remembering all those fucking golf terms."

"I only got to the 'G's in the glossary," he said, then he

brightened, as if suddenly realizing he had just made what, by any definition, was a very tricky connection. "Game on!" he exclaimed.

"Right now, I bet he's checking out Brian Seton on-line. And he'll find our perfectly swell cover story!"

So, we acted all excited, amped up like kids before gift-opening at their birthday parties. But not lost on me was the realization that we were gleefully celebrating the fact that my best friend was about to meet a murderer at his house, alone, at night.

CHAPTER 27

I found Hoffner's place, parked two homes past his, reckoning that the tall cactus in the front yard would create a prickly visual barrier between me and his house.

I wished Steve good luck again.

"This is kinda fun," Steve said. "Going all Hardy Boys and all."

But the last look on his face as he opened the car door told me he thought this was anything but fun. And that, of course, got me more nervous than I already was.

I stood by the car, smoking. Fifteen minutes went by... then twenty minutes. It was twenty-two minutes and four cigarettes later when I suddenly saw Steve running towards me.

"Start the car! Start the car!" Steve shouted at me, as if he had just scored the bestest deal ever at Ikea.

I scrambled back into the driver's seat faster than those Chinese fire drills—musical chairs with a car—we used to do at stop lights back in my high school days.

He was shaking as I tromped the gas and shot out of there.

"He made me! He made me!" Steve yelled.

"Settle down. Let's get outta of here."

"Fast!"

As I floored it, I could plainly see a figure in my rearview mirror. He was standing in the middle of the street, clearly illuminated by the streetlight.

No time to chat as I was busy beating a hasty retreat through the labyrinthian streets of the housing development while Steve was busy calming the fuck down. By the time we took the entrance to the hotel (on what felt like two wheels), he had stopped furiously rubbing the tops of his thighs and endlessly repeating: "Jesus, Jesus, Jesus!"

"Still having fun?" I asked.

"Fuck off."

In the hotel parking lot, I turned to him. "We're going to check out right now. Five minutes to pack up."

"Why?"

"He knows your fake self is fake staying here. How long do you figure before he turns up?"

"Yeah, but the room I booked will be empty. I'll be in yours."

"For the rest of our lives? He's probably going to sit and watch from the lobby."

"Oh," Steve said.

I could see that Steve's dread was subsiding, replaced with a sort of catatonia, almost as though he were sleepwalking. I'd been there before. The adrenaline runs out and you're left shell-shocked. With my continual urging, we were packed and gone in about four minutes.

"OK. Where to?" Steve asked as we left the parking lot.

"Gunnison...well, Denver first. He'd have no reason to think that's where we're headed. He doesn't even know who "we" is."

"Driving?"

"No. We have to ditch the car."

"I don't understand. He can't track it."

"Alamo can. All their cars have GPS. If he's got the plate number, he just calls them to report that one of their cars was in a hit and run. Then he screams at them for updates."

"Maybe he didn't get the plate."

"Maybe. Wanna take that chance?"

Steve didn't answer. I pulled a U-ie and drove away from the airport.

"What the hell are you doing? I saw the signs; we're almost there."

"If they do give Hoffner an updated location," I said, "he'll know to look for us at the airport."

I could feel myself becoming exasperated with having to

explain our every move to Steve. I parked the car on a residential side street several miles from the airport. We sat in silence for a bit.

"Steve, look at me," I said, trying to get him to focus. "Your only job right now is to get us to the airport. We're at 1404 Hillside Drive," I said, after noting a nearby house number.

As though he were on autopilot, Steve ordered up an Uber.

We said little as we waited for a Prius. Finally, sitting in the backseat, Steve leaned over and whispered to me.

"I got him."

"Sure?"

"Sure."

We didn't say anything else on the drive to the airport until Steve, after fiddling around on his phone, told me he had booked us on a 7 a.m. Delta flight the next morning to Denver, the soonest we could get the fuck outta Dodge. At that point, he hadn't played his recording, and we agreed not to do so at the airport lest we be overheard. And all I cared about just then was if a) the airport stayed open all night and b) they had those comfy padded benches.

Yes, to both and we stretched out at our departure gate and grabbed some fitful shuteye.

We were still bagged as we boarded the early morning flight, so we dozed again. But not before scanning the passengers getting on the plane as they inched their way down the narrow aisles. No sign of Hoffner. Sleep came a little easier. When we woke up, Steve seemed to have shaken off the fear and shock he had been experiencing and was back to normal.

I had yet to listen to the recording. I didn't think that anyone on the jam-packed plane needed to hear it. Again, Steve and I said little. Except for:

"You're absolutely sure you got a confession?" I asked.

"I did. Trust me. I've been in enough courtrooms to know what counts. Oh, and he mentioned he whacked some guy in Colorado Springs recently."

"Holy shit! Albert Lee Robertson."

"Who?"

"His road buddy to Florida."

"I guess some friendships just aren't meant to last."

It was a swell feeling walking through the Denver Airport, not looking over our shoulder. Safe. Steve took his own sweet time buying a replacement for the phone he was about to give Bellini. Finally, while Steve's rented car warmed up, we listened to his recording together.

A doorbell rings, a door opens.

"Come in," a voice I recognize now as Hoffner's says.

"So, you're the guy who knows a guy who knows a guy," Steve says.

"I am. Have a seat."

Time passes maddeningly slowly as they settle in to talk.

"I see your construction business is doing well," Hoffner says.

"You know about that? It's doing great. We just won a big contract for a shopping mall in Vaughn. You keeping busy?"

Hoffner sort of chuckles at Steve's awkward question.

"You were pretty drunk this evening," Hoffner says. "Sober now?"

"I am."

"Good. I'll ask you again: Are you serious about using my services?"

"Yes. Let's get something out of the way first," Steve says. "What kind of money are we talking about?"

"Twenty grand. Half up front, half when I've done the job. Plus expenses."

"Ouch."

"I don't discount. Take it or leave it."

"OK, OK. But it's gotta look like a mugging."

"It will. Oh, and the money has to be in cash," he adds.

"I can't get that kind of coin down from Canada."

"Bank draft then. US dollars, made out to RH Logistics."

"Fine. I can run it through my company."

"I gather this isn't your first rodeo."

"You know about that too?"

"Yes, Mr. Seton. So, you really want to try this again with your second wife?"

"That's why I'm here. I stupidly hired locally last time.

Did nine years because the amateur asshole couldn't keep his mouth shut."

"Nine and half years, if I'm not mistaken."

"You've checked me out pretty carefully. Now it's my turn."

"What?"

"Right now, I'm just taking your word for it that you do this sort of thing. How do I know you aren't just bullshitting me, looking for some easy money? I mean, if you stiff me, it's not like I'm going to the cops."

"You have to trust me."

"Actually, no, I don't."

"Alright. I did a guy in Colorado Springs last week and I had a contract in Florida just recently."

"Name of the Florida guy?"

"I didn't say if it was a man or a woman."

"I...I just assumed...," Steve says, obviously tapdancing.

"Why do you want to know?" Hoffner asks.

"Like I said, I need to be sure. I can probably find the story on-line to confirm it."

"Stan Harding. Satisfied?"

Steve and I looked at each other. That was the money shot.

"Yes. Do you want to know why I want the bitch gone?" Steve asks on tape.

"No."

"How soon can you do the...job?"

"As soon as I get paid. Within that week. I'll need a picture and an address."

"I'll have to get you the picture. And I live at...um...4... Highland Place, Rosedale."

There's a slight pause and then Hoffner says: "I'll be right back. I have to get something from the kitchen."

Then a longer pause and I could imagine Steve fidgeting away.

"I changed my mind!" Steve announces suddenly and loudly.

The next thing I hear is the front door slamming. I can fill in the rest from the time I saw him running towards the car.

"You did great, buddy!" I said and I meant it. He had.

Steve was visibly proud of his achievement. He was positively glowing.

"You just might have a future as a reporter," I added.

"Arsehole."

"Tell me about the end."

"I wanted so badly to play it cool. But I was sure he had busted me. Suspicion in his eyes when I hesitated about my own goddamn address. I figured the 'something' he was going to get in the kitchen was a big fucking knife. I panicked."

"No, you were smart," I assured him. "Sounds like he figured out you were bogus. Stumbling over your own address probably cinched it for him. By the by, he was trying to fuck you over for your 10K downpayment."

"How do you figure?"

"I had an eternity to think about it sitting in the car. Brian Seton might not have known but, for sure, Hoffner knew that he couldn't cross the border with a felony conviction on his record."

"That sonofabitch."

"Sad day when you can't trust contract killers."

"So, what's next?"

I gave him a number to punch in. If me and my sausage fingers had tried to do it on his phone, I'd wind up dialling a pizza joint in Topeka.

"Detective Bellini," the gruff voice answered, as I took the phone.

"Frank!"

"Who's this?"

"Your favourite Canadian."

"You're not Geddy Lee."

"Strange choice, but funny."

"What do you want?" he demanded abruptly.

"I want you to listen to something."

"New version of *Tom Sawyer*?"

"Better. I'm sending it now. Call me back at this number."

I hung up. Two can play this terse game.

Steve sent both recordings. We waited.

After about twenty minutes, the phone rang in the heated car. I answered.

"Jake?" Bellini asked.

"No. You've reached Alex Lifeson."

"Stop fucking around! How'd you get this?"

I told him all about our plan, perhaps going overboard a bit with details of how we tracked Hoffner down and engineered Steve's meeting at the Tucson golf club.

"So, it's useful?" I asked.

"It's solid."

"Can you pick him up now?"

"Not yet."

I nearly lost it.

"What do you mean 'Not yet'?! If he knows his jig is up, he's going to fuck off! Or he'll track us down!"

"Settle down. We have to vet the phone recording. I'll forward this to Tucson PD. They'll watch him. Where are you?"

"Parking lot. Denver Airport."

"I'm coming to you. I need that phone. I can be there in three hours."

"Fuck that, Frank. We not gonna sit here like frozen sitting ducks. See you at RMHH Enterprises. Two and a half hours."

"Get moving," he said and ended the call.

We got moving.

CHAPTER 28

I walked through the terminal, thinking of how much I cared for Steve. People may say that I have trouble expressing genuine emotion. Bullshit to that; it's no trouble at all. People whom I loved and who, for some reason, loved me back, just seem to *know*. And that's all that matters.

The early afternoon flight through Charlotte to Tampa gave me loads of time to replay the high- and low-lights of the soon-to-be-famous Colorado Clusterfuck. It had mostly turned out alright, although there were a couple of people who, if they were not behind bars or dead, might disagree. And nothing was going to bring Stan back. That sad reality cast a pall over the entire enterprise.

I know I sound callous about the fact that some bad guys lost their lives, but who gives a fuck? I don't spend a lot of time worrying about it. I figure—for all time—that if you decide to sign on to any venture that requires breaking laws and hurting people who've never harmed you, all in the quest for a better payday, then you have also signed on to *all* the possible consequences of that job opportunity. It's right there in the small print: "In addition to financial rewards, be advised that you might be arrested or killed." Or words to that effect.

IT WAS DARK WHEN I FINALLY WAS HOME-FREE IN INDIAN Rocks. In the four days I'd been gone, it was evident that Alex had been busy-busy getting the joint ship shape for the winter season. Not just the spic n' span interior that I knew would greet me. But, going by the solar lighting, I could see she had taken over my job of keeping the outside pretty. She would've spent a day getting rid of the dead palm fronds on the ground and the half-dead ones still attached, plus pruning the rest of the shrubbery. And another day on her knees, painstakingly separating the mulch from the river rock.

Much fierce hugging and kissing ensued as I came through the door. The beer and wine were chilled, the conversation warm as we sat at the patio table and caught up. And Alexandra looked sexy as all get out in short shorts and a gauzy wraparound beach cover-up thingy. It was hard to concentrate as she peppered me with questions about my doings in Tucson, while brushing a tanned and shapely calf against one of my old man chicken legs.

She refused to believe me when I grudgingly revealed that I had golfed. I could hardly believe it myself. Among other things. In turn, I told her about what Bellini had found —the addresses and names of all his grow houses, the detailed spreadsheets on each one, with some having the strange 'ABC Action?' notation. I saved the worst for last.

"The dope empire's been hurt badly but it could make a comeback," I said. "McGrath had a partner, maybe even a boss."

"How did you find *that* out?"

"From the hired killer. He told me this mystery partner had ordered the hit on me."

"What hit on you?!"

Shit! I thought. Why the fuck, Jake, did you have to include that little detail?

"Nothing to worry about, babe," I assured her. "They didn't know where I was."

"Oh, well then, I'll just erase from my memory, the fact that someone wanted my husband contractually killed."

"You gotta be used to that by now," I said, trying to josh her out of her alarm.

"I am, but it should be my job," she joshingly said. "Do you think Bellini will find this other guy?"

"Maybe. Or the local cops. Or the FBI. But it just pisses me off."

I saw that Alexandra had drifted away (people often do that when I'm speaking). She was staring into the distance, thinking. Then she snapped to.

"Alan Bigelow-Carter! ABC!" she exclaimed. "That's the name of the nervous professor I interviewed! The one who refused to pick his top student. There was something off about him."

"How?"

"I thought about it afterwards and couldn't understand why he was being so fidgety. If he was taking this principled stand of not singling out a student, why be nervous, instead of proud or confident? And he couldn't look me in the eye."

"He was nervous because he was worried that we were closing in on McGrath! And also, that's why McGrath couldn't give me a quick answer on the counteroffer; he had to check with Bigelow hyphen Carter! By George, I think she's got it! Way ta go, babe!"

"Thank you. So, *I* can claim *Now*, it's over."

"You must be thrilled to finally contribute something to this case," I teased.

"I may have mentioned this before, but you are *such* an arsehole."

"Care to take this discussion inside?"

We did but, turned out, there wasn't much discussing. Instead, a whole batch of shenanigans ensued.

THE NEXT MORNING, WE BOTH GOT UP EARLY—AS WE USUALLY do. Alex always has an extensive shit-to-do list, so she likes to get a jump on the day and needs the time to get things done. I get up before the sun does so I can justify napping later on. One of us clearly doesn't understand the concept of retirement.

With my first cup of coffee, I fired up my shitty laptop and sent a short note to Bellini:

Look for Alan Bigelow-Carter. He teaches in the UCCS School of Business. He's the ABC on the spreadsheets. McGrath always conferred with him before calling up Hoffner. Now, for Christ's sakes, do your job and leave me alone!

AS THEY SHOULD'VE, THE LOCAL AND NATIONAL MEDIA WENT big on Professor Bigelow-Carter's and Hoffner's arrests, the solving of the UCSS double homicide, then the apprehension of everybody named on Richie's spreadsheets soon after as the FBI-DEA-CBI dragnet was rolled up. Over a hundred arrests and, literally, thousands of charges and the confiscation of millions of dollars' worth of illegal weed as well as the promised return of actual millions of dollars from McGrath's dirty Canadian law firm.

Law enforcement played right along, feeding the media frenzy with all sorts of tantalizing information—the names of some prominent Coloradans who were hosting pot farms in their houses, and the details of four murders, including Stan's.

Although it was dwarfed by the magnitude of the weed and murder busts, the arrest of former Sergeant Loretta Moseby of the Montrose Police Department made the local news, when they learned of Moseby's connection to P.K. Back then, apparently, Miss Moseby—soon to become Sgt. Moseby—was a swooning admirer of Pete's when the boy was big man on high school campus.

With trials months away, everybody charged was *alleged* to have *allegedly* committed their *alleged* crimes.

The story had legs that grew to giraffe length when Steve, the media whore, kicked in his first-person accounts to a couple national media outlets. My name even came up, although, at my request, it had been changed to Mr. Unnamed Source.

Special Agent Franklin Bellini got his share of the limelight. It was an absolute joy for me to watch him squirm and mumble under the camera's glare, looking more uncomfortable than if he had just been asked by a reporter to account for rumours of his bedwetting into his teenage years and his enjoyment of shit sandwiches.

I of, course, had to send him a note:

Franklin, you old media superstar you! Caught your perfor-mances on CNN, ABC, NBC, CBS, NPR, FOX and Wsomething or other in Anchorage. You're a goddamn natural! No need to reply. But I will assume that your 'Fuck off, Jake' e-mail will be forth-coming anyway, ya big lug.

What seemed like a media maelstrom to us had, of course, negligible impact on Indian Rocks which continued on being a charming beach town mostly unaffected by the frenzied Florida building boom and we continued on being invisible to everybody but the few people we knew. Just another couple of retirees living the good life.

Bellini did write back, but not exactly with the note I was expecting:

Just wanted to let you know that all the press got the State Legisla-ture excited or scared they weren't doing their job. They've authorized millions more for us to step up the fight against the illegal growers. So thanks for that. It was almost worth having to deal with you two.

Now you can fuck off, Jake!

Frank

P.S. We arrested Jeremy Brown for attempted murder of – you'll never guess – you and/or your lady. On a hunch, I sent a Forensics Team out to the Harding place. On that side of the river, they found the rock scored by the bullet, figured the trajectory and found the likely shooter site. There was a pile of cigarette butts that turned out to be Brown's brand, with his DNA on them. We interviewed Joe Harding who admitted to innocently telling his buddy weeks ago about you house guests and your habits.

I wanted to be in on the investigation to really nail the bastard, but mostly to prove that you were a dumbass for saying there was nothing there and that I was a dumbass for listening to you.

PREDICTABLY THE TORRENT OF NEWS STORIES TURNED INTO A trickle within a week. Maybe it went on for a bit longer. I don't know; we stopped watching the news and instead, we enjoyed the hell out of each other.

We finished some minor renovations, we ate out at some pretty swell restaurants, as well as a few pretty swell dive bars. We spent a lot of the time at the beach, reading, illegally drinking. We didn't ever wear fucking socks. Alex got me walking more and I got her drinking more so that was a fair trade. I corrected some of her gardening mistakes and took the high hard one to the head from her for pointing them out. She gave me a haircut that I still haven't forgiven her for. We made love. We laughed. We were living in grace.

Then she left me.

Just for three days though, to attend a conference on ethical investing in Chicago where she was to be the keynote speaker and seminar leader. I was merciless, complaining long and hard about how she was *always* abandoning me to charge off to dangerous situations—I mean, it was Chicago after all.

On the day she left, I got a longish note from Steve telling me how everything was coming up aces for him. He'd turned in the final draft of *Deadly Growth,* apparently to rave reviews from his editor; his publisher informed him that they were planning to double its first print run over his previous book, and they would rush it to publication. His agent had re-negotiated his contract very favourably so his publisher could avoid the risk of losing the book at auction.

I was all smiles reading about how jacked my best friend was. He deserved it all; he'd come real close to being awarded a Peabody posthumously. And now he was living exactly the life he wanted.

He was back in Toronto but only long enough to make his exit from the *Sun* and get his pea brain-around not having a job anymore.

Then Steve's note took a turn for the worse as far as yours truly was concerned. He wanted to know if I'd be his full-fledged partner for a meeting with the Netflix folks in Los Angeles before Christmas. Owing to the public's unquenchable thirst for true crime series, they were prepared to throw buckets of money at his insider story. Sight unseen, they had optioned the book and Steve had finagled his way into getting first crack at writing the TV adaptation. He wanted me at that meeting, and he wanted to write the thing with me.

My instant reaction? I didn't want to do either. As generous and tempting as his offer was, it would come with a trade I didn't think I was prepared to make. I was at least smart enough to see a boatload of complications ahead. And I fucking hate complications—almost as much as I fucking hate socks. More travel, legal documents, arguments over writing, squabbles over producers' demands, fucking deadlines, budget spats, production issues, PR schedules. And above all, the passage of time.

Weigh all that against the simple and superb life I had with Alexandra. No contest, pal.

I didn't want to spend any time twisting the night away with pro and con arguments. Go with your hunch, Jake.

I wrote Steve back:

As nuts as it sounds, I'm gonna pass on your kind offer. I'll play the hand I got. And besides, what the fuck do you know about writing screenplays?

Within minutes after I hit send, he wrote back:

The same amount I knew about hiring hitmen and that turned out OK.

And then he immediately called. He was in full badgering/hectoring/cajoling mode. He almost sounded like an auctioneer, breathlessly rhyming off all the reasons why I'd be a fucking moron to turn him down.

"Sure I'm gonna get a deal with Netflix—But need you at the meeting—Leaving LA to go to Mexico for Christmas then the rest of the winter to write it—Rented a sweet 2-bedroom casa with a pool outside Puerto Vallarta—It's in San Pancho —I remember you talking about it—Would be a gas for Alexandra and you—Would be a gas writing with you—You think in film—You watch TV—Money could be huge—Establish a name for yourself—Bust down the door for your own fiction writing—All sorts of options and opportun—"

"—Steve, Steve, Steve, slow down, buddy. You're probably right about all those things. But you're knee-deep in the hoopla. You get jazzed about that kinda life. I get jazzed if the Raiders win a fucking football game or if I make it to my favourite bar in time for happy hour. But mostly, I'm jacked about spending all the time I want with Alex. We're just different and at different places."

"But I need you to do this job with me."

"I'm gonna break my rule about not getting maudlin. Steve, your friendship means the world to me, and I had the swellest time with you in Colorado, just like I do every goddamn time we hang around together. But you don't fucking need me. You got this!"

The conversation hung there. Long enough for me to have an idea.

"Steve? You know that deal we've had with your books? You give me what you think's fair for my contribution."

"Yeah. But what's the price for saving my life by getting us out of Tucson? If you recall, I was paralyzed."

"How about you not be an arsehole? I almost *cost* you your life first, sending you to meet Hoffner."

"Jake, my confession time. I don't think I've ever felt more alive in my life."

"Yeah, well, you almost weren't. The guy who pushes somebody off a subway platform then pulls them back to safety just before the train creams them doesn't get a hero biscuit. Now, as I was saying: why don't we cut the same deal over the series?"

"How would that work?"

"We can talk about it. You send me drafts to shit on. Hell, I might even do it in person for a couple of weeks in San Pancho with Alexandra. Then you give me what you think's fair."

"I believe we have a deal, my friend."

"Great! I'll have the legal department at Jake Lydon Communications Inc. draft it up and send you the paperwork."

"Fuck the fuck off, buddy-boy."

I DON'T BELIEVE IN ANYTHING LIKE DIVINE SIGNS, OR astrological predictions or any other such bullshit. I even think the idea of karma is a crock as the Raiders still haven't been rewarded for all the times the refs fucked them over in big games. Near as I can tell, the universe is universally bored by, completely uninvolved with, and totally disinterested in the doings of humans.

But within 24 hours of my call with Steve, I received two coincidental reaffirmations that I had made the right choice by not going all in with him.

That night, Alex called me from her Chicago hotel. She told me she had finished reading the draft of *The Sixth String* she had taken with her on her iPad. She said she had cried over, in her words, "the beauty and tragedy" of the book. That was good enough incentive for me to keep at this fiction thing. Alex is a tough crowd.

The day after that, I got an e-mail—found it in my Junk folder—from a literary agency based in Minneapolis, of all places. I recognized Treadwell & Brodsky as one of the targets I'd aimed at a couple of months earlier. The agent who wrote to me was Nathaniel Halston. His note wasn't the usual response of "Our roster of authors is full. Now fuck off" that I was getting used to. After being excited by the outline and chapter I'd sent, he said he now wanted the full manuscript and hoped I hadn't signed on with anybody else to represent me. That easily could've been bullshit, but he claimed to be fascinated by the Romani (Gypsy) culture and believed that the horrors inflicted on them by the Nazis had been underexplored. And he asked me to call him. That level of interest intrigued me, so I looked him and his agency up to remind myself. Completely legit. Not heavyweights, but they had writers I'd heard of, some prize winners among them. Let's call them promising, young middleweights. Except for Mr. Halston. To strain the boxing analogy: He was closer in age to Burgess Meredith's role in *Rocky* as the trainer.

I gave my fucking head a shake as I asked myself: Exactly how picky can you afford to be, Mr. No Name? How about you throw your lot in with Mr. Halston, a transplanted Brit who, going by his website photo, looked like Kelsey Grammer's dad.

I replied to Nathaniel (Nate and Jake? I liked it!), sending the entire book, along with a note thanking him for the interest and suggesting we chat after he's read the thing.

Boy, oh boy, did I have news for Alex. We were halfway across the causeway from the airport to The Beaches when I exhausted recounting my hopefully glad tidings.

Then, girl, oh girl, did she have news for me. The publisher of a stock market e-magazine approached her after she had delivered her speech. He wanted to know if Alex would be interested in writing a book about her adventures in ethical investing, her struggles in the early years, and her thoughts on the current state of so-called "progressive" corporate policies.

"And...?" I said.

"And I don't know," she said. "Are you going to keep writing?"

"Yeah. Weird, but it feels like I don't have much of a choice."

"I thought so and I'm glad. I'm going to tell them 'Yes.' But only if you and I keep on the same morning writing schedule."

"Agreed! Christ, I'm happy for you, babe."

"Ditto, old man."

By the time we pulled into the Hovel's driveway, we were awash in being happy for each other.

THE NEXT MORNING NEAR DAWN, BEFORE THE PICKLEBALL monsters started in the park across the street, Alex and I walked down to the beach with our coffee and were lucky enough to witness one of those rare and astounding natural moments you can sometimes see if you just look. The full moon was going down, not its usual ghostly outline but a solid, bright white disc in the blue sky, like a second sun, bright enough to create a stream of glitter over the calm Gulf waters to our feet. Not something you see every day.

I could almost watch the solid moon move as it sank behind a distant low cloudbank that stretched across the horizon. Then the second instalment of our morning show began as the rising sun behind us elected to decorate that cloudbank with pink and yellow frosting. For an added high-light, it lit up the froth of the occasional small wave tops.

We held hands, stared at the scene, stared at each other, And we smiled because...well, because we couldn't help it. Smiles that said we were goddamned lucky in so many ways.

Leastways, that's what I was thinking; I can't speak for Alex (although I'm pretty good at sensing what's on her mind). But, for all I truly knew, she was smiling because she was secretly happy remembering that I hadn't asked her to sign a pre-nup. All she had to do was to whole-heartedly encourage me to set out on my next clumsy and possibly fatal misadventure and, voila! both the Hovels—and my goddamned Hawaiian shirts—would be hers!

The witch.

ACKNOWLEDGMENTS

A cargo load of gratitude goes to JoDee and Lou Costello for a bunch of reasons. But to sum up: thanks, you two, for being helpful, smart, funny, good sports, and wonderful people.

Big thanks to Tyler Owens for the inside dope on the legal dope business.

And, as usual, a gargantuan thank-you to Glenn Torresan for designing and shooting the covers and laying out all the pages of squiggles between those covers. And for his genius in somehow getting a part of him on every cover of my books except one.

I also appreciate the hell out of publishing overlord Ron Corbett.

Thanks have to go to Stephen J. McGill who has allowed me to continue writing by allowing me to continue breathing.

Same to Maggie for rescuing me from a Dominican ICU – while at the same time watching me destroy her Christmas and her vacation. I'm such an arsehole.

ABOUT THE AUTHOR

John Owens is the author of seven Jake Lydon mysteries, as well as two works of historical fiction, *On the Rails* and *The Sixth String*.

He recently celebrated his tenth anniversary living in Morrisburg, Ontario with his saintly wife, Maggie.

You can reach him on Facebook by searching:
John Owens Ottawa.

www.ingramcontent.com/pod-product-compliance
Lightning Source LLC
Chambersburg PA
CBHW021848010726
47493CB00005B/1603